# Also by D-L Nelson

# Murder in Edinburgh

A Third-Culture Kid Mystery

Editor: Cynthia Brackett-Vincent
Book design: Eddie Vincent
Cover design by Deirdre Wait, High Pines Creative, Inc.
Cover photographs: © Getty Images

Published by: Encircle Publications, LLC
PO Box 187
Farmington, ME 04938

Visit: http://encirclepub.com

Sign up for Encircle Publications newsletter and specials
http://eepurl.com/cs8taP

Printed in U.S.A.

# MURDER IN EDINBURGH
## A Third-Culture Kid Mystery

# D-L Nelson

Encircle Publications, LLC
Farmington, Maine U.S.A.

# 1

## ST. PETERSBURG, RUSSIA

**"I don't usually do this."** James Morella looked at the woman standing in the Grand Hotel elevator next to him. In his travels to all parts of the world hookers had approached him, probably because when he was on the road—which was far too often in his opinion—he ended up in hotel bars to nurse a single scotch. He didn't like alcohol all that much but sitting in bars watching people was better than a hotel room with little English on the television or just one or two Anglo-news stations telling the same stories over and over.

He'd also been approached by business women and ignored them too, although more politely. He had categorized this woman as a business woman. Hookers didn't have a white streak blending into steel gray hair with a perfect cut. Nor did they wear Armani business suits. If he needed one word to describe her, it would be senatorial.

Alice La Russo, as she'd introduced herself, had the skin tone of a woman in her early thirties at most with no trace of a face lift. He didn't doubt her when she said she was from Boston. She had the bearing of a Boston Brahmin with the correct accent substituting the letter R for the letter H.

In his room, James and Alice chatted about Cambridge where he'd gone to Harvard Business School as they sipped a good French Bordeaux. Like him, she told him, she was on business in Russia, but whenever he asked her more about her work she turned the subject back toward him.

He was happily married, more or less, despite his job as a vice president of a Boston-based multi-national. It took too much time away from his family and not just when he was on the road. He put in long hours at the office and even when he went home, he would lock himself in the room set aside as his office there.

His wife, Marianne, a doctor with an HMO, was too occupied to complain. They did manage to schedule two-week vacations together each summer and a week at Christmas where they renewed their marriage. Since it worked for both of them, he accepted it as life— full stop.

As for his son, from the time he came home from the hospital, a screaming little mass of flesh, nannies had taken care of him until he was stashed at Phillips Academy in Andover.

He wasn't given to committing adultery. A good Catholic school education kept him faithful, mostly. He knew it was childish, but the couple of times he'd strayed, he was convinced Sister Marie-Louisa would appear with her ruler, screaming "Jamie Morella, you will go straight to Hell!"

If he hadn't been so horny and Alice so striking, he probably would have just gone back to his room and prepped for tomorrow's meeting rather than follow up on her suggestion. On one hand, that they were both from the same area was not a reason to do what he was about to do. On the other, it was a touch of home, where he had not been for the past three weeks.

There was still time to back out, but what the hell… why not? No one would ever know.

Each time he unlocked his hotel door, he felt he had walked back in time. The brocaded wallpaper and antique furniture were far more upscale than his usual on-the-road accommodations, although his job title allowed him to travel in comfort-plus. His upbringing in a good Italian family—where his father, a factory worker, grew vegetables in their modest back yard, and his mother doled out his salary in envelopes marked mortgage, electricity, food, etc.—made splurging hard for him even on an expense account.

At the same time, if he didn't take the perks that the other vice presidents did, his co-workers, those he competed against, would sense it as weakness. Competition for the next step on the career ladder made the Super Bowl look like kindergarteners playing with a Nerf ball in a sand box.

Often, he felt as if he'd been two people in one body: the kid growing up in Reading, Massachusetts, and the executive on the career ladder. It was as if his early life was a movie that he had half slept through.

This room, which cost in the four figures per night, was to impress the oligarchs that he would meet with in the morning: the expenditure, high even for his firm, was okayed by the CEO, himself.

"La Russo sounds French," he said as he unlocked the door.

"Huguenot, like Paul Revere."

He allowed her to go first. Maybe they should have gone to her room. How would he get rid of her after sex? What if his wife called, although she almost never did?

"I'll show you how the Russians drink vodka, if you let me make myself at home," Alice said.

He gestured with his hand.

She went to the minibar and brought out four small bottles, placing them on the tray which was on top of the bar, and carried it to the gold-leafed table in front of the blue silk two-seater couch.

"I'll be back." Jamie went into the bathroom and brushed his teeth. He just wasn't as good at adultery as others in his firm. At times, he felt like a total misfit. He'd had the drive to parlay a Harvard B School degree into a good job and then another good job and another and another so that at forty-nine he could be termed successful. Sometimes he wondered what it all was for.

The other executives on the team boasted about their road conquests. He'd made-up a couple to stay part of the boys' club, wondering if the others' stories were as much fantasy as his own.

Probably not.

When he returned, the bottles had disappeared. The vodka was in the crystal glasses provided by the hotel. Four-figure rent bought quality.

"You exhale, swallow it all and exhale again." Alice demonstrated with one of the glasses.

He didn't say, like my wife when she uses her asthma inhaler. The thought of his wife gave him another vision of Sister Marie-Louisa. The vision didn't stop him exhaling, swallowing and exhaling again.

The second the drink hit his tongue, he remembered he how much he hated the sensation of strong alcohol except for scotch. Yup, he was a misfit in the world he had joined. Every time the CEO praised him for a new deal, he felt he'd escaped discovery of his inadequacies.

The vodka hit hard. As he fell unconscious, he didn't see Alice wash and wipe her glass and return them to the position where the hotel staff always left them. Nor did he see her wipe everything she had touched.

But first she put on surgical gloves and touched his neck to see if she could find a pulse. There was nothing.

She went to his laptop on the desk. Against company policy, Jamie had not shut it down when he'd gone down to the bar. With two clicks she brought the laptop to life.

Going into Word she typed in the Russian she'd gleaned from a computer translation program finding the characters that she'd located in the symbols file. "I'm sorry... I had no choice but to poison him."

That will drive the police crazy, she thought as she let herself out the door into the corridor and down the elevator and back to her own hotel. Her flight home wasn't until tomorrow at noon.

# 2

EDINBURGH, SCOTLAND

**"He was murdered. It wasn't** an accident." Chantal Bosset MacAndrew poured a cup of coffee for Annie Young-Perret, her former Swiss neighbor, and then gave herself a second cup. Chantal had never developed the tea-for-every-important-discussion typical of Edinburgh dwellers although she'd lived in Scotland for fifteen years. Her French accent had melted into an almost brogue making both English and French hard for Annie's concentration.

Annie's slowness in responding wasn't in understanding the words but following the story behind those words. The phone call two days ago from Chantal asking her to please, please, please come to Edinburgh to help her combined with the "I will explain everything when you get here," made Annie fly out two days later.

The women had been neighbors in Corsier Port, a Geneva, Switzerland suburb, throughout their years at the *lycée*, but they were never close friends, despite staying at each other's homes when their parents were away. They had some overlapping courses and they crammed for exams together. Chantal had a more business, practical bent, where Annie could never take enough history courses to satisfy her curiosity about the past.

Now Chantal was the curator of a still-to-be-opened, small Edinburgh museum by the Early Scottish Poets Memorial Foundation dedicated to the preservation of national poetry before the 1600s. She was also a new widow.

Annie Young-Perret was a part-time tech writer and amateur historian, who was married to the Argelès-sur-mer, French retired police chief Roger Perret. They had a small daughter Sophie. Annie was more a friend than step-mother to Roger's university-student daughter, Gaëlle.

Annie understood Chantal's desire to go into museum curation although it was badly, badly paid. "It's a stepping stone to a larger museum and I love every minute of my day," Chantal had told Annie, who considered enjoyment of work more important than payment.

One of the reasons they hadn't been better friends back in Switzerland was that Annie had thought Chantal too predictable, too unadventurous. Later she had discovered how wrong she was when in her second year at the university, Chantal had gone camping, met Duncan MacAndrew and had what the French call a *coupe de foudre*: love at first sight. She'd finished her studies at Edinburgh University. Duncan was at nearby Napier University where he'd studied human resource administration.

Chantal's parents had been less than happy to have their daughter in another country but consoled themselves that it would never last. But unlike many *coupe de foudres* that burned out as quickly as a lightning bolt disappears, the couple had grown stronger and stronger over the years. Annie's mother, Susan had commented as Annie was packing to catch her flight to see what the problem was, that when she was with Chantal and Duncan it was like being with one person.

Annie watched Blane, the MacAndrew's two-year old son, push a truck around the kitchen floor making zoom-zoom sounds. Anyone, who thought there are no gender differences between boys and girls, would just have to watch her own daughter and Blane to see how pronounced those differences could be even as toddlers.

Thinking of Sophie made her wish she hadn't come without her, although she knew the baby was being more than well-cared for by her parents.

Sophie was a quiet baby, a year younger than the long-awaited Blane produced by fertility treatments after years of postponement while the MacAndrew built their careers and years of trying for a pregnancy without results.

Annie had become pregnant by accident.

"Why me?" Annie had asked Susan, her mother, about why Chantal had been so insistent she come. Her mother had gone to France to pick up the baby and took her back to Geneva.

"Why not?" Susan had asked. "You've solved other murders, but I do wish you would find another hobby. This one can be dangerous."

Annie felt discombobulated: the phone call, the flight to Scotland all happened so fast that she had to force her thoughts back to the why and now.

Chantal's kitchen was cozy. One wall was brick. The cabinets needed refinishing. Even if the house was old and only partially renovated, it felt like love had been there that even mourning could not hide.

"I tell you he was murdered." Chantal blew on her coffee. Steam fluttered around her face. "That was no regular hit and run."

Annie picked up her own newly-poured coffee, although she would have preferred tea. She was almost sorry to have given into Chantal's pleas, but there was no reason not to come that she could have thought of. A moment of nostalgia for her own kitchen in Argelès-sur-mer enjoying a few days of singledom hit her.

Her husband Roger was at a reunion of detectives at the 36, the famous Parisian crime unit where he'd worked for years before transferring to Argelès-sur-mer as police chief. After the reunion, he was going hunting with a couple of his old colleagues.

When she told him about Chantal's request over Skype, he encouraged her to help her friend. So much for the hope that he would discourage her. His disapproval of any of her mystery-solving activities was often and strong. She ignored them—except when she wanted an excuse not to do something.

As they had settled into their marriage each accepted the other's traits far more than they had when they were just dating. What had been a series of huge battles followed by making-up was no longer a cycle more predictable than the seasons before climate change. Now it was more a resignation rather than waste the energy to try and change either themselves or each other.

"I'll pick up the baby from your parents, join you in Edinburgh or go back to Argelès depending," he'd said.

"A hit and run is murder," Annie agreed trying to concentrate on what her friend was saying rather than thinking about her daughter and husband.

"The car that hit him was stolen from a car rental agency."

"Kids joy-riding? Drunk? Drugged?"

Chantal put down her cup and stared into Annie's eyes. "The car was wiped clean. Wiped clean. Spotless. Nothing."

"Smart kids joy riding?" Annie didn't want to appear glib. She was aware that Chantal had lost her *âme soeur*, her soul mate. Despite the disparities between Roger's world view and her own, she couldn't imagine life without him. She'd gotten a taste of what that might be when he had had his almost fatal heart attack that forced his early retirement.

"And he'd nearly been hit before. Four times total."

Annie looked confused.

"Three times before he was killed a car tried to run him over. I was with him once, about a month ago. We were on a sidewalk and if there hadn't been a driveway that we ducked into, I wouldn't be here talking to you now."

"The car came after you on the sidewalk?"

Chantal nodded. "And when I mentioned that the driver must be drunk, Duncan said it had happened to him twice before, but both times in the morning when people shouldn't have been drunk. I can show you the places in Edinburgh, but not the one in London. I don't know where that is. The local one is a residential neighborhood when we were coming back from dropping some of Blane's outgrown clothes at some friends."

Annie had to admit that multiple near misses were strange.

"Also, Duncan had been acting strangely, very withdrawn, and that never happened before."

"Did you ask him?"

"Repeatedly. He just said work, Duncan did."

Annie knew that Duncan was in human resources at a large multi-national company, although when he started there it had been a Scottish company only. AGG had bought out the company. She had no idea what AGG stood for. Duncan's company had been in magazine publishing, mostly trade magazines for different industries. According to Chantal, they were still doing the same thing.

"I want you to investigate."

Shit, Annie thought. "Why?"

"Well I know that you were indirectly involved in solving a couple of other murders and that Roger was a police detective and together..."

"I wouldn't know even where to start." Annie had never thought she'd come across one murder, never mind more than one. As for solving the crimes—she'd always felt that it was by accident that she'd found the guilty person. It hadn't been that much different than searching through historical records or deciphering old manuscripts. If anything, she was more interested in learning about the lives of the poets who would be represented in the new museum where Chantal was curator.

Chantal went to a drawer next to the one where she kept the spoons and brought out a newspaper clipping. On the top was a date from three days before, the day Chantal had called her. Circled in red was a help wanted ad looking for a translator on a short-term contract multi-lingual translator at Duncan's old company.

"I think the company had something to do with it," Chantal said. "He loved his job before AGG bought his company. Than he changed."

"Companies don't go around murdering their employees." Annie put her hand over Chantal's to try and balance her negative attitude to the theory.

"At least apply for the job," Chantal said.

# 3

## EDINBURGH, SCOTLAND

Annie checked the AGG address written on a scrap of paper. Grocery List was written on the top and there were drawings of vegetables at the bottom.

The company, where Duncan MacAndrew had worked before his death, wasn't housed in a modern office building in one of those soulless industrial parks just outside the city as Annie had expected it would be. Instead it was two blocks from Princes Street, the main shopping drag.

AGG had taken over a circle, which wasn't a real circle, just like Piccadilly Circus in London had nothing to do with a circus. It was, instead, a semi-circle of gray-stoned, three-story attached buildings that once had been mansions. A driveway with a landscaped garden that was between the main road filled the space between the street and the company.

Annie hadn't accepted Chantal's offer to loan her the car, partially because she didn't like to drive on the left and because it was a short tram ride. She could have walked, but a drizzle made her decide better to arrive dry. In rain her long, red hair frizzed even more. Despite wrestling it into a French twist, tendrils had sprung out all over her head. She described it as her Medusa look.

Half of her thought that if she were interviewed looking like a frazzled witch, they wouldn't hire her: she could tell Chantal, she tried her best without lying. It would put an end to Chantal's misconceptions that Annie being on the inside of Duncan's company might find out about his murder, if it were murder. About the only reason Annie gave any credence to Chantal's murder theory was that the number of near accidents were above logical chance.

Her conscience wouldn't let her lie. Damn her conscience. More than one time in her life it had landed her in trouble.

She wasn't surprised at the speed of the response to her résumé. With her English, French, German and Dutch fluencies, companies realized she could do the work of several translators, saving them money, although she demanded a higher compensation. Almost every time she applied for a job she would get the contract. However, this wasn't a contract job but a full-time post, something she had avoided all her working life. Not having a regular job was one of her goals.

Within a half hour of emailing her résumé, the phone had rung. That was yesterday. Because the last thing Annie had expected to do in Scotland was anything professional, her jeans would have been inappropriate. She'd rushed to the charity shops for something more businesslike.

She'd found a green suit in the first Oxfam shop where she'd looked. It would do her for years. Her black turtleneck looked as if it had been picked to match the oversized black buttons. Annie, who wasn't ever overly concerned with her appearance, thought she looked dynamite and super-professional frizzy hair or not.

Damn it!

Why *am* I getting involved, she wondered as she sat in a semi-comfortable, stuffed chair upholstered in a floral chintz outside human resources. A woman emerged, smiled and stretched out her hand.

"Fiona Clark. Please call me Fiona."

"Anne Young-Perret, but everyone calls me Annie."

"Annie it is."

Annie found herself liking this woman immediately whom she guessed was in her mid-thirties like herself. She usually thought of HR people as Human Remains, caring only about rules and not thinking of development of staff or personalities.

"I'm so glad you could come in so quickly."

Annie guessed the HR suite had once been an apartment by its reception area which would have been the entrance hall with four closed doors off it. A fifth, partially closed, showed a kitchen sink, cabinets and half-sized refrigerator.

As she looked around, she wanted to comment on the arrangement, but before she could, Fiona asked, "Are you thinking this is a strange set-up for a company?"

Annie nodded.

The woman opened the door with a bronze plaque with the word Fiona Clark HR Director engraved on it.

The room was more like a living room. A fire burned down to coals in the marble fireplace. The rain-streaked bay window had a cushioned window seat in front of it, which would be perfect to curl up with a book. There was a circular table but no desk. Folders, color-coded Annie guessed, filled the built-in oak bookshelf. A couch and coffee table with a bouquet of flowers made the room cheery.

Fiona waved Annie to a seat on the couch and sat next to her, tucking her legs under herself. "Part of the building has been completely rebuilt to be more like regular offices, corridors and all that. However, in HR we wanted to maintain a friendlier feel so our employees wouldn't be as intimidated when they came to see us. I shouldn't say this but corporate keeps threatening to make my department change to a more corporate look, but we keep delaying."

As Fiona talked, Annie found her liking increasing. She almost had to pinch herself to remember that she was here to become an insider and to prove to her friend that Duncan MacAndrew hadn't been murdered by AGG.

No, she was doing this more to put Chantal's mind at rest that the company he'd worked for wasn't responsible directly or indirectly. That Duncan worried about his job made him like most office workers in today's world.

A few days weren't a big sacrifice to make.

Fiona explained Edinburgh was AGG's European headquarters. Annie wasn't surprised when Fiona said that Delaware was their official international headquarters, although most of the bigwigs worked out of Boston. So many companies used Delaware for tax advantages operating a postal box while existing elsewhere.

"Here's the project. The company is doing major changes to all its HR policies to bring the new acquisitions in line with the other subsidiaries. We have offices in Germany, Holland, Italy, France, Sweden, Romania..." She went on to name at least ten more countries. "We want all our documents in the local languages for all the companies. Most of the policies are the same, but there are differences for local laws, of course where they don't conflict with the European Law. We won't discuss Brexit. For security, we don't want to hire translation services."

Annie knew what was coming next. Anyone multi-lingual would save the company money.

"When we saw that you could do three of the languages we needed, we wanted to talk to you."

"Because I went to school in Holland, Germany, and francophone Switzerland, I speak, read and write like a native in all three."

"And you're a dual Swiss-American citizen."

Annie knew that meant she could work in any European Union country even if Switzerland wasn't part of the European Union. At least that was true for the moment. A recent vote by the Swiss had limited immigration into the country, which meant that as soon as certain details were worked out, the Swiss might not have the same employment rights in the EU as before.

Not for the first time, Annie wondered if she should go for a French passport, too. She'd been there five years. Her husband was French. Her daughter was French. That wasn't today's decision. She had to get the job, find out that Chantal was wrong, quit and go home.

"Later we can do paperwork to bring on staff full time, assuming we like you and you like us. Do you mind taking a test?"

"Not at all?" Annie said.

The language exams were computerized. Fiona had brought her a cup of tea and a chocolate biscuit and told her the test wasn't timed. Annie found the vocabulary and grammar parts simple. Short essays in each language did not take more than fifteen minutes. As a tech writer, brevity and clarity were encouraged.

As she was getting ready to find Fiona, the woman stuck her head in. "I'm through." Annie pointed to the computer screen.

"I was going to ask you if you wanted a break. Now let me invite you to lunch while my assistant looks at the results."

\* \* \*

Lunch was at a healthy sandwich bar that had only four tables. The menu was on a board behind the counter. Because Fiona chose an aubergine and mint sandwich, Annie did too as much to ingratiate herself than desire.

Fiona asked several questions including why Annie wanted to move to Edinburgh from the South of France.

"In my spare time I write books, usually with a historical figure. Edinburgh has such a rich history to choose from."

Her lie made her wondered if Quentin, her editor and publisher, might be interested in a book about Scottish poets. He had been pleased with the sales on her first two books, although the one about the seventh century nun hadn't sold as well as the one about the woman who swam to shore after the Brits had bombed the ship she was on toward the end of the World War II.

Annie wouldn't have bought the second book either. She'd detested the woman and had never understood why Quentin had been so gung-ho about it.

"I grew up here, I agree. I'm disgustingly in love with this place despite the weather. What about your husband and daughter?"

"They're moving here as soon as Roger winds up some details." Annie knew that a permanent move to Edinburgh would be about 3,873,563 on Roger's to-do list. He wanted to be in a francophone environment in a warm climate and for all of Edinburgh's charm those two characteristics weren't on the city's advantages list. Annie wasn't about to share that information.

Fiona's phone dinged. Annie left the table to let the woman talk privately and went to the counter to order a second up of herbal tea. She hand-signaled a question if Fiona wanted a cuppa too. Fiona nodded.

When Annie returned to the table with the two cups of tea, Fiona was smiling. "You scored in the ninety-eighth percentile. Congratulations, you have the contract if you want it. Three-month trial through your company, but I think there's a good chance that IT will want you after that. Don't take it as a promise. I can't speak for them or their future needs."

"I won't. I do want the post. Let's talk salary."

"Eighteen pounds an hour."

"That's a lot lower than I usually make. And remember I'm doing the work of three people." Annie wasn't going to say no regardless of salary. Money wasn't her purpose for working there, but without a little negotiation, she might raise suspicions.

They settled on twenty pounds, still lower than Annie was used to, but three months maximum in a city she loved, was fine with her: Roger would be a different story. If things dragged out, he would have to bring the baby maybe staying through Christmas, not something that would make him happy.

She stuck out her hand and Fiona shook it.

"I'll email you the contract this afternoon. Can you start Monday?"

"Yes."

Fiona apologized that she had to get back to the office. "If you need any help settling in, we'll be glad to help."

As soon as Fiona was no longer visible through the snack bar's window, Annie dialed Chantal to tell her that she had the job. Then she called Quentin.

"Quentin Taylor." His voice was as sexy as his appearance with his wavy hair always grazing his collar and his eyelashes that would be considered fake on a woman. What Annie found the most attractive about him was the smile which never seemed to leave his face. Maybe because his publishing company, EP standing for Esoteric Publishing, was a labor of love, that broke even—but barely.

"Hey Annie," he said when he realized who was on the phone.

She explained her idea.

"Go for it. I can't pay an advance, but I'll up your percentage on sales once we cover costs."

Annie herself wasn't profit-motivated so she understood Quentin was operating on half a shoestring with his father's threat of demanding the startup loan he'd issued his son hanging over his head.

"Works for me," she said. It would be another tick in the "I've got to convince Roger this is a good idea."

# 4

**"Jesus! Mary! Joseph! Annie, you** *want* to take a job in Edinburgh?" Roger Perret's voice over Skype grew softer and softer until it was almost a whisper, a sign he was angry. She didn't have video.

"It's to help Chantal." Annie tried to keep her voice slow and low as well. Normally, in a situation when she wanted Roger to agree to something which he didn't want to, her speech went a hundred miles an hour.

She'd started the conversation asking about his hunting trip. He'd bragged that they would have venison all winter, although winters in Argelès-sur-mer were mild.

Venison seemed to her as a cold-weather food. Winters in Argelès were nothing like the winters she'd grown up with in New England, Holland, Germany or Switzerland as she moved with her father's work assignments. At the time, she'd hated it, always being not just the new kid but the new kid that had to learn a new language.

"You'll be grateful someday," her mother had said as the two of them would sit after dinner memorizing verb forms.

As an adult, Annie knew they had been right, and now she was even adult enough to admit it to them, but only once.

When she was wrong in her marriage, she would admit it. Deep down, she felt she was wrong to ask Roger to go on what she felt was a useless mission, but she wasn't ready to admit it. She promised

17

herself if she had to in the future, she would. If she could avoid it, however, she would also.

Her attention came back to his conversation about his old colleagues.

"So many of them had grown old and bored with retirement."

"At least you aren't bored or boring," she said. "What else happened?"

Only after he finished did she raise the subject of Edinburgh again. "It won't be more than three months if that."

"Jesus! Mary! Joseph!" Roger exhaled.

"And I talked with Quentin."

Roger sighed. "And what crazy project does he have in mind?"

Annie bristled at the word crazy, but this wasn't the time to react. Quentin with his long black curls and perpetual smiles wasn't someone Roger had taken to. He didn't understand how the man could be so happy working so hard to publish books that so few people cared about nor did he understand how he could be content with so little money.

Roger wasn't particularly materialistic, but Quentin, in his mind, relied too much on his father's wealth. Nothing Annie could say could convince him that the father was only a backstop for the business and Quentin would take a second job when necessary to make his living expenses.

Any suggestion that Annie seek a "real" publisher would have made Annie laugh because what she wrote for Quentin would not interest "real" publishers. That anyone read her books pleased her.

"He wants me to write about Scottish poets throughout the centuries."

"A guaranteed bestseller," Roger mumbled. "What is about you that you find cold places to stay in fall and winter when Argelès is so beautifully warm?"

Annie mustered her arguments. Sure, last year at this time she'd dragged her family to the Swiss Alps where there had been snow on the ground in October. This she would *not* bring up.

She debated saying, "It's only September, not winter," but thought better of it. Last year she'd had them spend much too long, according to Roger, in Schwyz while she completed an assignment writing a family history. It had come with a murder of one of the owners.

The word "murder" would not make Roger happy. Even as an ex-detective with many solved murders to his credit, he did not understand why and how his wife tripped across so many crimes—nor did she.

She chalked it up to having many friends all over the world because of her upbringing: it wasn't her fault that those friends had bad luck.

"I haven't taken an assignment away from home for nine months." Most of her projects were done in the small office set up for her in their smallest bedroom.

Last summer was the first where they enjoyed the tourist area as a family. He'd always worked extra hours during June–August when the police were busy with tourist problems: a missing child, accidents, a stolen car and the usual drug sales by dealers who came down from Paris.

Just before Chantal called, they had sat in a café along the beach. Roger leaned back in his chair and said, "I never had time to just sit and drink a—fill in the blank—coffee, beer, sangria, Banyuls, wine."

Annie wasn't going to remind him of that either. "I'll do my research at the same time." She refrained from using the phrase about two birds and a stone. Despite Roger's excellent English there were clichés she often had to explain, and she didn't want to get sidetracked. "But I'll be bringing in some money."

"We don't need the money. My pension is more than enough." After his heart attack, Roger's pension had kicked in. Because they lived modestly, they lived well without spending much money. His house was paid for, because of the high sale price of his Parisian apartment sold for the move south compared to the lower southern prices.

The couple enjoyed just sharing space, walking on the nearby beach, which made Annie think of all the "looking-for-a-man ads" she'd read making the claim about beach-walking pleasures. She'd never followed up, because she hadn't wanted to be married. Falling in love with Roger caused her a sharp right turn in life which never ceased to surprise her.

"And Chantal thinks her husband was murdered." Time to throw that into the conversation pit.

Annie timed the silence. After ninety-one seconds Roger spoke. "Well at least tell me why Chantal thinks her husband was murdered."

"A hit and run... they found the car... stolen... wiped clean of prints." She hoped that would catch his interest. "More important he'd had other hit and run attempts earlier in Edinburgh. Also a car came after him in London."

"And the others?"

"I don't have the details. You would be good at ferreting them out."

The silence told Annie she'd piqued his interest, so she pressed forward.

"Chantal says we can stay with her. The company will do her good. And Sophie will love playing with her son..."

How much further should she press? The words "don't over sell" came to mind. Definitely she would not say that Roger could take care of both children, saving Chantal money. AGG did have a small policy as one of their benefits, but £25,000 pounds would not go far.

"And it will give you something to do. Maybe consider Chantal's theories." If that didn't do it, nothing would. Roger missed working. Even after he left 36, the famous Paris Police headquarters for the calmness of Argelès, he had missed the murder investigations which, instead of having several to deal with at a time, were rare.

Annie shut up and waited and waited and waited.

"I know you are waiting for me to agree," he said after what seemed like many minutes had gone by. "I'll pick Sophie up at your parents and book a flight ASAP."

Annie gave an arm pump. "I love you."

"You'd love me no matter what I said."

"I know," she said, anxious to end the call and tell Chantal the good news.

# 5

**A**nnie liked the Edinburgh airport. It was not like the gigantic Heathrow or Frankfurt airports, which seemed more like large malls. This airport had the requisite few restaurants and shops. Decorations included photos of the long-haired cows and men in kilts playing bagpipes. So many airports were almost impossible to tell which city one was in until a sign revealed its location—not so here. The air was almost tartan.

Chantal had offered her the car, but Annie was uncomfortable driving on the left side of the road, although she had done it when she'd researched that stupid nun's life for her second book. Chantal had enough worries without Annie smashing up the MacAndrew's vehicle.

Chantal had kept saying how sorry she was that she couldn't go herself but there was a board meeting at the museum.

Annie understood.

The direct bus to the airport was only a couple of blocks from Chantal's home.

The arrival board said that the Perret plane had landed. She knew that Roger would have checked luggage taking longer than if he only travelled with carry-on. His carry-on was the baby and as much of her paraphernalia which the low-cost airline allowed.

Annie sometimes wished that when she went anywhere all she only had to do was to throw a few essentials into her backpack like

21

in the old days but not if it meant giving up Sophie and Roger. She'd seen kids with mini backpacks shaped like ducks or penguins and someday she'd buy one for her daughter and teach her to travel light.

It seemed forever for them to appear, but then, there they were. Roger held the baby as he pushed a caddy with two large suitcases and a stroller balanced on top with his free hand. Sophie spied her mother before her father saw his wife.

Annie swooped her daughter into her arms breathing in her still baby smell. No diapers to change immediately.

Annie tried to gauge his mood at being here.

Roger leaned over and kissed his wife. "Chilly."

Annie's antenna went up, afraid of a potential fight. She did get tired of their disagreements over her working assignments which took her all over Europe.

For years, she had managed to work only part time by doing translations and tech writing. The part-time Roger liked, even though he knew she'd worked out the schedule long before he was in her life. He also had learned to accept her absolute passion to explore different historical topics.

What he couldn't see was why she couldn't find work closer to home. Both had grown weary of all their argument's variations. At one point, Annie had said to Roger, "I can tell exactly what you are going to say, you can tell when I'm going to say. How about switching? I'll pretend I'm you and you pretend you're me?"

He'd agreed. It had been the watershed conversation leading to acceptance of the other's point of view without changing his own. Neither could explain how it worked or why it worked, but the couple had grown closer.

Roger's heart attack almost two years before and his forced early retirement created a new dynamic. He was free to travel with her.

Sophie's arrival, completely unexpected and unwanted, was also a major change to their couple. Now, neither could or wanted to imagine life without her.

"You or the weather?" she asked.

"Both." He kissed Annie on the top of the head.

Annie was amazed at how much she had missed the baby. She was never a woman who oohhed and ahhed over babies. Babysitting had not been considered a source of income no matter how desperate she might have been for extra money.

Roger, who had raised one daughter on his own, was rediscovering that sleepless nights were worth the delights of a smiling baby—almost.

The bus came quickly. "Okay, so brief me on what is going on. In detail."

Good, she thought. She was counting on his love of the hunt for a criminal kicking in. Annie told him about Chantal trying to set up a new museum for Scottish poets, her financial problems left by Duncan's death, which Chantal was sure was murder, and why.

"Hit and runs are murder," Roger said.

"I told her the same thing."

"Maybe he should look both ways before crossing the street?"

"What about cars coming up on a sidewalk?"

"More than coincidence," Roger said.

# 6

EDINBURGH, SCOTLAND

**"T**his was where Duncan and I had to jump into this garden."
Chantal said.

Annie stopped pushing Sophie's stroller or push chair, as Chantal
called it. Roger pushed Blane in his. Both had a plastic cover to keep
the kids from the mist. The adults wore plastic raincoats with hoods
and hats but carried no umbrellas.

They were on a residential street of individual brick houses, close
together with either small gardens of yellow and orange flowers:
Annie knew the names of none. "Pretty" was the way she'd described
most flowers, adding red, violet, yellow, small and/or big.

A few homeowners had paved half their space with flagstone or
concrete to park their cars reducing the amount of floral displays. All
houses had some type of garden, as if everyone was competing with
their neighbors to produce the best-looking one.

"Why was he here?" Roger asked.

Annie and Chantal had only told him they had something they
wanted to show him and "bundle up."

"Two reasons. He was checking on an allegedly sick employee,
whom the company thought was faking. I was dropping off some
baby clothes Blane had outgrown at a friend's living nearby."

Chantal rummaged in her bag for her phone and snapped several
pictures. "You can still see where the car damaged the hedge." She
pointed at broken branches the width of an automobile. The garden

24

behind the hedge was one of the more elaborate on the street.

Roger used his phone to snap photos from various angles, including a close-up of the tattered branches. "How long ago was that?"

"Duncan died a month ago yesterday and it was three days before that."

A man, overweight and with a comb-over, stomped out of the house. He wore an Irish knit sweater with leather-patched elbows and dusty-looking brown cord pants. A newspaper, its masthead hidden, was stashed under his arm. "What the hell are you doing photographing my property?"

Roger spoke in a French accent, far heavier than normal. "*Monsieur*, we are tourists and are fascinated by what the Anglos do to their gardens."

The man was probably about Roger's age and Annie guessed he was some middle-level manager who had developed a middle-level pot belly. She guessed his staff didn't particularly like working for him.

Chantal picked up Roger's idea. "We mean no harm. We live in the north of France where the weather is not, how do you say, not different from here. We were hoping for ideas… and…" she swept her arm up and down the street. "You are one of the few *maisons* that have not hidden part of your yard with bricks and stones."

Annie could have used a machete to hack through her accent. Even when Chantal was first learning English, she'd never had such a thick accent.

The man frowned, but not from unhappiness. He hadn't understood. Chantal repeated.

"Please stop taking photos." He turned and as he stamped back into the house he muttered, "Damned froggies," or that was at least what Annie thought she'd heard.

"*Nous parlons en français,*" Roger said, "*Jusqu'à il fermera la porte.*" The door shut.

"A car could have come over the curb easily," Annie said as she pointed to the intersection directly opposite the man's damaged hedge. There aren't any trees to stop it and I don't see cars parked on the street."

"No skid marks," Roger pushed Blane across the street and was followed by the women.

Chantal said. "The skid marks would be long gone by now. But you can see the force if the hedge is still damaged. I'm surprised the old grouch hasn't replaced it."

"What about the other attempts?" Roger asked.

If he used the word attempts, he believes, Annie thought.

"The London one was when Duncan was there for a meeting. He'd parked his rental car in a garage. As he walked down one of the aisles, a car almost careened into him."

"Did he say what kind?" Annie asked. She and Chantal had already been over all this, but she knew her husband well enough that dishing out information in small doses would increase his commitment level in a way that just telling him the entire story at once did not.

"He said it happened too fast other than remembering it was a gray sedan. He jumped out of the way and fell, hurting his shoulder," Chantal said.

"So, if someone really wanted to kill him, how would they know where he was?" Roger asked. "Witnesses?"

Chantal shrugged. "Duncan said no one was around. I can't think of anyone who might hate him enough to kill him, before you ask."

The rain had increased. They ducked into a pub with a clichéd blue plaid rug and a dark, mahogany high-backed seating built into the walls. Only one couple was sitting in the dining area which had a small fireplace with a blazing log. More logs were stacked to one side. The couple was maybe in their late fifties and didn't seem to have anything to say to one another judging by the pursed mouth on the woman and the man looking at anything but his wife.

Annie hoped she would never reach that stage with Roger. She also hoped he would live to be as old as the man. She still realized how lucky he was that he was alive at all, and although that would never stop her from disagreeing with him, it did help her sort real issues from unimportant ones. Time together was no longer limitless.

"Pub grub. I'm hungry. I'll have the jacket potatoes," Roger said.

By the time the waitress had brought their food, both children had fallen asleep in their strollers. Annie prayed that Roger wouldn't disparage the meal. His French sensibilities when it came to cooking were always on high alert, as if he felt he had to live up to some stereotype. She needn't have worried: he tucked into his food.

Roger asked, "Annie told me that you think it might be work-related. Why would anyone from his job want to kill your husband?"

"I can't think of any," Chantal said. "He's in HR. HR isn't a high security job in a publisher of trade magazines. No IT secrets. Nothing governmental. *Rien.*"

"What about an unhappy employee?" Annie asked.

"He never mentioned any. He was more involved in benefits, training, development. I don't think he ever fired anyone at AGG. That was left to Fiona," Chantal said. "His assistant."

"She's the one that hired me," Annie said to her husband.

"And the other try?" Roger asked.

"He wouldn't talk about it seriously other than saying he was tired of ducking cars. Duncan was one to make jokes about everything. It was his way of coping with problems," Chantal said.

Roger and Annie stopped eating to listen.

"I knew he was scared when he said he was going to buy more life insurance. He even said he hoped they paid out more for people who were run over." Her smile was more wistful than anything else. "He died before he could."

Blane started to stir in his push chair. Sophie stayed asleep. Chantal handed her son a piece of bread. He nibbled it and fell back asleep.

"Did he have a lover who wanted him to leave you? Or a lover with a jealous husband?"

Annie wished that Roger had prefaced the question a bit more diplomatically. She knew that Chantal had really loved Duncan and his loss was too much an open wound.

The question didn't seem to bother her. "If he did, he hid it well."

"Any change in his behavior?"

"For the last six months he kept saying he wanted to change jobs."

Annie cocked her head.

"Duncan had a strong sense of ethics. He felt the new owner of the company was unethical, but it's a tough job market. He sent out a few résumés, but he didn't really have time to search thoroughly."

"Unethical how?" Annie asked.

"He never wanted to talk about it. He told me I had enough on my plate trying to get the museum up and running."

# 7

## EDINBURGH, SCOTLAND

Chantal's Notes: *William Dunbar (1459?-1520?)* *poet, satirist, court something or other under James IV of Scotland . . . May have had some nobility in his blood line (note: check other sources).*

Almost 100 poems extant . . . Attended St. Andrews starting most likely at age 14 . . . Earned two degrees by 1447 and 1449 (whoops) that meant he got the degrees before he was born . . . Make that 1477 and 1479 . . . May have been a priest.

Fairly sure he went on a diplomatic mission to Denmark and Norway in 1491. He might have gone on a second mission to England with the Bishop Andrew Forman, whose mother's family name was Blackadder (no relation to BBC comedy series).

Was given a huge pension of £80 (check modern day value) . . . One contemporary doing about the same thing only had a pension of £26.

Has high place rating among the makars (explain that means Scottish poet or bard).

\* \* \*

The only kitchen sound was the clock ticking. Chantal capped her felt-tip pen, frustrated yet again that she couldn't find more about some of the poets to be featured in the museum. Sure, they had their writings, but little on their lives to make a good biography.

She'd scrolled the Internet and the universities. As one scholar had answered her e-mail request, "I can't tell you what doesn't exist." She supposed she was lucky to have what she had.

Her notebook had a cover resembling a medieval manuscript. She wasn't anti-computer, but she thought more slowly when she wrote by hand. Unlike many people, her handwriting was not only legible; it was a work of art.

She wanted a cup of coffee, but at 1:22 a.m. that would be stupid. She'd never get to sleep. She envied everyone in the house sleeping.

Blane and Sophie were tucked into the nursery. She'd given Roger and Annie her bed.

She'd made up the day bed in the alcove just off the kitchen where the clock was making so much noise. The windowless alcove was her office and a bit of library with floor to ceiling books shelves covering one wall. The wall over the day bed had tacked easel-sized paper covered with rough sketches of floor plans and displays.

A laptop was on a small table. The printer was on the floor under the table in front of the day bed.

Chantal might have been an artist, but long ago she'd decided that her talents were better used displaying art not creating it. A gallery job had led to her working at the Castle, the city's landmark perched on the hill in the center of Edinburgh. She'd overseen rotating displays, a job she'd loved.

It was at the Castle where she'd met the people who wanted to set up the new museum and tapped her for the post of director. Duncan had told her to take it despite a pay cut. He felt enjoying work was more important than money, easy to say when he was bringing in a good salary. It was Duncan, who earlier had insisted that she get her masters in museum management in Glasgow, encouraging her to do the daily commute between the two cities.

Now without Duncan's salary, her pay packet would barely cover Blane's sitter, although at this point, she could often take him with her to work. Later, when the museum was open and the presence of a toddler wouldn't be accepted, what would she do? She watched every pence, cancelling her television subscription, never letting a morsel of food go to waste.

Those problems were too huge to think about. Although she'd never been one to procrastinate on the difficult, right now, it was necessary.

Since Duncan had been killed, she couldn't sleep through the night. She did fall asleep early, but woke before midnight, staying awake until dawn. Rather than rest in bed thinking and worrying, she used the time to work.

How long she could afford to keep this job as director of the future Early Scottish Poets Museum, she didn't know.

She couldn't even guarantee they would be able to get the doors open between funding problems and internal wrangling by the board, most of whom she might have liked individually. When they were together fantasies of throat-slitting peppered her imagination. How grown, talented people could babble for hours over the inconsequential was beyond her.

However, this job was a big step for her. If she made it a success she might be able to move to a bigger museum. If it failed, she might have to leave museum work all together and find something more lucrative. The thought made her shudder as she imagined herself stuck behind a desk day after day doing something she hated.

She wondered it Annie was aware of how desperate for money she was. One of the first things her friend had done upon Roger's arrival from France was a major shop for all kinds of things that were luxuries: apples, bananas, ice cream with chocolate sauce, something she didn't even dare to dream of.

When the couple had carried in bag after bag, Chantal worried about how to pay for her share. Annie had told to her to forget paying; the food would keep Roger from moaning and groaning about Scottish food and the peace was worth the price. Besides, Annie added, "You're giving us a free room," while ignoring that they were there for Chantal's benefit.

God, she missed Duncan. He was the love of her life, as trite and like sentimental claptrap it sounded even to her. From their first date, they had been as one person.

Not that they always agreed, but they had worked out a way of negotiating, even playing rock, scissors, paper to find a compromise.

It wasn't that they were always joined at the hip either. They went off and did other things—him to his sports, her to her gospel group—then they came back together and talked about the shot he'd missed, the note she'd sung flat, the people they saw—those little details to laugh and moan about.

His last couple of months, he'd stopped sharing. When she'd asked what was wrong, he'd just said, "something at work." His worries were more than the close calls with cars, she knew. She tried to give him as much support as she could, the cup of tea when he was hunched over his computer or a back rub when she could see the tension in his face.

Enough! The museum was what needed concentration now.

She was due to meet the artist and builder at nine tomorrow morning to work on the recreation of the William Dunbar room, which would require some fake walls stretching the museum budget.

Concentration was hard. Had Duncan been alive, she'd be telling him her ideas, and he'd be giving her feedback—sometimes he had been totally off the mark, but more often he'd led her to forge better concepts.

Her notes may have been in her beautiful writing which looked as if it belonged on a medieval manuscript, but the content was tiring: create model of St. Andrews, copy of ship, type of clothing worn. So much research left to do. She wished they could afford to hire Annie to do some of it, but there was no budget. She was lucky that Annie, et.al. had come to help with Duncan's murder.

The police had not done their jobs. She was furious that when they found the stolen car which had proven to be the death car. They had chocked it up to joy-riding kids while ignoring Chantal's stories about the earlier attempts. If anything could infuriate her, it was not being taken seriously not just about Duncan's death but any time she knew what she was talking about. At least Annie and Roger believed her.

Maybe she could illustrate some of Dunbar's poems with photographs of place where appropriate.

Before Duncan's death she never had any trouble concentrating. "Don't punish yourself. You lost your soul mate," she said aloud.

"Are you talking to yourself?"

Chantal jumped at Annie's voice.

"Didn't mean to startle you. I just had to go to the bathroom, and

I saw the light from the top of the stairs." She looked at a sketch Chantal had started for the Dunbar room hanging on the wall. "It should be a great museum."

"It's hard for me to get it together. My thoughts bounce from the museum to Duncan and back again. I get so bloody sick of my mind cycling."

Annie put her arms around Chantal, who for a moment froze. Except for Blane no one had touched her since the funeral. Her family hadn't been touchers. After a few seconds, she let herself melt into the warmth. "What are you smiling at?" she asked as she pulled away.

"You using the very, very English word, 'bloody'."

Chantal nodded. "Like you, I've become a hodge-podge of different countries. I'll make tea." It was a good excuse to break away before she started crying.

With teacups in front of them, the two women, in their thick robes against the chilly house, didn't say anything for a few minutes.

It was Annie who broke the silence. "You said Duncan was different in the last few months before he died. Tell me as much of the how as you can."

"When he was first with the company he would talk about the people, the programs with enthusiasm. But after AGG bought out the company, he grew more and more silent. He didn't like his boss."

"Who was?"

"Senior VP HR. Duncan was just a vice president. No senior, just VP. The guy wasn't based in Scotland, but Boston. Still he was a micro manager."

Annie cocked her head. "Do you know where the main problems and dissatisfactions were?"

Chantal twisted her head left and right, up and down to loosen her neck muscles that often tightened when she spent too long at her desk. "Duncan thought HR was there to help the personnel, to help them develop their careers as they helped the company grow."

"And..."

"He said AGG thought employees hurt the profits needed to keep the shareholders happy."

"Why didn't he quit?"

"Too soon after he joined the old company. It would look bad on his résumé. He wasn't high enough to get one of those golden handshakes, although he'd joke that he'd take a bronze or even a copper one."

"With the price of copper, these days, I agree with him."

Chantal smiled—something she had done rarely of late. Having people, adult people, around, did help, she thought. "Do you think you'll be able to find out anything when you start work?"

"I don't know, but I'll try." Annie blew on her tea. "Roger's not a great computer person, but he's going to be looking on the Internet tomorrow to see what he can find on AGG."

# 8

A nnie sat at her desk of the AGG tech writing/translation department. Desk touched desk. Annie felt she could ask any of her neighbors to reach over and scratch the itch on her face and they wouldn't have to stand. HR should test for claustrophobia as well as technical skills before hiring.

Whatever charm the space had before the company occupied and converted into office space, had been destroyed.

Annie knew from being in other buildings of this type that there were decorative moldings, fireplaces and bay windows that must have ended up in a garbage heap.

They were also set up to make sure that no worker had access to a window by erecting cloth dividers between the desks and outside world. She suspected that building regulations were the only reason that the windows hadn't been blocked. A small amount of light filtered in over the dividers.

When she peeked into other offices on the way to her own, she found that it wasn't much better. There the cloth dividers created a mouse-maze atmosphere.

She'd been cautioned that chatting with co-workers was forbidden unless it was work related. Yes, that was the word they used, F-O-R-B-I-D-D-E-N. Had Annie not had Duncan's death as a reason for being there, she would have laughed, said, "You've got to be kidding," and walked out.

35

The room was on the cold side, but she was used to everything in England being under-heated. Why should Scotland, which was even further north be any different?

She glanced at her area-mates. The heads of the three men and one woman were bent toward their computer screens. One man thumbed through a dictionary, which surprised her. Why didn't he check on-line? The rest had papers to the left of their keyboards. From time-to-time, one person or another would put their finger on a word, cock their head and sit for a moment.

Annie wondered why the documents weren't already on-line and why they didn't use one of the on-line translators to convert them into the languages they wanted and then clean up the wordage.

Whenever anyone asked about the value of on-line translators, she would give them the example that when she tried to say in English that she was a fan of Sting, it came out on the screen as in French that she was a *ventilator* (a cooling fan) of an insect.

"We expect a minimum of fifty pages daily, which is less than the others?" The supervisor, a man probably a few years younger than Annie, balding and overweight, swept his hand around the room. "That's because you'll do it in Dutch, French and German. It's so much easier after you translate the first time."

"How many languages do you speak?" Annie asked.

He paused as if he debated answering. "Only English."

"American English." It wasn't a question. His accent was US-Mid-West, but Annie wanted to establish something between them, but she wasn't sure exactly what besides not being willing to be cowed by him.

There were other questions she wanted to ask, such as why was he in Scotland, why did he go along with such a sweat-shop like atmosphere. That wasn't why she was sitting here.

Thus, he disappeared into his half cubicle to one side of the office area without her challenge. If he moved slightly to the right or left from where he sat at his desk, he would be able to see his five direct reports.

As Annie worked on her first document which were descriptions of things allowed in and on a desk of all employees, she realized not only were the measures draconian, the person who wrote the text was a terrible writer. Sentences were convoluted. She quickly did a Fogg count, a simple mathematical formula to determine the reading level needed to understand content. It came out as twenty-six years of education. Annie, with her masters in medieval history, and who considered herself intelligent, found what she was reading almost impossible to understand. Middle or even Old English would be as easy or perhaps easier.

In other assignments, she would have gone to the supervisor and offered to put the material into readable English before translation. Even if she thought it might be appreciated, this wasn't her mission.

She glanced across the room where her supervisor, "Mr.-Berry-not-Jack, we don't encourage first names here," was sitting at an angle watching everyone. He picked up the telephone.

Good Lord! Annie didn't believe that workplaces like this still existed. No wonder Duncan had decided to quit as soon as a quick job change wouldn't be a black mark on his career.

When Mr.-Berry-not-Jack, hung up, he came over to her. "HR wants to see you." He looked at his watch. "I still expect your fifty pages. If you have to stay later…"

Annie didn't ask if she would be paid overtime. She wasn't sure about UK law. Most of her contracts had outlined terms in very clear terms. This one did not.

As Annie walked through the building attached to the one where she'd been stationed to the HR offices, she observed that most of the original interior had been destroyed. Although none seemed as crowded as translations services, faces looked tense. Smiles were non-existent.

A sign on a door said, "IT ring and wait." A man, carrying a large printer did just that, using his elbow to push the buzzer.

Annie didn't see anyone answer, but she wasn't about to dawdle. During the hour that she'd been working she had only done five of her required fifty pages and those weren't in order. She'd thumbed through the paper and picked out the easiest, the lists, the ones with photos or diagrams where there was less type. Her desire to rewrite into simple English was swallowed along with the cup of coffee that she was allowed to drink at her desk, but she was told "no food" under any circumstances.

HR had its own receptionist, a young girl with half-blue, half-blond hair. She wore a sweater that showed off her breasts and a roll of flab under her breasts. Annie had not seen her when she was interviewed.

"I'm Annie Young-Perret. Mr. Berry told me to come down."

The girl smiled. At least in HR smiling wasn't considered an offense, Annie thought as the receptionist searched through a pile of folders. She pulled one out and Annie saw her name typed on the identification tab.

"Have a seat. Just go through and sign everywhere it says to sign. There are red x's so it won't be hard."

Annie opened the file. A quick count revealed twenty-one sheets of paper.

"Just sign, you don't need to read them… they're just the stuff the government wants."

Annie, in principle, read whatever she signed, even when she was on-line, and you needed to check "I agree to…" boxes.

The phone on the receptionist desk rang. "Hmm, hmm, I'll be right in," she said to whoever was on the other end.

The girl stood up. "My boss needs me. Just leave the folder on my desk."

Annie looked around the office. There was no sign of Fiona Clark, who had interviewed her.

There was a copy machine in the corner, but she didn't know how long the receptionist would be gone. She'd passed a copy machine outside, but it looked as if it needed a key card to operate.

Instead she took out her pen and her smart phone and began snapping each sheet, all the time holding the pen in her hand and keeping her back to the door where the receptionist had gone.

When she heard the handle turn, she put the phone into her jacket pocket and began writing Ann Yaung Parrot. Her legal name was Anne Young-Perret. She sloped her signature left instead of right, changed the A, Y, g and t completely formed the letters differently from her normal signature. Although she didn't know English law, she hoped if it ever came to court, the documents would be illegal. Why it would come to court, she wasn't sure.

"Not done?" the receptionist asked.

"Almost," Annie said. She had had time to notice that some of the pages were part of a whole document. One had to do with confidentiality. Another was about health and safety. She hoped she'd be able to read what she'd photographed as much as she wished she'd been able to photograph them all. The one about insurance she'd only been able to snap the first page of three.

When she was done, she went back to her cell as she was beginning to think about it. She noticed one of her co-prisoners, the only other woman, was talking with Mr.-Berry-not-Jack, who nodded several times than turned his back on her.

The woman, who was taller than Annie would have thought now that she was standing rather than hunched over her keyboard, then walked over to Annie who had just started on her next page. "I'm having trouble with a certain phrase. Can you check what I've translated from the French to make sure it makes sense?"

She put the page in front of Annie. On it was written, "Everything we do is filmed by cameras, our computers are monitored. Even the cafeteria has recording equipment. Can you meet me after work at Costa's, the one on Princes Street?"

"Of course, I'll help." Annie put her fingers on the note and nodded. "This should work." Then she read the translation below the note, made a couple of suggestions to the text. "That should do it. It was the subjunctive. I hate French subjunctives."

"So do I," the woman said.

The woman smiled. Annie smiled back.

Annie took it as an agreement on time and place.

# 9

## BOSTON, MA

**Rita Rizzoli Richardson knew that** she should go home to work on a proposal. Instead, she'd put her laptop in her car trunk, left the garage and walked across Copley Plaza past the Boston Public Library. She'd practically lived there from her first year at Boston Latin. Even when she received a full scholarship to Boston University, the library had been more than where she did her research, but her refuge from her warring family.

Behind her were the offices of AGG where she slaved each day. Slaved was the right word. However, her goal of being a vice president was in reach. Even potential VPs needed a night off, a heretical statement she would never utter in the office. Sometimes, she wondered if it was worth it.

So many days that she wished she could stay home, crawl into bed with a book and look out their floor-to-ceiling window at the tiny lake—well it was more like a pond, that bordered their property. In winter, it froze solid enough to skate, although she never had the time.

As a kid, her dream had been to be a speed skater, but she never knew how to follow up nor would her parents known if she'd asked them, which she didn't.

Her mother was a housewife. Her father worked at the local bottling plant, which took orders from big drink manufacturers. They tried to be good parents, sending her and her four brothers to Catholic school, but weren't much for encouragement for her to be anything other than what they were: lower middle class, hard workers, towing a line.

It was her passing the exam for Latin then having a great guidance counsellor that secured her the four-year Boston University scholarship. Her education had caused jibes from her family about her becoming too big for her britches, rather than any sense of pride. Although she wished it had been different, it wasn't. She'd accepted it.

More of the time, rather than thinking about her parents and siblings, she wondered why she and her husband had bought a house so far out of Boston. It wasn't because they'd yearned for a country life.

They were like guests in their own home. Tom often slept at Brigham and Women's Hospital: she worked too early and too late at the office. At least with their off hours, their commute was usually only about forty-minutes rather than the hour plus in rush-hour traffic on routes 27, 128 and the Mass Pike.

At times, she had to remind herself how lucky she'd been to even get in the door of this multi-national with businesses worldwide. A few carried the AGG label. Other companies were so twisted through a variety of legal systems that it would be impossible to trace back to the Boston headquarters.

It had taken her almost ten years to work it out herself, despite being second in command in the controller's office. Some of the ramifications worried her, especially when she'd read headlines about a disaster tied to a subsidiary of a subsidiary of a subsidiary.

When she mentioned it to her boss in passing, he'd told her, "Not to worry your pretty little head about it."

She'd weighed his misogyny against his upcoming retirement and his vacant chair that might be hers if she behaved and didn't worry her "pretty little head" that she knew was a damned smart pretty little head.

Tonight, she didn't want to think about anything work related. Tonight was her night to be a human, not a person-chasing-a-VP-title night. She and Tom would be an ordinary couple at Symphony Hall listening to the Boston Pops.

The program featured gospel, Tom's favorite music. For that reason alone, she expected him to find someone to cover until he received his text. "A patient is about to deliver twins. It will be difficult delivery. I won't leave her in the lurch." He never used text abbreviations.

"Leaving her in the lurch" to Rita meant he would make the mother-to-be have the babies on her own probably in a field somewhere instead of assigning the birth to another very competent doctor, but she didn't say it. Tom called her sense of humor, sarcasm. She called it realism.

They had season tickets for the Boston Ballet and the American Repertory Theatre. Half the time some woman went into labor either before the performances or during them. Rita couldn't understand why her husband almost never let another person cover for him, but never asked. What little time they shared, she wasn't going to spoil with unpleasantness. Besides, Tom's occupation with his work made him unaware of her occupation with her own. It gave her freedom.

She slipped into a bar across from the Boston Public Library to order a Kahlua sombrero and a serving of potato skins. She planned to walk to Symphony Hall on this unusually cool June night. The Boston heat and humidity from last week had seemed to go on holiday. As far as Rita was concerned, it could stay away forever.

In New England, anything was possible with the weather. Tom, who came from California, complained about it. Especially during a vicious snowstorm, he threatened to move back. She would cite her career track at AGG: he would kiss her and the subject would be dropped—at least until the next Nor'easter when the man they hired to plow didn't arrive when Tom was already late for his shift.

She noticed a gray-haired woman at the bar who had come in right after she had found a seat. The woman's features were sharp, but her face was far younger than her hair color would suggest by a couple of decades—maybe even more.

The woman got her drink and walked over to Rita's table. "Please don't think me rude and if you're waiting for someone, I'll go away. I hate sitting alone at a bar, but I can't face another night alone in my hotel room."

Rita didn't mind. Within a few minutes they were exchanging histories.

Alice La Russo said she was here on a business trip. She lived in New York.

Rita, who often acted too much on impulse, according to her husband, said, "I'm on the way to a Pops Concert. I've an extra ticket…"

"I'd love to go if you're offering."

As they walked down the street, Rita noticed that Alice was wearing gloves. She debated asking, but before she could Alice said, "I've a rash on my hands. I have to keep them creamed and the gloves keep me from getting things greasy."

"Can't be pleasant? Allergy?"

"Poison ivy. The itching drives me crazy. I should have known better than to pick the flowers next to the ivy."

\* \* \*

"I'm not religious," Alice said, "But 'Amazing Grace' always gives me shivers."

The two women had separated themselves from the concert goers milling toward the Green Line and headed toward where Rita's parked car at the Westin Hotel where Alice said she was staying.

The temperature had dropped even lower. Although they were shivering, they chose to walk rather than play sardine on the T.

"Let me pay you for the ticket," Alice said.

"Not necessary. I would have thrown it away otherwise. I'm just happy someone enjoyed it." Her phone beeped showing a message from Tom. "Complications. Won't be home tonight. See you in the morning, I hope."

Rita realized that Alice had read it.

"I'm sorry, I should have looked away."

"Don't be. Nothing earth shattering. My husband's a doctor, an obstetrician."

"Women pop into labor all the time, right? Usually at the worse time for whatever you want to do." Alice scratched her gloved hand.

They had reached the Christian Science Monitor building. As a girl, the Mapaporium, where one felt they were inside the globe, was one of Rita's two favorite places in Boston. The other was the garden at the Isabella Stewart Gardner museum. She always appreciated that the woman who built the palace in Boston had a name that matched with the beautiful garden. "There are two places you might want to look at tomorrow, if you're not too busy."

They arrived at the Westin Hotel.

"Would you like to come up for a thank-you drink, before you go? It could be tea. I bought some awesome cookies at a bakery today."

Rita was tired but wasn't looking forward to a drive home. "Maybe coffee to keep me awake."

She knew the Westin well. AGG kept six rooms on a full-time hold for visiting VIPs or for their officers who worked late. She'd crashed in one during a late spring snowstorm just two months before. Add to all the lunches she'd eaten there, she felt she could almost be put on staff.

Rita, as soon as she saw Alice's room, knew that her new friend was well-paid for whatever she did. It was furnished with a queen-sized bed, a three-seater couch with orange and beige cushions a desk, dresser and night stands. A window offered a view of the red-brick buildings of the Back Bay which were barely visible at night except for the small glow from the faux gas electric street lamps.

An open suitcase showed a nightgown still folded and a toiletries case. Both were in a shade of soft gray often called pearl as was a small suitcase.

Alice busied herself with the tea kettle left for the comfort of guests. "I know you said coffee, but I've a special blend of tea I travel with. Wanta try it?"

"Sure." Rita kicked off her shoes and settled on the couch. Alice's back was to her as she made the tea.

"It's a smoky tea," Alice said.

Rita took the cup and cookie that Alice handed her. She noticed that Alice didn't touch the cookie with her gloved hands but had used a tissue.

"Sorry, I don't have a proper plate."

"I've been in enough hotel rooms to know they aren't like home." The tea was good, nothing like she'd had before, but she only bought

44

regular boring tea bags at the supermarket.

God, she was tired. Hey eyes were closing.

\* \* \*

Alice watched Rita fall asleep. She took a syringe from her case and filled it with succinylcholine, sux as it was often called by the medical profession who used it to relax muscles often before things like an endotracheal intubation. The strength in this syringe would bring down a horse.

The white blouse that Rita wore was short sleeved. Alice didn't have to unbutton it to reach the unconscious woman's armpit, which needed a shave. Wonderful. The hair follicles would hide the prick mark, when the pathologist did an autopsy. She would seem young for a heart attack, and Rita doubted that they would test for sux.

Her review of this project showed her that Rita had had rheumatic fever as a child, which meant a heart weakness was more than possible. With luck this would not be considered a homicide. Even if it were, she had no connection to this woman. The project was merely another assignment.

Too bad in a way: Rita seemed nice. She didn't understand the woman's desire for a corporate career. The idea of being stuck behind a desk X hours a day was too stifling to even contemplate. But then again, few people chose her occupation, if you could call it that.

This had been far easier than Alice thought it would be. The room had been rented in Rita's name with an AGG company credit card. When Alice had moved into the room that afternoon, she wore a wig resembling Rita's hairstyle. That wig had been stashed under the mattress.

She hadn't been sure how, when or even if she would be able to get Rita up to the room. That it had happened the first day was a bonus. She would be able to finish this assignment and then take some needed time off.

This project was made so much easier because women dressed corporate like men dressed corporate. Boring, but helpful, she thought. One corporate exec was almost indistinguishable from another unless they were exceptionally beautiful or exceptionally ugly. Rita was neither.

When she'd arrived, she'd put on the surgical gloves before opening the door. Then she'd taken off the wig, replacing it with a gray one, and changed into a pants suit.

She'd set up the cookies, the sedatives. A syringe was filled with more of the same succinylcholine. She wondered why when the state executed a murderer they couldn't do it like she did or like the vets did with cats and dogs: fast and usually pain free.

Enough thinking about the last few hours: this kill was her best yet, but she couldn't let herself feel too confident. It wasn't over. This assignment had gone much more smoothly and faster than she thought it would. It had been her luck that Rita's husband had stood her up once again and she made contact much sooner than expected. On the other hand, it hadn't given her time to check, double check, triple check all the details she normally did.

She pulled off her cloth gloves replacing them with a surgical pair. When she touched Rita's neck there was no pulse. Should she risk giving her one final shot in the arm pit? No, the woman was one-hundred percent dead.

Time to clean the room. She washed her cup but left a second uneaten cookie near Rita's half eaten one. She left the prescription bottle of sleeping pills next to a half-drunk glass of water. She had had them prescribed for Rita by a doctor located in Back Bay, not that far from the office and she had assumed the Rita disguise when she did. The smoky tea had disguised the taste.

There was one more chore she needed to do. She took the woman's phone praying it was still open. It was. Bringing up the text from Rita's husband, she typed:

"Have a mean headache and am exhausted. Will stay at the
Westin tonight. I'm taking something to make sure I sleep.
Love you.
R

When Rita had sent her husband an email when they first arrived in the room, Alice saw how she'd signed, "Love, R." Rita had held the phone on her lap.

Alice's skill in reading upside down paid off.

His last word from his wife would be one of affection. Alice felt good about that.

The mention of the sleeping pills would make the death look accidental if the heart attack theory didn't fly. The dosage was not enough to have killed her. Alice considered confusing coroners almost a hobby.

This was truly an easy, easy assignment.

Back in her own home, also in Boston, she reviewed her actions, making sure she had left no fingerprints, although as far as she knew there were no record of her prints anywhere, Of course any hotel room must carry hundreds and hundreds of prints, but that was not a reason to grow complacent.

How delightful it was to be in her own bed. Travelling was beginning to wear on her: yet she knew to give up work would be boring. One could read only so many books. She'd get a good night's sleep and check out in the morning in time for her flight to Colorado Springs where she would go hiking for the weekend, fulfill another assignment and then back home to Boston, her own place, her own bed for a while.

As she fell asleep, she thought how much she deserved the mini holiday.

# 10

**"I'm having coffee with someone** I don't really know," Annie said on her cell phone. "Someone I work with who wanted to meet me off-site."

She was sitting in the designated coffee shop. Only a quarter of the tables had occupants, most with only one person who sipped coffee or tea while reading the newspaper or a book.

She had resisted the chocolate éclairs and brownies to not spoil her supper or her tea as Chantal called it. God, that woman was becoming more Scot than the native-born. A person walked by with an éclair. Despite being in her thirties, her mother's oft-repeated rejection of something sweet close to meal time had been imprinted in her psyche.

"Male or female?" Roger asked.

She knew it was curiosity behind the question, not jealousy. Blane and Sophie were chattering in the background. She would have much preferred being with the three of them.

Chantal had a board meeting for the Poet Museum and had told them not to wait for her along with her thanks to Roger she needn't worry about a babysitter for Blane.

"Female. It's all a bit mysterious while talking about something else."

"And work? How was it?"

"The word sweatshop comes to mind. Ooops, here she comes."

"I'll have 'tea' for when you and Chantal make it home. Bye, *je t'aime*."

Annie observed the woman better than she could at work because of the placement of their work stations. She was average height with shoulder length brown hair, brown eyes and a few freckles on her nose. The woman pointed to the coffee counter. Within three minutes she was seated across from Annie with a scone and a cup of tea.

"I'm Louisa MacLaughlin," she said. Annie already knew that. Louisa took the battery out of her phone before she spoke. "I've been with AGG for a year. It is probably the worst place I've ever worked in my life. And I suggest you remove the battery too."

Paranoid, Annie wondered, but maybe not. With her limited experience of the company, horrible was probably the kindest word. Before speaking, she removed her battery. "Yet you stay there."

"Single mom, two kids. I mass mail résumés. I've had a couple of phone interviews. So far, no luck. Not a good job market now."

"You're a translator."

Louisa's brogue was like a melody. Annie had to concentrate on what she was saying rather than be lulled by the sound.

"Yes, but I started as a tech writer with the IT department. Not much call for translation work here in Edinburgh. I do freelance for two international lawyers. Letters and stuff. It's not a living." She sipped her tea. "That's a secret by the way. I'd be fired if they knew I was freelancing."

"Trust me."

Silence followed.

Long ago, Annie had learned silence often brought more information than questions. She applied the technique by blowing on her own tea although it was no longer hot. Good God, wasn't this woman ever going to break down and talk?

Louisa ate half her scone.

Standoff, Annie thought. She saw a clock on the wall and she figured she'd give it another minute.

Fifty-eight seconds into the minute Louisa said, "I saw you at The Co-op with Chantal."

Annie nodded.

"How do you know her?"

"We used to be neighbors."

Louisa nodded. "Did you know Duncan?"

"Yes."

Why had Louisa wanted to meet with Annie if she didn't want to share information? Had Louisa been more than just a co-worker? She couldn't imagine Duncan being unfaithful to Chantal. Their couple had seemed so rock solid whenever they saw each other, although infrequent, usually for a drink around Christmas when both couples were visiting their respective parents.

"He was a good man: a good manager too," Louisa said. We'd worked together before at another company for almost six years."

"I never knew what he was like professionally."

"I wondered if you came to work for AGG because of Duncan."

"Why would you think that?"

"Duncan was my friend. He told me that he'd almost been run down before he was killed. I don't believe in co-incidences. I don't believe his death was an accident."

Annie was startled that Louisa shared Chantal's opinion that Duncan was murdered. She felt slightly better about pulling Roger away from home. "Did you talk to Chantal about this?"

Louisa drank more tea. "I was waiting. I wanted to give her time before telling her about the other attempts."

"Attempts?" How much had Duncan shared with Louisa? Would it match with what he had told Chantal?

"I believe someone wanted Duncan dead. He believed it too, or at least he told me he believed it."

"Did you ask him about it? Details, I mean."

"He said he didn't want to talk about it at work. We were in the cafeteria."

"Did you talk to the police?"

"I called them. They brushed me off." Her hair fell over one eye. She reached into her handbag for a clip and swept it back and fastened it at the nape of her neck.

"So why are you here?"

"I thought if you were a friend, you might convince Chantal to push the police to investigate further. Save me from having to talk to her." Chantal sighed. "I'm not very good at these things… broken china… shops… raging bulls and all that."

"Why me?"

"And I checked you out." Louisa didn't look at Annie when she said it but finished her scone instead.

"Checked me out?"

"I saw you when HR brought you around and turned you over to the asshole."

Annie wasn't surprised at that. What had surprised her that no one had introduced her to anyone including the four other employees in her cubicle.

"The notice came around about an hour later that you would be joining our staff. Of course, everyone feels sorry for you."

Annie frowned. "Because…"

"We're sorry for another person's suffering. I looked you up on the Internet using my phone when I went to the toilet. They monitor all computer use. Don't do any personal stuff."

Annie had already decided not to mix personal and work, and certainly not any detecting on her work station.

"I read the interview you did when your book came out. The one about the swimmer and the murders in Germany."

Annie made a mental note to check herself out on the Internet when she got home but not when Roger was around. She frustrated him enough without any reminders of her past escapades.

"AGG is an evil place. Bad things happen to employees." Louisa looked at her watch. "My God, I've got to run. My babysitter will kill me. Let's pretend we don't know each other at work, but we need to meet again. Maybe over the weekend?" She grabbed her coat, purse and scarf and was out the door.

# 11

EDINBURGH, SCOTLAND

Chantal's notes on Robert Henryson: *(birth and death dates unknown. (Guess 1462 and late 1490s). We've copies of his thirteen Fabillis. His room will be devoted to drawings done in a medieval style and Aesop-fable like. Recommend the size of three-feet high, two-feet wide. On the left will be his story in 15ᵗʰ Scots and on the right modern English.* She picked up her pen and added: *"We need listening posts where people can sit and listen to all the tales in both forms of English."*

Chantal suspected when the museum was done, the Henryson room would be her favorite place. The dearth of information on the poet's life and lack of originals of his work had pushed her abilities to come up with imaginative ways to show the times he lived in. She would continue searching, but held out little hope. She'd put out every feeler possible to archives and private collectors worldwide. Most had laughed at the mere idea.

She glanced at her watch: an hour before the board of directors filtered in. Her office space was cramped with its desk, file cabinet, drawing board and a couple of chairs. She suspected that it once was a pantry because it was off a very, very old-fashioned kitchen. My God, the only stove burned wood. Imagine trying to set a temperature in something like that for a cake. Yet in all the BBC period dramas, cooks brought out great pastries. She wondered how many cakes failed to rise in the old days.

The budget to turn this house into a museum came from the

Scottish government and donations. Edinburgh had many writers with worldwide reputations and international best sellers who supported the project. They gave money while cajoling everyone they knew.

Board member Maximillian Rhodes (pen name) sometimes used by Hamish Brown in his younger days when he wrote what he described as pulp fiction to pay the bills, joked that instead of The Early Scottish Poets Museum they should call it The Shoestring Museum.

The house itself had been free, left by a wealthy local poet, Anna Reed, who never published a thing. She read her work in open mikes across the city. When she was about to read, the pub would fall silent and all that could be heard was her cane tapping on the wooden floors as she shuffled to the mike.

Like Van Gogh, she became popular, well, as popular as poets can be, after death.

She hadn't lived in the house, this house. She had a modern apartment near Haymarket Station. Chantal never discovered why the woman had not renovated the house and turned it into income-producing property. More research to do, to make the building's history part of the museum's exhibition.

She wished she had income-producing property. She also suspected that creating this museum would be one of her greatest professional pleasures. Leaving it would be painful.

Or maybe she could rent out her third bedroom. Mostly, she wondered when she would begin to make decisions on her future rather than ruminate over alternatives.

This was not the time to concentrate on personal problems. The board was due to arrive far too soon. The meeting would take place in what had been the dining room. New lighting had replaced gas lamps—imagine gas lamps now.

She had insisted that the new lighting mimic the old but with the advantage of electricity. To be truly authentic they would have to light the museum with stinky, tallow candles. She could just imagine the fire inspector's face when he saw those—never mind the darkness.

She a wrote a note to consider placing a mannequin in the lobby sitting in a small cell-like room, straw on the floor, a quill pen, a tallow candle and three sheets of paper made in India in the late 1200s. Of course, that meant that the display would have to be behind glass. All they needed would be for some kid to decide to write a note on the ancient paper.

She mentally began to discount the board's objections as she readied the dining room for the meeting.

The walls had been stripped of inches of wallpaper, each ghastlier than the one under it. The walls' bumps had been sanded smooth and painted light beige.

The board would meet around the workman's table balanced on saw horses. Chantal had thrown beige printed cloth over it—her own— bought for drapes she would never make.

Paper pads and pencils were at each place. She placed several types of cheese and crackers strategically on plates so all five board members could reach them. Going to a box she pulled out two bottles of wine, one red, one white and removed the corks to give them time to breath.

"Anyone around?"

Chantal jumped. It was much too early for the board to arrive.

"I know I'm early." J.J. Harris, the artist who hopefully would get the contract to do the Henryson murals, was standing in the doorway. "I didn't scare you, did I?"

"Only a bit."

Chantal had found J.J. through a friend of a friend of a friend. The board had debated having a city-wide contest. They'd lost four months' time on that debate, Chantal thought. That none of the writers had time to publicize nor judge the entrants was the only reason, that she'd forced the issue and went searching for an artist herself.

When J.J. had taken her through his atelier three days after Duncan's funeral, she knew he was the right person. She had not said anything to him about her loss, until he mentioned that she looked upset.

"It's not you," she said.

"I've big ears and a small mouth," he'd said.

She told him. He'd put his arms around her not in any sexual way as she'd cried as she'd not cried since the policeman, looking distressed, had stood at her door. Jason had no tissues, no handkerchief, but supplied her with toilet paper.

When she apologized for breaking down, he told her no need. If they didn't become professional colleagues, they could be friends. "I won't be a predator," he'd told her. "You'll find it will happen with some of the couples you and Duncan knew. When my wife was widowed, several of her first husband's alleged friends offered to comfort her with their penises."

J.J.'s way of phrasing his wife's predicament amused Chantal despite her grief. She reminded herself that her decision must be a professional one, not one based on empathy. That was not difficult. Although, or maybe because J.J. earned his living as a children's book illustrator, his own work was magical both in design and subject.

The two of them appreciated that they were kindred spirits although not sexually, for J.J. was quite content in his marriage. Chantal remained at the stage where she still couldn't face cleaning Duncan's clothes out of his closet much less going to bed with any male. She hadn't washed the pillowcase where Duncan had last slept although the smell of his shaving lotion had long dissipated.

"What chance do you think I have?" J.J. placed his large, black portfolio on the table being careful not to disturb the cheese plates.

"I can never tell with this group," she said. "Something I think will pass without question causes them to rage on for hours and hours about some little point such as whether to put the ticket booth on the left or the right of the entrance. But the cost of a new roof they passed without even inhaling."

"Roofs are necessary."

"It could have waited a couple of years. Never mind."

J.J.'s drawings of foxes, sheep, roosters and even a nun created a world that Chantal would have loved to enter. She looked at her watch. "We've time to hang them against the walls."

"But they are only quarter-size."

"We'll make sure they are well lit."

They finished just as the first writer entered. Jackie Ferguson was almost sixty but was fighting aging with every trick possible including surgery that hadn't been as successful as the shopping-novel writer had hoped. The operations had left her expression permanently pained. The only part of her face, which the surgeons had left alone, were her lips. In moments that were less than kind, Chantal wondered when she would have them Botoxed.

Despite her vanity, there was nothing much about herself that she took all that seriously. She considered her success a fluke and accepted the jibes of another board member, Peter McEnroe, in stride.

Peter took everything about himself seriously and more than once suggested that Jackie, if she couldn't consider being on the board a great honor, might make room for someone more inclined and with more literary talent, someone like himself.

Chantal suspected had they brought on someone whom McEnroe considered his caliber, he would bristle at what he would perceive as competition in his superiority quest. She played a game with herself by timing how long it would take him into the meeting to mention he had been nominated, not once but twice, for the Man Booker prize. Chantal had been tempted to buy him a T-shirt with the words "Man Booker Nominee" emblazoned in tall letters. Prudence won out, but she imagined him wearing it to meetings with other writers.

The other board members were all mystery writers at three different stages in life. David Jones was a Welshman who'd gone to Edinburgh University and wrote a teen mystery to avoid doing a paper. He had created a character that caught the public's attention, a fifteen-year-old girl. When he received a contract for two more books, he showed his professor, who said he was a terrible writer, and withdrew from classes. At twenty-five he was content to spend time at the pub, picking up women, jogging every day after writing five hundred to a thousand words daily.

Janis Aiken had been an anthropologist from London who had written her first mystery to prove to a friend it wasn't difficult. However, she had a deep appreciation of everything in Scotland and was determined that the museum was going to be so entertaining that people would learn to appreciate the poems even if they had never read a poem in their lives. Chantal found her the best ally on the board. The two women often strategized on how to move things forward.

The last writer, Hamish Browne, had just tripped into his eightieth year and had several mystery series to his credit. His memory was less than perfect. Chantal thought of him as a lovable old dog one delays putting to sleep because there's some quality of life left.

By the time were all seated, the wine poured, the cheese nibbled, the battle began, little of which had to do with the quality of J.J.'s work and more to establishing their own egos.

Chantal did her best in not screaming at them that with all the problems in the world, with her own personal pain, it really didn't matter how realistic was the color in the foxes' fur nor the type of frame that would set off the art work, the size of the poems versus the size of the art work.

By the end of the meeting, the board had given J.J. the commission. After the members had left, Chantal sat back in her seat. "I don't believe we did it," she said.

"Sometimes things work." J.J. gathered his things.

Chantal hoped he was right.

# 12

## EDINBURGH, SCOTLAND

To leave the women alone to clear out Duncan's clothes and other things, Roger had taken Blane and Sophie to the zoo, although Sophie was much too young to appreciate the animals. She would be happy just being pushed around sitting next to Blane. Every time she saw him, her face took on a sunshine quality.

A full roll of large, black, plastic sacks was in Chantal's lap. She was sitting Indian style on the couple's bed. Periodically, she turned it over and over, without unrolling it.

"This is hard for you, I know." Annie sat next to her, and reached for her hand. "We don't have to do this today. We can go to the pub for lunch…"

"I feel a but coming on."

"…*but* if you want support to go through Duncan's things with a support team, now is the moment. If you don't, I understand."

Annie hoped they would find something, anything, that might lead them to a real reason to investigate the accident slash murder. After talking with Louisa, she gave more credence to the murder theory but had little, make that no idea how to proceed. Chantal might have confidence in her, but Anne believed that her luck in solving murders was more accident than ability. If she were a TV series, it could be called. *The Accidental Detective.*

"It has to be done." Chantal stared at her hands and the roll of plastic bags.

"I'll start." When Chantal didn't stop her, Annie opened the top drawer in the dresser designated as Duncan's. His shorts and undershirts were neatly folded. Annie noticed they were a variety of colors and were jockeys not boxers. Two matched sets were silky and bright red. She looked at Chantal.

"We could take these to a shelter. A charity shop wouldn't be interested." Chantal tore off one of the bags from its roll. A sheet of labels was on the oak night stand next to the bed. She tore one off and wrote shelter on the one in the top left corner and stuck it on the bag.

Within two hours the bags were filled and labeled: cleaners, charity shop, shelter, trash.

Annie had insisted they put on music, music from their growing up years in Switzerland including Francis Cabrel, Johnny Halliday, PowWow, Stephan Eicher.

"I know this sounds stupid, but now that his clothes are no longer in the drawers and closets, I know he's not coming back. I mean I knew it before but *know* in the sense of feeling it deep within me."

"Not stupid at all. When his things were everywhere, you could pretend he was on a business trip, or late getting home from the office." Annie put her arm around her friend who melted into her embrace.

"What about his desk?" Annie asked after several minutes had gone by, "Unless you don't want me to see personal stuff."

"I'm not worried about the personal stuff. But I've had enough for…" Before Chantal could finish, they heard the front door open and Roger call, "We're back."

"Saved by the bell," Chantal said with a half-smile that Annie knew cost her friend.

The women went down stairs to the entry where Roger had two children asleep in the double push chair they had borrowed from one of Chantal's neighbors whose twins had outgrown it.

Each woman lifted her own child and carried them upstairs to their beds. Neither woke as they were being poured into pajamas which were thick enough that they didn't need to be covered with blankets.

"I will get to the desk, I promise." Chantal said as they returned to join Roger who was dialing the Indian Takeaway around the corner.

"I'm here to support," Annie said, "not judge." However, she was hoping that Duncan's desk might give her some useful information because his clothing had advanced nothing.

# 13

Carol Dixon turned the key of her studio loft overlooking Boston Common. It had once belonged to an artist who had bought it back in the fifties when it was considered unusable space. Carol had lucked out when she bought it from the woman's granddaughter who had no business sense, hated cities, especially Boston.

Later the girl had sued Carol for "tricking" her into the low price. Carol had kept all their emails where the girl even lowered the price without Carol asking at one point saying, "I just want to get rid of it," she'd written. The suit was dropped when the girl's attorney told her, she didn't stand a chance.

Carol had revamped the loft turning one end into a state-of-the-art kitchen with dark red appliances and soft gray tiles. Only a couple of friends were aware that Carol really had a domestic side and was more than an accomplished cook.

The rest of the flat was decorated with English antiques, except for an eighteenth century Chinese screen with its mother-of-pearl designs against a deep ruby enamel background hiding a queen-sized headboard-less frame backed up against the wall.

When Carol wanted to sit up in bed, reading and drinking coffee, she used her many overstuffed pillows to prop herself into comfort.

She adored her loft, keeping it neat without it looking artificially ready for an interior design magazine photographer on a shoot for the next issue.

Ethan, her non-boyfriend, boyfriend (he'd like to be more: she was content with their sometimes meeting up in and out of bed) called the place "textured" with its wooden floors, and hard glass skylights that left it luminous even on the grayest days and brick walls. He told her she should be an architect like himself.

Carol was drenched. Even though at the building's entrance three floors below she had shaken herself, she was still dripping as the antique elevator made its squeaky climb to the top floor. When wet dogs shake themselves dry, they made it look easy. Carol wished it was the same with her.

The grocery store on Charles Street, a non-chain with specialty everything, was at the other end of The Common. The rain had caught her about half-way home.

Leaving her shopping basket on the kitchen counter and draping her coat over a chair to dry, she went into the bathroom area to towel dry her short, highlighted blond hair.

No place like home was more than a saying to be cross-stitched, framed and hung on a wall, although she wouldn't have had a piece of embroidery anywhere in the loft preferring paintings by unknown artists who should have been known. If they became famous, it would add to her assets: if they didn't she still would enjoy their work as well as feeling good about supporting their talent.

As a child she never thought of what her life would be like as an adult. Throughout school, including her high school at the demanding Phillips Academy in Andover, she had top grades. She'd graduated Magna Cum Laude from Harvard with a degree in international relations. Her law degree came from Yale and she passed the bar on first try.

She'd never practiced.

Carol didn't need to work. Her trust fund covered all normal expenses and she was amazingly frugal. However, she'd learned long ago that doing nothing was boring, that playing the society debutant was even more boring. It was up to her to make her own excitement, which she did with the same dedication as she had in getting top grades.

She saw her telephone light beeping. After putting down the bag of groceries, she started playing the messages.

Message 1: Hi, this is Ethan, Carol. If you're back would you like dinner and a movie and anything else Saturday night? I tried your cell, but you haven't returned my call.

Message 2: Carol, ring me please. (Carol's mother never left her name.)

Message 3: Since it's Saturday morning, and I haven't heard from you, I assume tonight is out. If you're away call me when you're back. I still love you. (pause) This is Ethan just in case.

Message 4: Call me. (mother)

Message 5: Call me. (mother)

Messages 6-10: Call me. (mother)

Message 11: You're doing this to annoy me. (mother)

She debated calling her mother back or putting away the groceries. The groceries won, as did running the vac over the wide-planked, wooden floors, straightening the magazines: *New Yorker*, *Nation*, *Harvard Review*, *Foreign Policy*. She was at least three issues behind in reading them thanks to her travels.

Maybe she'd take the rest of the weekend to stay home and just read and relax. She had a new painting bought on her last trip to London, which she wanted to hang. In her imagination, she was dressed in sweats, curled up on the couch, a pot of black dragon pearl black tea in ready reach.

Despite being caught in the rain, she hoped it would continue. The water beating on the skylight brought her comfort in the same way that after a snowstorm she would wake and instead of seeing blue or gray in the skylight above her bed, there would be a white blanket.

Although she could have easily afforded a cleaning woman, she didn't want anyone in her apartment, especially when she wasn't there. Sometimes she allowed Ethan to stay over, although she preferred staying at his place because she could control when the date was over. A Friday night date might run into a weekend if there was something interesting to do. When he stayed in her loft, she would have to make up excuses to get him out in the morning, had he not left after they'd had sex. He called it making love. She called it sex.

When she stayed overnight at Ethan's or any man's and was left alone, even if he only went downstairs to make coffee, she would look through his drawers. If he went out before she did, she'd add his desk and even his computer to her investigations.

The bathroom was the only closed off part of the loft, behind a half red-brick wall with the top half being thick, opaque glass. Carol dropped her clothes as she went to the shower. She'd pick them up after her shower. Her neatness had begun when she went to boarding school. Before that, her nanny or a maid had picked up her things.

No sooner had she stepped out of the shower that had erased the tiredness around her shoulders that she always felt for a twenty-four-hour period after coming home from a so-called business trip than the phone rang.

As she dried herself off, she listened to her mother, "Carol Catherine Dixon, enough is enough. Call me or I'm coming over to that ridiculous place you call…"

"Hello Mother."

"It's about time."

"I was in the shower."

"I mean, I've left message after message on that horrible machine."

"I'm sorry, I've been away."

"AND…"

Carol waited for the rest of the tirade that was sure to follow in her mother's Boston Brahmin clipped accent. And it came "never call… don't care… your stepfather says… if you would only tell me when you go out of town…"

Carol put the phone down on the antique trunk and lay on the couch next to it, saying "hmm hmm" whenever it seemed reasonable. She closed her eyes and almost fell asleep.

"Carol? Carol? "CAROL?"

Carol grabbed the phone. "Yes, Mother, I'm here."

"Well are you coming to dinner on Sunday or not? Your stepfather went to a lot of work to make sure Jonathan should come."

Jonathan? Jonathan? She was too tired to immediately think of whom her mother was speaking. Probably Jonathan Webster, the attorney that her parents would like for a son-in-law. He worked for her stepfather. She'd never had told them Jonathan was gay, because it was his business to share or not and because both were amused at parental attempts to pair them off.

More than once she acted as his beard. He was a great tennis partner. However, she hadn't seen him for several months. Hope burns eternal in the hearts of match-making parents, she thought.

Her parents had never been introduced to Ethan. They never would be unless they happened by accident to bump into each other when she was with him, which is unlikely. Carol stayed clear of anywhere her parents might inhabit.

Their snobbery limited them to a small number of places around Beacon Hill in the fall, winter, spring and Kennebunkport in the summer. Carol seldom went to the family compound and when she did it was for special reasons such as unescapable family event or heat so hot that her air conditioning couldn't fight it.

If Carol had any regrets at all about her loft, it was the proximity to Louisburg Square where her parents, grandparents, great grandparents and great-great grandparents had owned the family homestead. "Riddled with history," Carol described it, not because she hated history—in fact she loved it—but because the personal family history felt like a prison.

"It's been over three months since you've been here," Annabel Barron Dixon Hancock whined.

Someone should tell the woman that whining unbecoming in a child was ridiculous in a woman in her sixties. Her mother must be slipping, Carol thought. It was four months and three days, but she wouldn't point that out. Carol imagined her mother sitting next to the telephone, a Princess model with push buttons. Her mother and stepfather were frugal New England Yankees personified despite their wealth. One did not replace things that worked.

Her mother also had a smart phone, although she ranted against the usage in front of other people when "One should be talking to the one they are with." On that Carol had agreed with her mother— about the only that thing the two women didn't argue over.

Her mother's hair would be styled in the same page boy she'd worn since graduating from Wellesley. Her sweater and cardigan would match and pick up one of the colors in her plaid woolen skirt. A string of pearls, handed down from her mother and grandmother, would be around her neck. No hanging around the house in jeans or sweats for her mother. Carol told Ethan once she suspected that her mother went to bed fully clothed and woke without a wrinkle in her outfit or a hair out of place. She gave that explanation as a reason he was better off not meeting her family whenever he asked.

She had met his, and although not of the same class, both his parents were full professors, his father at Boston University and his mother at Simmons. Their conversations were full of left-wing politics which would have made Carol's parents cringe.

More than once she imagined a dinner with the two sets of parents and her own totally confused by the amount of laughter and the frequent touching of the professors.

If there were a museum for old-fashioned Boston Brahmins, her mother would be a relic on display.

She hadn't seen Jonathan for a while. He would deflect her parents' criticism of her since they were pushing for an engagement. They knew the game. She'd arrive late. They would leave together. He would walk her home and they'd dissect the evening and catch up with the part of their lives not to be shared with the parental generation. She'd never have to be alone with her parents.

"What time Mother?"

# 14

**A**nnie wrestled her kinky red hair into a scrunchie. The bathroom mirror was steamed from the shower finished minutes before. Steam had congealed into droplets. Good thing she didn't wear make-up because putting it on through the fog might leave her looking a bit weird.

Outside the rain battered against the window: rainy days and Monday. Shit!

Annie didn't often swear and not just because it was a go-to-your-room offense when she was a kid. She felt she could communicate better with other words. Nor did she mind when others issued shits, fucks and God-damn-its. She credited herself with having more originality in showing her displeasure. People tended to be startled when she did swear giving her cursing more weight the rare times foul words fell from her mouth.

As she brushed her teeth she thought, shit, *merde* and fuck. AGG's toxic atmosphere made the nasty words, any nasty word, one hundred percent applicable.

How long was it since she had so dreaded Monday mornings?

Ages!

Most of her assignments had been varying degrees of pleasant no matter how challenging and/or how tight the deadlines. Even where there was tension, the atmosphere was nothing like it was at AGG. She had to remind herself for the five days that she'd worked there that her only reason for being in that shit hole was to discover anything she could about Duncan's death.

In her heart of hearts, she thought there were no wild geese to chase in the company. Even with Louisa's suspicions, Annie thought that companies, even AGG, did not go around running over their employees.

Duncan might have gotten himself involved in something not related to work, but what that would be was also hard to imagine. He was such a good person, but then maybe the good person was only on the surface and underneath he worked for the Mafia. She shook her head at the absolute stupidity of *that* idea.

Chantal had never been that good a friend, but there were afternoons after school when they'd studied together. They suffered through the *maturité gymmasiale bilingue* in French and English at Le College Calvin. As they drowned in homework, it was hard for either to muster any pride in being at a five-hundred-year-old high school. The most they could feel was gratitude that they didn't follow the curriculum during the time of John Calvin with Latin, Greek, grammar, logic, Bible and rhetoric.

Annie supposed that surviving was a bond in itself: the bond was why she hadn't booked her family on the next flight home.

Why was she still fighting believing?

Because she wanted to go home, that was why. Well, if she wanted to go home, she better get serious about finding something or proving there was nothing.

"Breakfast." Roger's voice drifted up the stairs.

Annie grabbed her new charity-shop suit jacket and headed down to the kitchen with its long, pocked-marked oak table.

Blane and Sophie were in their high chairs, the second being borrowed from the same neighbor who loaned the twin stroller. Roger had laid out scones, oranges and bowls of Earl Grey tea.

Chantal came into the room. She was dressed in jeans and a sweater. With construction still going on in the museum and no meeting to pry money out of potential donors, her outfit was professional for the circumstances. "Good morning."

"Roger makes scones better than you, *Maman*," Blane said. "He puts lots and lots of jam on it."

"My son, the food critic." Chantal took a bite of one. "I'm already late. What the hell?" She sat, reached and unpeeled an orange and sat down to drink her tea.

"Let's walk together," Annie said when they'd finished.

On the street, light filtered through heavy clouds. The air smelled of rain that would probably go from spitting to drizzle to downpour if the weather forecast could be believed.

Once inside, AGG she headed to the cubicles with the five translators' desks. The three men were already at their computers. Louisa MacLaughlin came in a few minutes after Annie, but earlier than the official start time.

Annie would have loved a forbidden cup of tea. A new rule had been issued last Wednesday. Tea breaks were confined between ten and ten fifteen. She had found the trip to the cafeteria and then long lines made it impossible to have time to consume anything.

Annie was the only one translating human resource material. The others worked on reports or translated newspaper and business articles back into English.

As she worked, she wondered how company rules would stand up against labor laws in other countries. Granted, the UK had opted out a lot of the ones that the EU had proposed and who knew what Brexit would bring, but the company needed to follow the same regulations in the countries where they set up offices.

Her first assignment was to work on family leave with a death in the family, which was two days. That included if the family member died far enough way that travel was required. Thus, if you worked in Stuttgart and your father died in Dubai, you would have to take unpaid leave. There was also a limit on the amount of time spent in the toilets both in terms of number of trips and the minutes in each. Egads!

The only chatter between any of her co-workers was to check wording. Tom Curtis, a stocky Welshman, who claimed his build came from his mining family's genes, had named their boss Simple-Simon-aka-Mr.-Berry-not-Jack.

Simple-Simon-aka-Mr.-Berry-not-Jack was the type of boss that hovered, waiting for any misdeed. He saw Tom sitting back in his chair. "You should be working."

"I'm thinking."

"Well don't think too long," Simple-Simon-aka-Mr.-Berry-not-Jack said.

"I'll make my quota." Tom stuck his tongue out at the retreating back of the boss, earning him a thumbs-up from the team.

Louisa, who was walking back from the copier at that moment, exchanged a look with Annie who rolled her eyes in response. What Simple-Simon-etc. didn't see, wouldn't bother them.

The only good thing about the fifty-page-a-day pressure was that the day passed quickly. The bad thing was that Annie's back ached from being hunched over the computer. When she stood up to walk around, Simple-Simon-aka-Mr.-Berry-not-Jack swooped down to "Why aren't you at your desk?"

"I need to stretch."

She deliberately stretched longer than she needed. Maybe she'd been lucky that she hadn't run into this type of digital sweatshop before. Maybe this was what had bothered Duncan. It's temporary, it's temporary, she thought. I need to escape as fast as possible. Maybe Roger can help.

Bells regulated the office: bells for the morning and afternoon fifteen-minute tea break and bells for the lunch break. At noon when the bells rang, Louisa followed her to the cafeteria located in the basement. Cement walls were institutional green Annie guessed it was once where the servants worked.

The two women sat side by side at the same table in a corner of the cafeteria with their fronts facing a wall. No one was at the next table.

Roger had packed Annie's lunch: left-over red onion quiche, a green salad with a small container of his own dressing and an apple he'd sliced. He'd rubbed it with lemon, sprinkled it with cinnamon and wrapped it tightly in plastic film to prevent browning.

Louisa took out a tuna fish sandwich. "I'd love to trade with you, but I bet you aren't interested."

"Sorry, I'm not."

Louisa looked around to see that no one was listening. "They haven't reassigned Duncan's office. Maybe there's still some information in there." She had her hand over her mouth. "Cameras are everywhere and who knows if they'll read our lips."

Annie couldn't see anything in the wall or overhead. To be on the safe side, although Annie thought Louisa was being overly cautious, picked up her napkin and held it to her mouth. "I'm sure they've cleared everything out."

Louisa dropped her napkin.

"No mikes under the table." Louisa picked up her tea mug in both hands against her mouth and blew on it. "I was in HR yesterday. I saw some boxes in his old office. I don't know if they have Duncan's stuff in them or not. We should look."

Annie wished she had asked her when they met up for coffee why she was so interested. She wasn't going to let the opportunity to slip by a second time.

Louisa held her tuna fish sandwich in her hands in such a way that her mouth was half covered but didn't bite into it. "Because he knew something was wrong. He questioned me like no HR person would under normal circumstances. He went beyond how working conditions had deteriorated after the AGG sale. He wanted to know more about the documents from the States." She put her sandwich down.

"Why do you care?"

"He was a nice guy and friend. More than just a work friend."

Annie frowned.

"I don't mean he was a lover or anything. He helped me find a babysitter when I had a problem. Twice he passed on free-lancing leads even if it is against company policy. Friends do that... or at least professional friends do."

Annie agreed. She noticed that Louisa was doodling on her napkin. When she looked closer she saw she'd sketched a camera with an arrow. Annie's eyes followed the arrow and she did, indeed, see a camera on the opposite wall.

"See! I told the truth. You didn't believe me. That was put in about two weeks before Duncan was killed. It was done at night. He told me he was against it. There was nothing he could do. Boston orders."

Annie stretched, allowing her to look at the camera which was very inconspicuous sticking out of a wall cabinet. One would have to know it was there to be aware of it at all.

When she'd been interviewed, she'd noticed several cameras placed around the building. She wasn't sure if they were turned on. Cameras could be used to intimate people who would worry they *might* be recording. She thought she'd found all their locations and had made a mental list adding the one in the cafeteria.

Louisa took her napkin and blew her nose and stuffed it in her pocket. She dropped her spoon on the floor. As she bent down to pick it up, "Let them think I'm really clumsy. Do you want to go with me to search his office or should I go alone?"

What the hell was going on, Annie wondered. This type of environment would have not been anything Duncan would have approved. Now his unhappiness with the job made sense. But unhappiness didn't lead to murder, being fired maybe, or made redundant as the inhabitants of the British Isles called it.

Annie took a final bite of her dessert and wiped her mouth. While the napkin was covering it, she asked, "When?" She had to admire Louisa's courage considering her precarious financial situation.

"Tonight. After everyone leaves. People clear out from this hell hole as fast as they can." Louisa reached around to pick up her purse hanging on the chair so her face was out of camera range.

As she headed back to her cubby, Annie felt she'd been cast in a bizarre movie.

# 15

EDINBURGH, SCOTLAND

When the end-of-day bell rang, the three men in Annie's work area put their papers away and shut down their computers before gathering their things and escaping.

Louisa finished with what she was working on a few minutes later before also shutting down her computer and leaving, winking at Annie as she strung the strap of over bag over her shoulder. She waved goodbye.

Annie, because she wanted to be the last to leave, continued working.

"Why are you still here?" Her boss's voice made her jump. No one had added anything to the idiot's nickname during the day. He had on his coat and was wrapping a scarf around his scrawny neck. He hovered over her as if he planned to strike her.

"I wanted to get a head start on tomorrow's work. It's a bit complicated…"

"You know we won't pay overtime. Americans expect that."

Asshole, she thought. "I'm not asking for it."

"Good. Clock out now and then come back *if* you must." He nodded and left.

Annie looked at her watch. The building was eerily silent, but she put her card in the time clock located at the entrance to the department. Each department had its own clock. She guessed the company wouldn't be responsible for paying for employee time wasted walking from the main entrance to their desks.

If Louisa wasn't coming back, she might as well go home. As she started down the hall, Louisa stepped out of a doorway. "I signed out, left, but came back. I ducked the cameras. I don't think they show all the way to the floor, so I crawled."

"Smart you," Annie said.

"Good thing that they're too cheap to hire night guards."

They made their way down the corridor. "Stick to the walls rather than the center here. A camera might pick us up," Louisa whispered although the building seemed deserted.

"Think any are hidden?" Annie asked.

They jumped when they heard a noise. Two women, wearing yellow uniforms, one with a ratty blue sweater, pushed a cleaning cart in their direction and away from the HR offices. The non-sweater wearer took a vacuum, or a hoover as Louisa would call it regardless of brand, rolled it up and down the carpet. The other went in and out of offices emptying waste paper baskets, lining them with new blue plastic bags before returning them.

"Talk about business and lean against the wall," Annie whispered.

"I'm not sure how many pages are due next week." Louisa's tone was slightly louder than conversational.

"If we don't have too many meetings, it shouldn't be a problem. Did you get the graph I sent you?"

"I haven't had a chance to study it, but as soon as I do, I'll send you my comments."

When the cleaning women were out of sight, the two women turned the corner to enter the HR section of the building. Annie expected the office would be locked until she spied a camera pointing at it. "What should we do?"

"The camera is on the upper half. Look at how it is pointed."

Annie wasn't convinced. Even if it only shot their top half, the door opening and closing would be caught on film. Then she saw a second door but no camera. She pointed.

The two women dropped to their knees and crawled to the second door. It wasn't locked. A bookcase was pushed against it. Together they found the strength to push it aside.

"No lights. The camera will pick it up through the glass," Louisa said.

Some light came from the street lamps but not enough to do a thorough investigation.

Duncan's office had been toward the back of the suite. That was the one that had a nameplate removed. She pointed at it, held up her hands as if she was questioning.

Louisa mouthed Duncan's.

"Cameras?"

"I looked. I never saw one," Louisa said. "Be careful! We don't want our shadows picked up through the glass."

Annie followed on her hands and knees, feeling foolish. It was if they were in some Grade B movie. Hell, Grade D.

There was no camera in Duncan's old office.

Annie dug into her purse for the flashlight she always carried with her.

"I didn't think of a torch," Louisa said.

A crate with personal possessions including photos of Chantal and Blane were under the big window. Only top managers were allowed windows, Annie had noticed. Peons were kept behind cloth barriers head-high or higher.

"I wonder why they haven't given these things back to Chantal." Annie ruffled through a crate. "Maybe they forgot." As she said it, she suspected it was more that no one cared. "Pens, photos, Duncan's diplomas and certificates."

Louisa picked the lock on the gray metal file cabinet opening and closing drawers in a file cabinet. "In this computer age, why do they have so many folders?"

"What's in them?" Annie asked.

"Personnel files?"

"I'd have thought they'd have it all on computer."

Louisa brought a folder over to her and held it under the beam of the flashlight. "Looks as if these are forms which need a signature, insurance stuff mainly."

"But they could have scanned... never mind." Annie had long ago learned that common sense wasn't common and where companies were concerned it was even less so.

Duncan's computer was on an extension to the right of the desk. As much as Annie wanted to turn it on, she knew that it would signal someone had been there.

The women started in on the desk. Mostly it was more pens and paper clips, menus from a take-away Indian restaurant in the neighborhood and a few notebooks, the type stenographers used in the old days. Duncan was a note taker, she knew.

Her telephone rang. Both women jumped.

"Where are you *Chérie?*" Roger asked.

"Still at the office: I'll tell you about it when I get home." He would be displeased at the risks she was taking, they'd argue, she would apologize and he would forgive her. Sometimes she thought maybe they should put a few of these types of conversations on tape and just play them back while they did something more rewarding. Or better yet, not give him the details.

"We'd better go," Louisa said.

Annie nodded and slipped the notebooks in her briefcase. She doubted that anyone had made an inventory of what remained in the office. She hesitated about the diplomas and photos and as much as she wanted Chantal to have them, she thought it was too dangerous. She'd tell Chantal to ask for them.

As they left the building, using the same camera-avoidance techniques, she thought, it might have been smarter had they worn gloves.

"I wish I'd time to look at my file," Louisa said.

# 16

EDINBURGH, SCOTLAND

**When** Annie let herself into the house the first thing she heard were the sounds of children laughing coming from the bathroom upstairs. She found Roger kneeling by the tub where Sophie and Blane were immersed in bubbles. Roger made a yellow rubber duck fly through the air, dive under the suds and tickle Sophie.

"Me next, me next, me next," Blane hollered.

Roger's grin and wet shirt told her he was having as much fun as the children. She swallowed the warning that if children were too excited they wouldn't fall asleep.

It took another hour to get them settled.

Downstairs, Roger nuked a meal he'd cooked earlier. Mac and cheese wasn't French. "The kids love it and I wasn't sure when you and Chantel would be home. It has reheat-capability." He produced homemade applesauce with his special combination of spices.

They were halfway thru eating when Chantal walked in. One look at her face, and Roger jumped up to pour her a glass of wine. "Bad day?"

"If any of my board members die of strange causes, don't ask me for an alibi." She took the wine and as she sipped, vented about changes after completion, budget limitations and how could anyone who sold their writing not understand marketing. When she finally finished, she sighed, "Tired of hearing me rave?" Before Roger and

77

Annie could respond, she added, "I'm grateful you listened. Blane is cute, but a rotten listener."

Later in bed Annie told Roger, some of what she and Louisa had done without mentioning crawling under security cameras.

She watched his face twist into disapproval. "What am I going to do with you?"

"You want to go home, don't you?"

He nodded.

"Then we need to prove how Duncan was murdered." She jumped out of bed. The floor was icy on her bare feet. "I forgot. My purse?"

"Downstairs. Next to the shoe rack."

The stairs were even colder on her feet than the bedroom wooden floor. She grabbed her purse and rushed back to bed.

"Ouch!" Roger said when she put her feet against his leg. He dived under the covers as she looked through the bag and rubbed warmth back into them as Annie ransacked her purse.

The notebook, a small 3x5 with a torn brown cover under her gum, comb, keys, hairbrush, Sophie's pacifier, tissues and change, was at the bottom, stuck in the torn lining.

"What is that notebook for?" Roger asked.

"It's Duncan's. We didn't have time to look at it."

Roger sat up and put his arm around his wife as she flipped the pages. There were notes about meetings, a grocery list or two. Certain amounts of money were written. Something had been written in pencil and smudged out. "Duncan must only like to write on a clean page."

Roger nodded. "There's a list of country codes, I think."

Annie tilted the notebook. "CH, D, F, N. Probably. Unless it is a code.

There was also a list of subsidiaries that Annie knew belonged to AGG and some companies that meant nothing to her.

"What does it all mean?" Roger asked.

"Unless we can get more information about what he wrote, I'd say it was useless."

# 17

**B** ob Johnson, (Ret. Air Force Colonel) angled his car from the car parking area at the Colorado Springs airport. It was good to be home despite freezing rain lashing his windshield.

He'd grown up in the Springs, went to the Air Force Academy there. He'd served more than one bout of teaching at the Academy. His wife, a local girl, had followed him on his different tours of duty to Japan, Germany and Texas and finally to D.C.

A light snow was falling: good for skiing. Maybe he'd get a chance to do a few runs before he had to return to D.C.

He headed up the mountain toward Manitou Springs where his wife had fled a week before saying she was fed up with Washington, fed up with him always working, fed up, fed up, fed up.

It wasn't the first time she'd walked out. Being an Air Force officer's wife with all the ass kissing of officer's wives whose husband's rank was above his was something she had hated, but to give her credit she'd played the game well.

She had stopped playing the day he retired. All she wanted was to go home to Colorado, to be near her grandson and to live peacefully.

Peaceful had worked the first two years. Then the Iraq war had started. Johnson hadn't wanted to get into that fight, but he was upset when he heard about lack of equipment the forces had had. His buddies still in told him that the services were so eager for bodies that they sent improperly-trained and ill-equipped people.

Tom and his best friend, Richard Copp, had started a contracting company, finding trained ex-soldiers and outfitting them properly. Through Ray Anderson, his congressman and neighbor, he'd landed contracts for Iraq, Afghanistan and Somalia. Copp told him to move to Washington to suck-up to the decision-makers because as a small contractor, he was up against some pretty big players.

His wife went along, but barely. As for sucking-up at cocktail parties, she refused, saying she'd done enough for several lifetimes. But contracts came with his sucking.

?to fill those contracts. At one point, he'd re-mortgaged his house putting him on a collision course with his wife.

Last month, he and Richard had sold the company to AGG. Part of the sales contract was for him to continue as CEO for three years at a ridiculously high salary. Money was no longer an issue with his pension and the sale cash.

When his wife heard three more years, she high-tailed it for their Colorado home, saying he would be welcome if he quit. "It's my turn now. I'm through being a puppy running after you waiting for a pat on my head."

The rain turned to sleet pelting faster than the wipers could clear the windshield as he drove up the mountain. He tested his brakes. The car skidded slightly. It didn't worry him. He'd driven just about every vehicle imaginable in his lifetime under almost every condition.

It was close to midnight. He hadn't told his wife he was coming. He'd call when he arrived in Manitou Springs. He couldn't imagine she wouldn't let him in on a night like this. She would want to know what he had to say at least.

It was getting harder and harder to see. He slowed. A car behind him had on its high beams, reducing his visibility. They were the only two vehicles on the road.

He felt a jolt from behind.

The following car tapped him.

Johnson sped up slightly. What was that bastard trying to do?

The other car sped up.

The next tap sent him over the edge of a small incline into a tree. The airbag inflated.

Johnson was stunned.

Looking out the driver's window, he saw a soldier dressed in camouflage. The soldier opened the door and grabbed his head and twisted his neck.

The last thought Johnson had as heard the crack of his own bones was, "Oh, my God, it's a woman."

The woman put two fingers on Johnson's neck.

No pulse.

She climbed the hill, got in the stolen car. Her next actions would be to change back into civvies and ditch the car near the motel where she would spend the night before taking a taxi to the airport.

# 18

Roger Perret decided to walk to the Edinburgh Central Station of Police. He'd left Sophie with Chantal, with a smidgeon of guilt. Both children would limit how much work she could accomplish. After all, it was her fault that he wasn't happily ensconced at home in France. It balanced the guilt.

His wife wasn't innocent in this entire caper. Annie was always ready to run off to help a friend. He appreciated her deep sense of loyalty but admired it more when it didn't impact him.

That Duncan had been nearly hit by cars before was suspicious, he had to admit. As a *flic* he wished there had been witnesses rather than just Chantal's secondhand information. Unlike when he was a detective with 36, he didn't have access to all the data needed to figure out the circumstances.

He turned off the narrow path between the brick houses toward the larger road by Haymarket Station. A soft mist dampened his cap. He hated umbrellas. Maybe living in Scotland would change his mind about them—or not.

Chantal had shown him on the map how close the station was. It made no sense to take a tram. He had been spoiled growing up and living in Paris with its Metro system where the major problems were strikes not limited access.

He was sure that this would be a wild goose chase. Strange English expression. How many times did someone chase a wild goose? Hunters shot wild geese. They made the shot or not. Since geese usually flew in packs, or whatever the word was, in their V-formations if a hunter missed one, there were others.

What was the best way to approach the police who had investigated the hit and run if—and it was a big if—they would even talk to him? Being an ex-cop didn't have much standing when he was from a different country.

He came to a park. On a warm summer day, which he heard was rare, sitting on one of the benches under the trees would be nice. Sophie would enjoy playing on the grass and would probably find other little girls with whom to play.

He spied the blue and white sign saying Police Scotland and the Latin *semper vigilo*, whatever that meant. He could just imagine the political battles that went into the selection of the motto. One thing he did enjoy about his retirement was the lack of departmental politics, up, down or sideways.

The building itself was non-descript—brown stone, an attempt at decoration with red pipes on one side was about the only thing that made it a bit different from other buildings nearby. Three driverless white police cars with blue and yellow markings were parked across the street.

The policemen, constables, he thought they might be, came out in black uniforms, got into one car and drove off. By the speed, or lack thereof, he decided it wasn't an emergency.

He looked at his watch: 10:47. He had timed it so he wouldn't be at the beginning of a shift when meetings could be taking place or lunch times.

Inside it could have been any police station in the world. A reception area had two benches in front of it.

Behind the desk was a young woman in uniform. "May I help you?"

He pulled off his hat and gloves, which were now sopping. "I would like to talk to the detectives who handled the Duncan MacAndrew hit and run. I believe it was from this station."

The woman frowned and said something. There were some Scots whose English Roger found incomprehensible, worse even than the Quebecois's so-called French. He remembered a Scottish movie in the original version he and Annie had gone to and afterwards he admitted he had to read the subtitles. She'd laughed and said that she had to too, which had made him feel better.

He asked the receptionist to repeat herself.

"You're not from around here," the woman said. He saw on her badge her name was Sarah Matthews.

"I'm French."

Sarah busied herself at the computer to the right of her desk.

"That would have been Inspector John Stewart, but he's not here."

Roger had to ask her to repeat it twice. He thought she'd added that he was at headquarters in Stirling, but he couldn't be sure.

"However, the sergeant that worked with him on it is here and she's in."

Sarah picked up a phone and muttered something followed by, "Take a seat." At least that he understood or thought he did. She didn't stop him when he settled himself on a bench of an unknowable wood. It was three people wide and hard.

When Roger had been chief he never thought of the discomfort of people waiting. There might be a psychological advantage if the person had done something wrong, but for those that were worried about someone else... stop it, I'm retired. These aren't my problems," he said to himself.

The clock behind the receptionist ticked off the minutes. Roger debated going back to ask when the sergeant would come, but he didn't want to piss her off. A man in a suit appeared from the back with a kid in a hoodie. The kid slumped toward the exit and left without any acknowledgement of the man who disappeared behind the closed door.

A young woman appeared. She was wearing a black suit, not a uniform, with a bright pink blouse and a scarf tied much in the way that French women did. Her hair was short blond, reminding him of a younger Sharon Stone.

In TV detective programs the women *flics* usually wore long hair, not practical if they were to get into a fight. Nor was it practical if you were running and hair was blowing in your face, or so he had been told by one of the women who had worked for him.

"Robina Collins. *Vous êtes Monsieur Perret?*"

He was taken back by the French with its distinct Quebecois accent.

"*Vous parlez français?*

"Do you prefer English?"

"Either." Roger thought maybe that she might be more comfortable in English so let her choose.

She led him behind the reception into a small, windowless room. Two chairs were upholstered in a rather worn green fabric that matched a couch large enough to sleep on. An old-fashioned bulky computer covered part of a coffee table of some fake wood.

On a small end table, there was a machine for tea and coffee. Milk capsules and sugar sticks were in two dishes. Sugar particles were scattered over the wood.

The furniture left little room to walk around.

Robina sat in one of the chairs and pointed to another for Roger to sit, which he did. "This is sometimes a room to relax or when we need privacy to talk."

"But not for questioning," Roger said.

"No. No two-way mirrors, no recording equipment, no cameras. Not good for interrogation. It does work for a quick nap when we go a couple of shifts." Her head tilted toward the couch. "Not comfortable for more than twenty winks or make that fifteen."

Had Roger not been married, he would have wanted to ask her out. She oozed charisma. Infidelity, in either his marriage to his first wife or to Annie, was not his thing, but a fantasy or two never hurt. She was a good twenty years younger. He was sure he wouldn't be interested in an old man with a bum heart.

"You asked about the MacAndrew hit and run."

Business like, he thought as he nodded.

A knock at the door interrupted them. A constable came in and made a cup of coffee and left after Robina nodded her head toward the door. "Thanks Hamish," Robina said.

Not only business-like, she was a woman who liked to control, he decided. Strong women had always appealed to him. Lord knows, he was married to one. Better back to the topic: he explained about why he was in Edinburgh and about Chantal MacAndrew's belief that her husband had been more than the normal hit and run.

Robina looked at her watch. "Almost too early for lunch, but let's go anyway." She left him alone, but returned fifteen minutes later with her coat, a stylish camel hair. The umbrella she carried sheltered them both as they walked to a nearby tea room. Roger was aware of her arm through his and her body rubbing against his. Calm down, he told himself.

The tea room had two stories. The overweight woman with stringy hair behind the counter, greeted Robina with a huge smile. They exchanged a comment about the weather and then pointed to the winding staircase leading to the basement saying, "If you just want to talk. You don't have to buy anything."

"Sure, that will happen," Robina said. "What'll you have, and I'll get it?"

Roger was not going to let her control the purchase. He bought two tuna sandwiches and two cappuccinos and carried them downstairs. Robina was seated at a round table with red-cushioned chairs. A fire burned in a wood stove in one corner. They were alone.

"I didn't want to take a chance that anyone would see when I gave you this." Robina opened her purse and pulled out fifteen sheets of paper, which she had folded in half. "This is a copy Duncan MacAndrew's file."

Although he was shocked, Roger took the papers and scanned them, including the black and white photos of the body. He assumed the originals were in color. The autopsy report was truncated into a list of injuries sustained the in the crash.

Robina waited until he put the papers aside. "My boss didn't want to pursue it and was happy to chock it up to hit and run."

"But the other attempts?"

"He ignored it. The murder rate in Scotland is falling. Only about sixty a year, nothing really."

"The whole country?" What was Scotland's population—around five million? His department at 36 in Paris handled anything from 150 to 200 a year with a population of 2.2 million plus. Argelès had had only one murder in the decade he had lived there. Annie came close to being the murderer's second victim.

Thinking of Annie reminded him not to think of Robina the way he'd been imagining her.

"The whole country." She bit into her scone. "I disagreed with my boss. He basically told me to shut up."

"Is there anything in the file, I should pay attention to before I give it back to you?"

"That's your copy and I've risked my job to give it to you."

Why, he wondered. "Why?" He had to ask.

"I'm an old-fashioned cop. I believe that those that commit crimes should be punished."

Roger wasn't sure what to say.

As she put on her coat, she said. "I do have vacation time coming. If you want any help, I'll be happy to take some time off."

With that she put down her card where she had added her personal phone numbers, mobile and land, before she descended the staircase leaving him with the papers.

# 19

**" Now that was dumb,"** **Robina** Collins spoke to herself as she cut through the park on the way back to the police station. For the millionth time, she doubted that she was cut out for police work, not that she didn't love it, but following orders was hard, especially when she disagreed with what her superiors told her to do. She had learned they, and especially her direct report, had no patience with correction from a junior person.

The MacAndrew hit and run had been one of those. She'd even gone down to London on her own time to check the garage where one of the attempts had happened What a waste of a free day and money. In the garage where it happened all the floors looked alike and tire marks, had there been any, were long gone. If she had told her direct boss, Inspector Stewart, he'd have laughed at her.

Her blond hair didn't help. Dumb blond jokes abounded. When she passed a drugstore with a hair color display in the window, she went in. The packages started with blond, went through brown, a few reds and then came blacks. She picked up the black. That would shock the station.

How stupid, she chided herself. I'm a natural blond. Women pay a fortune and worry about roots and all I have to do is nothing. She returned the box and walked out of the store.

What she'd done in giving that hunky Frenchman the copied file would get her fired if it were discovered. What excuse could she use?

Writing a paper for the on-line course she was taking? She'd have to show them the paper, which she could cobble together fast enough. And she'd have to find a course and then explain why she hadn't asked for reimbursement. Still no one had seen her take the file, although Joe, who had worked in to the copy room and asked her to let him know when she'd finished. He hadn't seen what she was copying.

The problem with a lie is that it can lead to more and more lies until it is impossible to keep track of what she'd said. Good when it was a criminal she was questioning, bad when she wanted to hide something. Her preferred method was to say nothing.

She'd always been a good student. Although she started school in Edinburgh, her family had moved with her father on various assignments. Of course, she couldn't follow him to Afghanistan or Iraq where his battalion, the Royal Scots Borderers, served. She had been able to go with him on that surprise assignment which had him first at the British embassy in Toronto and then to another special assignment in Montreal.

There was something secret about what he did, which she never understood. He wasn't able to tell her anything about it either.

If she were to blame others for her failings, it would be her father with his mixed messages. Like most military, he believed in rank, order, which meant following orders. But he also taught her the regiment's motto, "no one assails me with impunity" and it was there where she ran into problems.

She felt assailed because of her gender and lack of recognition of what she contributed. All the clichés like hands tied, not rocking the boat, would infuriate her, but she would hide her reaction and accept the command.

Her friends who worked in various corporations said the same thing. The top decisions by the men and women who were paid incredible amounts didn't seem to have much to do with the reality of running the company.

Come to think of it, she didn't have one girlfriend satisfied with her work. Wait a minute, that wasn't right. Elena had opened a tea room and although she was always on the edge of going under, she loved every bit of the process of decoration, menu planning, service.

Robina had tried to forget the MacAndrew case, tried to forget his wife and baby, but she had failed. Inspector Stewart had told her over and over that a good copper had to be objective, couldn't let emotions get in the way. He didn't tell her how to do it.

Hiding her emotions from others was easy. Hiding them from herself?

Impossible.

It was like some of the kids that they arrested, usually kids from the slums, those who didn't have a chance, implanted themselves in her memory. If their lives had been different, would she ever have had to arrest them?

She and her brother had had a good upbringing. Her mother was one of those cookie-baking moms, who listened to her stories when she came from school. There wasn't a school performance when her mum wasn't in the audience cheering her on. The woman even smiled through her first violin concert when the screeches far outweighed anything that could be called musical.

Not that her mum was easy. Certain rules were as strong as anything Moses brought down from the mountains on stone tablets. Rooms were to be picked up at the end of the day, politeness was necessary even to those she disliked, although she was allowed to vent her real feelings to her mum when the object of the dislike wasn't around.

Such was the case with Sadie Costello, an American Colonel's wife. She was one of those cheek-pinching women. Robina hated it when her mum had other regiment wives in for bridge. Sadie would swoop down and pinch-pinch-pinch.

"I want to bite her hand," Robina had told her mum after the third time with all the indignation a seven-year old could express.

"Let's pretend I'm Mrs. Costello and you can pretend to bite me when I go to pinch," her mum had said. And they did. "Now next time try and stay out of her way."

Her mum had also been a great support during their time in Canada. Robina had been scared starting a new school. Her mum had the habit of drawing cartoons with Robina as the heroine whenever she faced a difficult task.

It had helped during her first week.

Once she discovered that many of the others were kids who transferred from place to place every few years, she settled in loving the dual-language international schools in Toronto then in Montreal.

She'd found it hard to go back to Scotland because she knew things the other kids didn't and vice versa. Because she was originally from Edinburgh, they had little patience with her lapses of knowledge.

However, despite her mum's strictness, there was also a whole question authority-avoidance mentality that Robina developed from who knows where, that was almost impossible for her to tamp down.

She saw the station but didn't want to go back in, where not just mountains, but mountain ranges of paperwork awaited her.

Monsieur Perret had thrown her off balance with his good looks. Too bad he wore a wedding ring. One of her rules was no married men. Many asked her out: all were refused.

It had been a year since she had a relationship, her last boyfriend having no patience with her erratic schedule, which also made finding anyone new difficult.

Time to get back to work, but she would follow up on the MacAndrew case and only about ten percent was because of Perret.

# 20

## EDINBURGH, SCOTLAND

**"Haggis and a good French** Merlot, a cross cultural experience." Roger lifted his glass in a toast to Chantal. The children were asleep. The three adults were almost as tired as the kids had been, but unlike a little child, they couldn't rub their eyes with the back of their hands or suck on their blankies to ward off grouchiness.

Annie wasn't sure if her husband was being sarcastic or not about the combination of the Scottish regional dish mixed with a good wine. Before she could ask the doorbell rang.

The kitchen was off to one side of the entry hall. Chantal excused herself to answer it.

Annie could hear Chantal saying, "I remember you. Why don't you come in?"

Robina Collins followed Chantal into the kitchen. She was wearing jeans and a Staffordshire sweatshirt under a blue wool winter jacket. Her ears were covered with a blue headband which she removed along with her mittens. "I don't want to interrupt…"

"You're not," Chantal said. "Please have something to eat. There's enough for all of us." When Robina mumbled her thanks, Chantal added a plate, flatware and a glass in front of the empty seat.

Robina pulled out the extra chair carefully to not hit the fridge. There was room for her to hang her jacket on the back, but not much. She looked at Annie. "You must be Mrs. Perret. Your husband came by today."

"Call me Annie. He was just about to tell us what happened," Annie said.

Roger poured wine into the new glass Chantal placed on the table. "I haven't had time to check out what you gave me. Our daughter needed a bath before Annie got back from work, and…"

Robina held up her hand. "No need to explain. I've been thinking about the case ever since I went back to the station."

"But you're doing this unofficially," Roger said.

Robina nodded. "*Very* unofficially." She accepted the haggis that Chantal offered. They lifted their glasses in a toast. "It's good," she said after taking a sip.

"Why are you doing this?" Chantal asked.

"I was never satisfied that it was an ordinary hit and run," she said.

"And…" Roger prompted.

"When I got back to the station today, I went over the file again. I picked up something everyone, including myself missed."

"And that was," Annie said.

"The vehicle we recovered that hit your husband, Chantal, was a rental car. Kids joy riding don't usually take rental cars. It was stolen from the rental service at the airport," Robina said.

"But those cars are well observed," Roger said.

"We never talked to the rental car company." Robina turned to Roger. "Are you free the day after tomorrow?"

"Sure. What time?"

"It's my day off. Nine? After rush hour?"

"Chantal?"

"I'm meeting with the artist. I'll take both kids with me to work."

# 21

EDINBURGH, SCOTLAND

**C**hantal's Notes: *Richard Holland (died* circa *1483) satirical poem Buke of the Richard Howlat. Birds, alliteration pokes fun at church but supports the Douglasses before, during and after their downfall. Do we want to get into those politics—maybe politics and poetry section???? Maybe show an excerpt of the poem with the Rs, Ds, Gs, and Ms, jumping out*

Sae come the Ruke with a rerd, and a rane roch,
A bard owt of Irland with 'Banachadee!',
Said, 'Gluntow guk dynyd dach hala mischy doch,
Raike here a rug of the rost, or so sall ryive the.
Mich macmory ach mach mometir moch loch,
Set here doune! Gif here drink! Quhat Dele alis the?

When he was exiled to Orkney and Shetland (use photos of the area?) Rector of Halkirk. Use maps?

\* \* \*

"Chantal?"

J.J. Harris stood in the doorway, his huge, black portfolio in his hand.

She jumped.

"I'm sorry I startled you." His discomfort at her discomfort showed

94

in the blush that caused his freckles to meld together all the way up to his red wavy hair.

"What's a decade or two taken off my life?" Her smile proved she wasn't upset.

"I'm sorry, I really am."

"It's okay. Tea?"

He nodded.

As Chantal prepared two mugs, J.J. unzipped his portfolio and pulled out a roll of paper about a foot high, that he began to unroll to reveal a scene was of a shepherdess being pursued by a knight.

Holding the mugs in her hand, Chantal let her eyes absorb his work. Only the sky was a soft blue, the rest were slap-you-in-the-face strong colors. The figures were small, but as she looked more closely at the roll, she saw the shepherdess' skirt was well over her waist showing a well-rounded bottom. The knight's expression showed appreciation of the view.

"A bit risqué."

"I can see this running around the room just above the wainscoting," he said. "But that's not all."

He then pulled out illustrations: a town and a country mouse were shown by background rather than the clichéd clothing. "I suspect these will pass muster, not the others, but I like to give a choice, one to be rejected making the other more desirable."

"No one on the board is puritanical, but..." Chantal began. The door creaked opened again and board member Janis Aitken walked in. The anthropologist/writer had taken off her coat and as usual wore a narrow black skirt touching her boot tops and a black sweater that came down over hips. Her red earrings were so large that they grazed her shoulders. "I hate to barge in," she said.

"Not a problem, ever." The board never came by except for meetings, although they plagued her with emails and phone calls. Janis, of all of them, was the most rational and could often turn a disagreement into consensus without ever adding her own opinion. She had a method of questioning that didn't even seem like questions that often included, "If we did it this way what do you think would happen," or other questions that led the person to the conclusion Janis wanted. Chantal considered Janis a mentor in conflict resolution.

Janis motioned for J.J. and Chantal to sit in the two folding chairs. "There's no way to say this without creating a shock. Hamish is dead."

"Dead?" Chantal echoed.

"Dead? Hamish?" J.J. said.

"What happened?" Eighty was an age when people could die, but when Chantal had talked to him on the phone, two days ago, he had been in top form, laughing at his own jokes as usual. He had even remembered small details from the last meeting and was asking her follow up. "How do you know?"

"I was out walking my dog and went by his house. They were bringing his body out. The housekeeper was standing in the door—She called me in." Janis picked up Chantal's cup and took a long drink. "She found him at his computer."

Hamish might have been in his eighties, but he'd adopted new technology as soon as it came out. He sometimes had trouble figuring it out, but there was a neighbor, a young boy who tutored the old man.

"The housekeeper said he was at his computer, his head on the keyboard. He was in the middle of a sentence for his next novel."

"Holy shit," J.J. said. "That will rock the publishing world."

Chantal nodded. Hamish had not only been a world-wide best seller, he'd never been chary with his opinions. His standards for his genre were high. A good comment from him on a back cover of a young writer would boost the author up several notches. A bad review might cause publishers to never look at the new writer again.

"He's the biggest donor to this museum." Selfish, I am, Chantal thought. The poor man is dead, and I'm worried that his death will mean the end of this job.

# 22

## EDINBURGH, SCOTLAND

To reach the door, Robina Collins walked through the high wooden gate up the path of the twenty-by-twenty garden, which was mainly rose and gray flagstones. She climbed the six wooden stairs to the kitchen entrance. All the attached brick houses looked the same and although she'd been there the night before, in the daylight she wasn't sure about the color of kitchen door. In the dark it could have been red or black.

She was relieved when Roger Perret answered her knock.

"Are you ready?" She was wet. Her raincoat thrown over a dark gray suit and a black turtleneck hadn't done much to protect her. The red and black print scarf that she had tied after watching a ?Z video called "25 ways to tie a scarf" was damp. She'd put it on because she hoped to look French chic, even as she was chiding herself for thinking that way.

She folded her umbrella, a prolly as she called it, that had failed to protect her from the rain. Twice it had turned inside out.

Next door a neighbor was moving her garbage can from outside her fenced garden back onto her property. Chantal's had never been put out, she noticed.

Roger followed her eyes. "I really should have done it for Chantal. I should do more around the place."

"Isn't trying to find her husband's murderer helping?"

Roger stepped aside to let Chantal enter the kitchen. She wiped her feet on a mat with a duck and the word "welcome" in the same un-ducklike orange as the fowl.

"The children?" she asked.

"Chantal has taken them to the museum. Last night she'd stayed up late talking with my wife, about the death of one of the poets involved in the museum and what it would mean. My wife is good at that, talking people through their worries."

Robina didn't want to hear about his wife. She asked to use the toilet and would have been pleased to know that Roger watched her climb the stairs and was thinking again how attractive she was. But he wasn't a cheating man like many of the *flics* he knew.

When the toilet door shut, Roger, reminded himself he'd been lucky with his two wives, although Annie was a handful as Virginie never had been. Every now and then he wondered what his life would have been like had she not been killed, and he'd stayed at 36. Probably he would have had his heart attack earlier.

Love was a strange, strange thing, but faithful didn't mean he wasn't allowed to appreciate female beauty. When it was combined with intelligence and a good personality, his appreciation levels went up.

Robina almost skipped down the stairs and back into the kitchen.

"Just let me get my coat," he said.

They walked toward Haymarket where she'd parked her car. Robina was taller than Annie... more stylish without being a fashion slave. She carried herself with a confidence. Mostly she didn't seem like most women *flics* that he knew. Stop it, he told himself.

"It won't take long to get to the airport," she said. She was right.

The car rental agencies, or car hire offices in the local vocabulary, were grouped together. The one where the hit and run driver had stolen the car was a local: Scotsman Drive-Away.

"Sexist name," Robina said. "Women hire cars, too."

The office was like most car rental places: a smallish office with a couple of desks, computers, and three easy chairs upholstered in a plaid. Roger didn't know enough about Scottish plaids to tell if it were a clan plaid or not. A coffee table was between the chairs with yesterday's *The Edinburgh Evening News* and *The Scotsman* and *Edinburgh Life*.

A man with hair graying at his temples was behind one desk, and a much younger woman with blond hair grazing her collar sat at the other desk. Both wore vests matching the upholstery. She asked, "May I help you?"

Before Roger could say anything, Robina asked, "May I speak with the manager?

The man put out his hand. "Ian MacCallister. How may I help you?"

Robina flashed her badge. "We're looking into a robbery and a hit run about three months back."

Ian frowned and turned his head slightly to one side. "You don't rush, do you?"

"This is Roger Perret, who is an exchange policeman, part of a program that gives us more help," Robina said.

"Jillian, please make them tea, you do want tea, don't you?"

Roger nodded, although he would have preferred coffee. Robina was certainly ballsy, acting as if this were an official call. Although he knew he had years more experience than she did, based on their ages, he allowed her to take over.

"Exchange from where?" McCallister asked.

"The South of France," Roger said. He wanted to give enough information to be convincing, but not so exact to encourage MacCallister to check.

"Go there for holidays, when I can," MacCallister. Nice to get out of the bad weather, especially in winter. I don't know how I can help."

"We were wondering if perhaps there was some film of the parking lot where and when the car was stolen."

MacCallister snorted. "Took you long enough to ask. I offered when it first happened. You lot didn't seem all that interested."

"Again, understaffed. It's what happens with austerity, dontcha know?" Robina's brogue seemed stronger, matching MacCallister's, Roger noticed. He remembered Robina saying that the police had overlooked following up on the rental car. He chided himself for being critical. Overworked *flics* often had too much to handle. He didn't know what else might have been on their assignment sheets and no one connected joy riding kids, car rentals and hit and runs.

"We usually destroy the tapes every couple of weeks." He was interrupted by Jillian putting down a tray with paper cups in a matching plaid.

Roger wanted to say, "Isn't this taking corporate identity too far," but resisted. God, four years ago, he would have only been concentrating on their mission. He was getting rusty in his retirement. "Do I take it you no longer have the tapes, Mr. MacCallister?"

"Call me Ian. Wrong. I kept that one, just in case someone decided to do their jobs."

Roger found the combination of hospitality with the tea and the jibes interesting. Before he answered a man and a woman in business suits, small suitcases on wheels and laptop cases slung over their shoulders entered.

Robina said, "Why don't you take care of your clients. We can wait."

MacCallister smiled. "Jillian can handle them. We'll go into the back room."

"Perhaps you'd like to go for a second cuppa somewhere in the airport, our treat," Roger said. "We can talk more privately."

Before MacCallister left his desk, he pulled out a disk. "I transferred the tape for the day you mentioned to this key. If you have a laptop we can transfer it."

"I've one in my car. We can stop on the way to the coffee shop," Robina said.

Roger noted that Edinburgh Airport is not one of those places that could be in any city in any country. When he arrived, he'd been too glad to see his wife and anxious to get Sophie home before she became overtired. He liked the photos of long-horn shaggy cow photos decorating the walls and the men dressed in kilts. A man, also dressed in a kilt, walked up and down the concourse playing a bagpipe. The duty-free shops had the normal international products but there were signs for real Scotch whisky and canned haggis as well. He'd pass on the haggis, but maybe a bottle of the whisky when they left, which wouldn't be soon enough.

MacCallister led them to a small food establishment with tables in front, but also a few behind the counter overlooking the runway. We can talk privately here."

"I'll be direct," Robina said, when she returned with scones and coffee. "We don't think it was ordinary kids joyriding who took the agency's car that killed Duncan MacAndrew. Teenagers don't usually steal cars from airport rental agents."

"Of course they don't. I told the police that."

"Do you remember who you talked to?"

"An arrogant bastard, excuse my French." He looked at Roger. "Sorry."

Roger waved his hand. "When French swear, they don't say, 'Pardon my English, though.'" He said it with such a big smile that MacCallister had to smile back.

"Take a look." He handed them the disk.

Robina fired up her laptop and inserted the key. The quality was grainy and in black and white.

"It's the far end of the parking for hire cars," MacCallister said. "The camera is not easily visible there. My idea. It peeps through a sign reporting space numbers for the cars."

The three of them watched a slim figure, five foot six, enter the frame and look all around. They could tell the height because there were markings on the wall designed to help identify the height of any vandal. The idea started with banks, but this was the first time Roger saw it used by a private business.

"Is it a man or a woman?" Robina asked. She hit the key and the picture took up the full screen.

"Dressed like a kid in jeans, a sweatshirt and a baseball cap," McCallister said. "I've looked at this at least twenty times, but the hips seem a bit more like a woman's."

"You should be a detective," Robina said.

She's flirting, Roger thought. MacCallister's smile told him that it was a good technique.

The young man/woman walked to the car. His/her back was to the camera so they couldn't see how the car was opened, but it started immediately.

"He or she had to have a key," Roger said.

"The key was missing from the office, but no kid or anyone looking like that was in the office that day. We didn't even notice the key was missing until the next day. That wasn't a reserved car."

"Now look at the car next to it," MacCallister said.

They did, but didn't see anything unusual.

"That car had been rented by a woman that morning. She took the key, the paper work and never took the car."

"Were you paid for it?"

"Yes. We checked the credit card company. Everything was in order."

"And the paper work?" Robina asked that question.

"Never got it back," McCallister said. "Again, I tried to tell the police that, but the idiot I talked with…"

"Do you remember his name?" Roger asked.

"John Stewart and right rude he was too."

Robina glanced at Roger. He was sure that was her boss but would wait until they were in the car to ask.

"And the woman's?"

"I'll have to check the database."

"May I copy the key?" Robina asked.

MacCallister nodded.

# 23

Carol stretched out on her bed. Had she been a cat, she'd have been purring in the sunbeam coming from the skylight above. She was reading a Jake Lamar mystery set in Paris, one of her favorite cities. The tea that she had prepared earlier was only half drunk and the blueberry muffin bought the day before was half eaten. Toasted, it didn't taste stale.

Her duvet kept her warm. She had installed under the floor heating but turned it off at night because the air became too hot. She had absolutely nothing she needed to do for the next month except enjoy herself.

Or at least she hoped that she didn't: no planned meetings with the man, her ex-lover, who doled out her assignments. Half thoughts of quitting and not for the first time sometimes jumped onto the pages. She didn't need the money, but she had loved the challenge.

She loved the excitement.

She loved working out the details.

Or at least she'd loved it all until now. The challenge was waning.

Maybe she'd catch up on movies, see what plays were in town. Most of her friends were married with children and lived out in the suburbs. Visiting to listen to them brag about how clever little Timmy was because he opened his own baby food jar—well that didn't interest her.

Once she thought she might have a husband and children, but

the word *later* kept coming out of her mouth when people were rude enough to ask her. She had wondered at one time whether her biological time clock would lead her to looking at strollers and cute little baby clothes, but so far it hadn't rung, or if it had, it was too soft to hear. She still had enough years before menopause would force her into a final decision.

The telephone rang. She debated not answering, but caller id showed that it was Jonathan Webster. Why not say hello?

"Do you have time for lunch, Carol? I haven't seen or heard a word from you since we ate at your parents."

Of course he hadn't. She only called him when she needed something or vice versa. Probably he needed something now, but he was charming, fun, and she had nothing to eat in the house.

A grocery shopping trip was on her to-do list. The list of ingredients for several meals that she planned to cook for herself was already in her purse. Being holed up with books and DVDs with maybe a walk around the Common was the most ambitious thing she had on her schedule at least for the next couple of days. However, a good meal without clean up? "Depends on where you might want to take me?"

"Name it?"

"TexMex?"

"Señor and Señoritas? At 1:30 when the crowd begins to go back to work."

"Fine."

She looked at her watch. She could read at least five more chapters before she had to shower and walk to the restaurant nearby on Tremont Street.

\* \* \*

Carol found Jonathan seated toward the back of the restaurant that had the typical faux Spanish décor: piñatas, sombreros, brightly colored ponchos, that sort of thing. The restaurant was half full and most of the remainders were finishing coffee, dolling out bills or pulling credit cards from their wallets.

"A seat near the back," Jonathan said to the maître d, who sported a striped green, yellow and orange poncho over one shoulder. "That one, if possible." He pointed to it. No one was around that table, but it had dirty dishes on it.

"As soon as we clear it," the maître d muttered. Carol guessed he was a college student or at least was of an age to care less about his job.

"What's up?" Carol asked when they were seated. "This is a first. We get together when you need a beard, when you want your parents to think you might want a woman in your life. Sometimes I go to a film with you and Seth, and by the way, how is he?"

"Adorable as usual."

"And your law firm still doesn't suspect?"

"Definitely not. The Chairman has never asked, but suspects, I think." Jonathan called his father The Chairman and had since Carol and he were students at Phillips Andover. He even called the older Jonathan Webster III, Chairman to the old man's face. "We pretend I'm 'normal' and he doesn't want my mother to know and certainly not anyone in the firm. They don't allow couples, even hetero ones." He looked up. "And speaking of Seth, here he is now."

After shaking Jonathan's hand, Seth hugged Carol leaning his head on top of hers. "Do I look straight enough?"

"Could have fooled me," she said. Carol flicked her hand toward one of the two empty seats. "I like the handshake bit."

"Good cover, hun?" Jonathan asked.

The waiter appeared. They ordered the daily special and sangrias.

"So, what's up?" Carol asked when the waiter had brought her sangria. He was about as caring as the maître d.

"What makes you think...?" Seth started.

He was the type of gay, Carol thought, that when women looked at him they thought, what a waste, which she knew wasn't fair. A gay guy would look at a handsome straight man and think the same thing.

"She's savvy, that's why she's asking," Jonathan said. "It's my father, he's made me a proposal. "He's offered me a half million if I would get married."

Carol frowned waiting for the rest of the story.

"As I said, he suspects I'm gay and he may think I have a thing with Seth. He doesn't want to know for sure. I suspect something in his twisted little brain tells him that a good woman would make me forget Seth."

Carol sighed at the wasted energy of people pretending to be what they weren't for any of a myriad of reasons. Stupid. At the same time, there was so much that she would never tell her mother or anyone about her life. Fortunately, no one knew her secrets—not her darkest secrets, not her lightest secrets. That was different. She didn't pretend to be something she wasn't except for work and that was a game.

Seth sat forward resting his arms on the table. "Worse than that. He wants a Jonathan Webster Cinq." He stared into her eyes.

Carol met his stare before realizing what he was thinking. "Oh, no, you aren't thinking?"

Both men nodded.

"Me?"

"Look, a half million will let us set up our own law firm. We can do gay law."

"Gay law?" Carol wasn't sure she'd heard of that category: human rights, family law that sort of stuff, but gay law?

"All human rights issues. We'll sell one of our flats and move in together." Carol had been to their apartments, condos located in the same building on the Boston-Brooklyn line, although technically they only lived in Seth's, using Jonathan's only when family visited. She had been amused once when she'd been there. The couple had brought dirty dishes up from the other apartment and left a basket of clean clothes near a set up ironing board to make the flat looked live in. The medicine chest had the necessary partially used toiletries. At one point, Jonathan had left mustache trimmings in the bathroom sink for his parents to see.

"My first reaction was to tell him to go to hell, as my father, not as my boss," Jonathan said.

"I've never seen him so angry when he told me," Seth said, "but when he calmed down, I tried to make him think of what we could do with the money."

Carol fiddled with her glass before taking a big sip of the sangria. "And you are telling me this because I could be your... your incubator?"

When both men nodded, she asked, "What's in it for me?"

"My father said he'd give me another $250,000 when my wife produces Cinq. That would be yours. When we have the money safely salted away… stupid expression isn't it… you can divorce me because I'm gay."

"It would be nasty to go for alimony, though," Seth said.

Carol didn't need the money for being a baby machine, much less alimony. Each of her assignments brought in close to $100,000. Admittedly the new international banking laws made it harder for her to hide the money, but she had safe boxes full of gold as well as digital currencies such as Bitcoin.

She didn't play the stock market, calling it a sucker's game. She owned three apartment buildings over near Harvard medical school, a total of nine units. All were rented to families who'd been there forever and appreciated a landlord who kept up the premises—all this besides her trust fund on which she could live without anything else.

However, $250,000 would buy more real estate, a single house. Her chosen career in a way was like a star athlete's. It had a time limit. Combined with her getting bored it could lead to carelessness.

She found it hard to believe that she was giving it some consideration. Her mother and to some extent her stepfather would be ecstatic that she was getting married. They'd be thrilled to have Jonathan as a son-in-law until the divorce.

But there was a big catch. The baby wouldn't go away. It would want to be fed, clothed, schooled, loved.

Jonathan picked up on her concern. "If you liked the kid, you could help us raise it."

"In other words, I'd be surrogate mother?"

"Or the real one."

"We want a baby." Seth put his hand over Carol's. "But love is love." When he saw her hesitate he added, "You could be as involved as you want or not at all."

Carol liked the two men. That Jonathan was gay, had been no secret between them since she caught him kissing another male student at Phillips. He'd been terrified she would tell, but she saw no reason to. They were friends and afterwards confidents on a far deeper level.

She had been happy when Jonathan had found Seth after a series of disastrous relationships that had left him crying on her doorstep.

Seth and Jonathan made a good couple. They would be good parents, and they'd be happier being out of the corporate law firm dominated by The Chairman.

"If I wanted to keep it... him... her?"

"You could live in the same building, or we could all get a house together." Seth said.

Living together was more than she wanted.

"And I would get pregnant how?" Sleeping with Jonathan was more than even she could imagine.

"Artificial insemination." The two men spoke as one.

"And if it is a girl?"

"We try again," Seth said.

"And again," Jonathan said.

And if I get pregnant with three girls, I could end up with three abortions. She wasn't pro-life, but the idea of aborting a healthy child for its gender and to earn a quarter of a million dollars made her uncomfortable. The discomfort itself almost amused her considering her work and that she never had placed a high value on human life.

"But we have a way around it." Johnathan took her hand. "We won't marry until we know you're carrying Jonathan Webster Cinq."

Once, when she was at university, she thought she was pregnant, and she'd debated getting an abortion. Fortunately, her period started before she saw the doctor, but she suspected that she would have gone through with it rather than be saddled with a child before her junior year.

Her parents would have been delighted to be grandparents and would have pushed for marriage to the father, a boy in a man's body and even less ready than she was to settle down. Adoption would be out of the question for her parents, so her only option would have been abortion. She and the boy/man had bought a bottle of champagne when her period arrived. That was the last evening they'd spent together, reinforcing Carol's belief that abortion would have been the right decision if she had been pregnant.

"The waiter brought their meals. Carol did not speak until he was out of hearing distance. "You're both crazy."

Seth looked disappointed. "You won't do it?"

"I didn't say that. Let me think about it. But don't get your hopes up."

# 24

## EDINBURGH, SCOTLAND

**Sophie and Blane had conked** out early much to the surprise of their mothers who had put them on the couch after their baths with their blankies and a Sesame Street DVD. About ten minutes later the mothers noticed them curled up on the couch with their thumbs in their mouths and their eyes closed. They carried them to their respective cribs. Neither child woke as the women closed the bedroom door and tiptoed downstairs.

"Do you think they might be coming down with something?" Annie asked a few minutes later as she set the table. Even after a year, she still was unsure of herself as a mother. Children had never been one of her goals, but she adored her daughter. At times, she worried that Sophie would not survive her own inept mothering.

Downstairs, Chantal took frozen pizza out of its box while Roger tossed a salad with his special vinaigrette. For all the years that Annie had known him, he was never willing to tell her how he made it. She had joked that when he was in intensive care after his heart attack, she had been tempted to badger him into giving it to her by making him think he was on his deathbed.

The microwave dinged. Chantal removed the pizza. "I can't believe we three Francophones are eating this."

"I like the brand of frozen pizza," Annie said.

"I can't believe I do too." Roger stared at his hands rather than look at either woman.

"So, what did you find out at the car hire agency?" Chantal asked, her mouth full.

Roger filled her and Annie in on what he and Robina had discovered.

"I want to see the video," Annie said.

"Me too," Chantal said.

After the dinner dishes were cleared and Chantal had made herb tea, Roger set up his laptop. "Do you recognize the thief?" he asked Chantal.

She shook her head. "I'm not even sure if it is a man or a woman."

"Robina and I wondered about that, too."

"How did the thief get the car out of the garage?" Annie asked. I rented a car there when I came over for a wedding about a year ago. I needed a special token."

"He must have had one," Roger said. "The manager had no idea how he would have gotten it, though."

They watched the video five times more, stopping it in places to look more closely at this or that detail.

"It's a woman," Annie said. "She'd hit stop. "Hips. A slight indentation for a waist." She put the point of her knife against the waist of the thief on the screen.

"It could be just the way the cloth breaks on a skinny male," Roger said.

"I agree with Annie. The legs, even in the slacks, look too skinny. Usually men have thicker legs."

"Not always," Roger said. "There's another thing. The man at the agency said a woman had rented the car next to the stolen one but never took it." He stopped the video again and pointed to the second car.

"It stayed in the parking lot?" Annie asked. When Roger nodded, she said, "Than they could have used the token to get the car out of the parking garage."

"He, the manager, didn't remember what she looked like… his assistant thought it might have had gray hair, but she wasn't sure either."

"No woman ever went near the car she rented?" Chantal asked.

"No, and that's strange." Roger said.

"You and Robina didn't think to ask the guy more about the woman, the one who didn't take the car... what she was wearing... did she have luggage?"

Roger shrugged.

Annie reached out and covered his hand with hers. She wanted to say something about his being out of practice but didn't. It was her job to help her husband find his stride in retirement, not undermine him.

"Tracing the woman will be next to impossible at this point," he said. "At least the guy at the agency said that all their records from that period were back at headquarters. He couldn't get at them and we'd need a court order, which Robina can't ask for because she's not officially investigating." He cut himself another slice of pizza after tilting his head to ask the women if they wanted more. They shook their heads. "I can't help but believe, though, there's some connection."

"Like the boy and the woman could be the same?" Annie asked.

Roger shrugged.

"So! It's another dead end." Chantal sat back in her chair. "I want to cry."

"The thing is that this car theft is so strange, and a missing woman who doesn't use a rental car is so strange, that I no longer doubt that your husband was murdered," Roger said.

"Thank you." Chantal whispered the words. "It's nice to be believed."

"The problem is," he paused and let out a long sigh, "I have no idea where to go from here."

Annie knew that Roger often reached that stage in an investigation, but he would niggle it and niggle it until something made sense to him. She hoped he would do it this time before his desire to go home overrode his curiosity in the case.

"We didn't find anything in Duncan's work stuff, either, that would make any sense," Annie said. She didn't go into what she and Louisa had done, breaking into the HR suite. "And when I went by today, his office was empty and they were painting it."

"Dead end." Chantal continued crying.

Annie looked for a tissue. There were none. She handed Chantal a paper towel, who used it to blow her nose. "Could there be anything else, anything at all, anyone who might have considered Duncan an enemy enough to want to kill him?" Annie wanted Chantal to think that they were covering all possibilities, but sweet, loveable Duncan and the word "enemy" did not go together.

"His rugby team, there was one man he didn't get along with." Chantal frowned. "I'm trying to think of his name. Jamie, Jamie… something Irish… O not a Mc or a Mac." She pulled out of Annie's arms. "O'Donnell. That's it."

"Did he and Duncan fight over something?"

"I never met him but from what Duncan said he was unpleasant to everyone. Chip on his shoulder. I can't imagine that he'd kill Duncan."

"Could it have been him in the video?"

Chantal shook her head. "Jamie is a big son-of-a-bitch. And broad. He ploughed through the other team."

"Do you want Robina and me to talk to him?" Roger asked.

"You could, but I think you'd be wasting your time."

Annie had an idea. "Did he come to Duncan's funeral or wake?"

"I don't think so."

"Do you know who did?" Roger last.

"I have a guest list: guest is the wrong word, people who signed the guest book."

"Maybe we can check everyone on it," Roger said. When Chantal turned her back to him to clear the table, Roger rolled his eyes at Annie.

# 25

Annie felt she should be happy. Roger was on his way to eliminate possible suspects and once Chantal believed they were at a dead end, she would be able to quit her suck AGG job. She wasn't even sure there was anything more to learn here, but just in case, she would hold on at least for another week.

She imagined herself with Roger and Sophie going to the airport to catch a flight to Geneva for a quick visit with her parents, then train down to Argelès. Sophie loved the train. Watching the other people and the swaying of the car amused her then put her to sleep.

However, Annie wasn't happy. Quitting, not the job, which she would love to do, but not helping Chantal get a sense of justice, bothered her. She feared there was no way they were going to find who killed him. Too much time had passed and there were no clues.

When she got out of bed, everyone in the house was still asleep. Her goal was to get into the office before anyone else. Maybe others had been killed in strange ways at AGG. There was an intranet supposedly to improve morale, but Louisa MacLaughlin had said since AGG took over it was more of a list of don'ts than anything else.

Other than Duncan being unhappy at work, there was no other reason to think that his death was work related. Her ability to see if there any financial misdoings existed was nonexistent. Still, nosing around the intranet might generate some ideas.

For the company to have an intranet for alleged morale, then

114

so overburden the staff that they didn't have time to look at it was corporate stupidity at its finest. Her feet touched the icy bedroom floor. She felt for her slippers without turning on the light then gave up and scuttled into the bathroom.

Chantal's shower had limited hot water. A long shower was neither fair to the next person nor to Chantal's bills.

It was still dark when she left the house. The days were growing shorter and shorter.

Before Annie had fallen asleep last night, Roger had asked her if she'd ever thought of suggesting that Chantal and Blane move back with Chantal's folks. "Not a good idea," she'd whispered and had turned over. Although it would have eased Chantal's financial pressures, she knew that Chantal's mom would make life hell with her bossiness and her constant reminders that if Chantal had stayed in Geneva and not moved to Scotland she wouldn't have the problems she was having.

Even if Annie had suggested it, she would have phrased it as, "Have you ever considered…" Telling people what they should do, just would never be her style.

When Annie arrived at the AGG building, the cafeteria was just opening. Annie waited for the coffee and tea lady, as she was called, to pour water into the huge heated container. Although in her mid-fifties, the woman scampered up and down the stepladder as agile as any Olympic athlete if there were an event for pouring pitcher after pitcher of water. Another of the staff, a woman also in her mid-fifties set out tea bags, sugar and milk cups. Did all the cafeteria staff belonged to the same decade?

A notice said that beginning January 1, cafeteria meals would no longer be company subsidized. Annie hadn't remembered seeing it before. Maybe she'd been unobservant, but she hadn't heard any grumbling either.

"Good morning." Annie tried to make her voice cheerful.

The woman smiled. "You're in early. Most people drift in just in time to start work."

Annie believed that. Yesterday she'd heard several people complaining they had to wait so long to clock in, that they were late and were afraid their pay would be docked. Woe be to the person who was constipated or had diarrhea. Bathroom breaks were clocked too.

She knew that her boss, if he discovered how early she was in, would remind her she was NOT, and he would repeat NOT, be paid for the extra time.

In her imagination, she pictured herself standing up after one of his criticisms and saying, "There's not enough money in the world for me to stay in this shithole," but today would not be that day. If there was anything else to find out about a connection between the company and Duncan's death she was better off here.

Damn it!

Her instinct told her there was a connection. That her instincts were right about 60-70 percent time only meant they were wrong 30-40 percent. Instincts weren't facts.

It wasn't just instinct. According to Chantal, Duncan had no enemies thus no one would have a reason to kill him. Sure, he played rugby with a local club with someone no one liked. Maybe Roger could question the members of the team, but Duncan had been playing with the group since he'd finished university. Chantal told her it was an all-in-good-fun team who liked winning, but weren't fanatic.

Lose and a beer at the pub afterwards where all mistakes were forgiven.

Win, and a beer at the pub was for celebration.

Duncan had been club treasurer one year but had handed that chore over three or four years before. Chantal couldn't remember exactly how long. The amounts of money were so small, that a murder motive made no sense.

All the other things that occupied Duncan centered around Chantal and Blane. He had been a family man who loved coming home at the day's end, trade his suit for sweats, play with his son, eat his tea and maybe watch the telly with his wife or read a book.

Chantal said her husband thought himself dull, but he was a happy man, or at least he had been up until the almost accidents had started happening. The change began when AGG had bought his company.

"He was so enthused at first," Chantal had said last night. They'd sat on her bed. "He thought that with the resources of a multi-national, he could do much more for employee development. That feeling lasted about two weeks. He would come home and say, 'I don't want to talk about it.'" Chantal mimicked her late-husband's tone. "Before we'd share stories about our work, but then he closed up. I mean closed up. It never happened before in our marriage."

Annie brought up her own work on the computer so when someone else came in she could switch screens instantly. She put the paper copies of one of the documents that she was working on next to her keyboard. She never understood why they wanted her to work from the paper copies when doing on-screen translation was easier.

Once the second screen came up, she went into the company intranet. Like Louisa had said, much of it was what wasn't allowed was written in negative terms. Annie mentally rewrote each sentence in positive terms. She loved the sign, "The grass thanks you for not stepping on it" vs. "stay off the grass."

There were pulldown menus for the different countries where AGG had a subsidiary. A lot of it was more blah blah about how wonderful the company was including a message from the CEO telling how profitable it was and the rosy outlook for the future, which was due to his wonderful leadership. And there was a sentence in different languages about the honor of being employed by such a successful, forward-looking multi-national.

The CEO's photo was against the backdrop of Copley Square in Boston where AGG was headquartered. Annie hadn't spent much time there, but it was the region where her parents had grown up. On visits to her grandparents, they had toured the city giving her a perspective about her birth country where she felt like a complete stranger. As always, she and her father would go off and explore the history while her mother visited friends.

She always felt smug when watching a TV show that she recognized a place in a foreign city that wasn't a major landmark and could think, "I had a cup of coffee there, or we ate at a restaurant around the corner, so-and-so died there in a revolution, or an (artist, musician, writer that she had seen, listened to or read) lived there.

On the Scotland page, there was an obituary for Duncan in the events heading that included promotions, marriages, resignations and new hires. Other deaths included retirees, but they were all within the last month. There was no archive for anything.

She flipped back to the headquarters and she noticed they too had obituaries and that a Rita Rizzoli had died in Boston—like Duncan's obit—there was no cause of death given. Considering how many people worked in the Boston area, for AGG was one of the region's largest employers, a death wasn't all that unexpected. Still Annie jotted down the name on her iPad to research later.

She went into the German site to discover that Henrich Müller had died suddenly of a heart attack at the age of thirty-five. He was the CEO of a subsidiary AGG had just bought. Stress, probably.

People started walking in. Annie changed screens and began translating the rules for emergency leave into Dutch that said, employees had to deal with emergencies on their own time. From living in the Netherlands and having had several assignments in Amsterdam, she knew that the Dutch were allowed this type of leave to care for a sick child, handle a broken water main, that sort of thing with full pay.

She went to the toilet, taking her iPad with her. Once in the stall, she searched the Internet to find the government site that gave the current law. AGG was in violation.

At lunchtime, Annie went to HR. Fiona Clark was at her desk eating a sandwich. No other employees were in the HR suite. She smiled at Annie. "Come sit down. Want part of my sandwich?"

"I'm on my way to the cafeteria."

"Too bad, it would mean fewer calories for me." Fiona wasn't fat, but she wasn't skinny either. "What can I do for you?"

"It's the emergency leave policy I've been translating for the Netherlands."

"What about it?"

"It doesn't conform to Dutch law."

Fiona put down her sandwich. She opened her mouth to say something, but then closed it.

"How do you know this?"

"I worked in the Netherlands. I double checked the government website."

Fiona gave a long sigh. "There's really nothing I can do about it. In this company... Did you say anything to your supervisor?"

Annie shook her head.

"Don't. It won't go well for you if you do."

Annie waited for more information. None was forth coming. "I'd better get to the cafeteria before my lunch hour is over."

As she walked down the stairs to the cafeteria that was clearing out as people headed back to their desks, she wondered if Duncan had known about the parent company breaking the law in other countries and that was what upset him.

Her imagination, no matter how vivid, couldn't find a connection between that and Duncan's death. People didn't get killed just because someone discovered a company was doing something wrong.

# 26

**R**obina Collins brought two coffees back to the table where Roger Perret waited. The clock, one of those kitschy ones of a cat with a pendulum tail, on the Kitty Tearoom wall read 10:19.

Two women, each with a baby carriage, were the only other people there. One baby whimpered as its mother, or a woman Roger thought was its mother, rocked the carriage with one hand. Whatever she and the other woman were talking about, it engrossed them.

"My boss comes back today. He won't be happy to find I've taken a day off. I'm happy it's one more day without him." Robina placed sugar next to the coffee cups. Those cups had faces of cats as did the napkins. Roger hoped the toilets weren't litter boxes.

"You don't like him?" Roger noticed how good she looked in the navy-blue slacks and navy-blue sweater, which fit extremely well. She'd thrown a plaid woolen suit jacket, which had a matching blue stripe over a chair. Or maybe the plaid should be called tartan. He'd been corrected once on using the word incorrectly.

"You know the saying, 'My way or the highway'?"

Roger nodded.

"That's my boss. And if I do get an idea that he does listen to and it pans out, then he thought of it."

"I've had supervisors like that. Probably everyone has, unfortunately."

120

"This may be the last day I can get off and then you're on your own except for my normal free days. My badge will get you in doors to talk to people, but if I'm not with you then…"

"I don't look enough like you to pass if you loan me your ID card, and I certainly don't look like a Robina."

She smiled, holding his eyes slightly longer than he was comfortable with but he let her be the one to break away. "Let's see the list."

Roger brought out his iPad with the name of those who had attended Duncan's funeral. With Chantal's help, each one had been put on a spreadsheet with the name, address, email, phone, profession where known and their relationship to Duncan. The five names on the top of the list, Chantal had indicated might be the most productive. Three names at the bottom, she'd written, "I've no idea who this is." On the last name, she wrote, "I couldn't even read the handwriting on this one."

Jamie O'Donnell was the first on this list.

"Chantal said that O'Donnell was hostile to Duncan, but she didn't know any more than Duncan didn't like him all that much either."

"Both on the same rugby team." Robina read the note. "We should start there."

They drove to O'Donnell's workplace, a factory specializing in cakes, pies and biscuits as Chantal called cookies. Good baking smells hung in the air.

The receptionist's eyes widened when Robina showed her badge. The girl was young, with long blond hair, probably only a slightly lighter shade than what nature had bestowed. As she talked, she twirled a strand.

"He's not in trouble," Robina said. "We thought he might have seen something as a bystander."

"I thought he might have done something wrong with his temper and all." The receptionist clamped her hands over her mouth, much like a small child who'd been told to keep a secret and said something like, "I was told not to say that daddy was drunk last night," and then realized what she'd said too late to retract it.

As they walked outside to the loading dock where they'd been told they could find him by the hair-twirling receptionist, they saw three men dressed identically in blue coveralls and matching red jackets.

As they approached, Robina explained why she'd been so careful to tell the receptionist, after flashing her badge, that O'Donnell was in no trouble, but they thought he might have information on a matter. "If we get him mad and he complains to my boss: then I'm in big trouble. Big, big trouble," Robina said, "Impersonating an officer on duty."

Roger had already guessed her reasoning.

Two delivery trucks with the yellow company logo on the side of the red truck were backed up to the dock. Men were loading pallets of boxes onto the back of the vehicles.

"Which one do you think O'Donnell is?" Roger asked.

"Any of them have the build to play rugby. And they are all about Duncan's age."

As they watched, Roger noticed two of the men were chatting and smiling. They wore blue coveralls with open jackets with the name of the company on the left pocket. Each had a name badge hanging around their necks with their photos, but the typeface was too small to read. A third man was working at the same rate as the other two. He neither smiled or talked. "How about the unhappy one?"

They moved forward until they were right below the dock looking up. Roger didn't like that position from a strategic point. He maneuvered himself onto the platform and pulled Robina up after him.

"You can't come up here. It's restricted," the non-smiling one said.

"We're looking for Jamie O'Donnell," Robina said.

"Who wants to know?"

Robina pulled her badge.

"What have you done now, Jamie?" the taller of the two smiling men asked. Only now they weren't smiling. They stood and watched, their arms folded across their chests.

"He's done nothing. We need some information about a crime that really has nothing to do with him," Robina said.

"Then go away." Jamie lifted another pallet and put it on top of the three he had put on the truck earlier.

"It's about Duncan MacAndrew."

"Never liked the git, had a big, fat head. Just because he's dead, I don't like him any better."

"You went to his funeral," Roger said.

"Hey, you've a froggy accent. When did the police hire across the water?" He shoved his hand in his coverall pockets.

"Exchange program," Robina said. "You went to his funeral. Accents aren't a reason not to answer the question."

"The whole team did. Wouldn't have been right not to."

"You two had a fight, we heard, shortly before he died," Robina said basing it on Chantal's notes.

"Nothing serious. I was mad. He kept missing practice. Said it was work. I told him if he couldn't practice, he shouldn't play."

"Did you hit him?" Roger asked.

"Are you crazy? If I'd hurt him, then he wouldn't be able to play. That would really make the team mad at me."

"Anyone else on the team who would want to kill Duncan?" Robina asked.

Jamie shook his head. "He was kinda too devoted to his family. Seldom had time for more than one beer at the pub after a… not something you would get killed for."

Robina and Roger thanked him.

Back in the car, Roger said, "I noticed you didn't give him your card."

"I don't want him calling at the station. What do you think? Suspect or not?"

"Not worth bothering with. Who is next?"

# 27

## BOSTON, MA

Carol Dixon walked back to her loft after her lunch with Jonathan and Seth. As she approached the Park Street Station T stop at the top of Boston Common and crossed in front of the Park Street Church, her mobile phone rang.

She had been remembering that when she was in third grade her class had sung, "My Country 'Tis of Thee" there commemorating the anniversary of its first performance ever in the church. She couldn't remember which anniversary. She didn't care. Her parents had forced her to go and she'd stood in the first row without opening her mouth.

"I despair of you," her mother had said, not for the first time and not for the last, after the performance. Her mother had taken away her dolls as punishment, not that Carol cared.

She disliked her dolls. They never had a pee pee like she did. She hated her fashion doll the most and had taken one apart to see if there was anything inside like a heart or stomach. That was the point that her mother sent her to a child psychiatrist, Dr. Childs.

"If your name had been Dr. Adult would you not be allowed to work with children?" she had asked. He had laughed not realizing that what she wanted to do was annoy him, not make him laugh.

Carol found she had a special talent for making adults uncomfortable by looking at them a certain way as if she could penetrate their lies. She considered it her revenge for the ills forced upon her.

She also learned how to play their game to get what she wanted.

That worked so well in school, that her grades were always tops except for math.

Her first private school for junior and senior high years was in Lowell, Massachusetts just off Route 38 as one entered the old mill city. The school had taken over several old Victorian mansions that once belonged to mill owners.

Most students came from wealthy New York families and were the girls that couldn't get into Phillips Andover or Exeter or any other top school. Yet thanks to the horrendous tuition, it could hire top teachers to bring out the best in each student.

After she put her math teacher in a position that he was forced to touch her breasts, her math grade was an A-. "Only A-," she'd asked. The rest of her As she'd earned and without a great deal of effort: history, literature, even the non-math sciences came easily to her. After one reading the material became part of her. Biology was fun because of dissection. She liked cutting up the cat best.

"It would look strange if you went from a D to A," her math teacher had said.

"You could say either I suddenly understood or that I seduced you. That would be bad for your job security."

She would sit in the front row and stare at him. He never touched her or gave her a low grade again.

As for the other girls at the school, she thought most of them stupid for caring about clothes, make-up and boys, although boys were forbidden. When she had joked that "nuns in a convent" had more male contact and more freedom, she'd won the friendship of her three roommates. She pretended to be interested in what they were interested in.

Her junior year she transferred to Phillips Academy in Andover where the courses were harder. She still pulled top grades and was commended by her teachers.

Dr. Childs and her mother were pleased that Carol finally fit in. Carol didn't care that they were happy or not except it kept them off her back.

She had no problem being accepted at Harvard between her grades and 1600s on her SATS and Achievements. Her math teacher, the one from the Lowell private school, wrote a glowing reference. Her essay on how she wanted to become a civil rights lawyer didn't hurt.

At Harvard, she convinced her mother and stepfather, for her father was now dead, she needed her own apartment in Cambridge. They bought one for her. It allowed her time to study without having to play the game of making friends with students.

She stayed in the flat through Harvard Law School. Once she passed the bar, and despite job offers from several top law firms in Boston, probably some at her stepfather's urging, she used the sale and part of her inheritance from her father and grandfather to buy her loft in downtown Boston.

It was at that point she had a much more interesting offer for work than putting in sixty hours a week, locked into a "cube farm" as she called the offices she'd visited and seen the new associates hunched over their computers.

Her memories were broken by her phone ringing again.

"Carol!" It was the voice of man for whom she freelanced and had since her last year of law school. He was a friend of her stepfather's, the same age, and her lover. A "what if conversation" after sex prompted him to hire her for assignments.

"I have another assignment for you. In fact, I have three."

"Too much, too close together."

"Think in terms of over the next nine months," he said.

"That should give me plenty of time to plan. When shall we meet up?"

"I need to be in Cleveland next week."

They seldom met in Boston, partially because of his wife. Carol would fly into a major city, not the city meeting place but one within a reasonable distance and rent a room, which she would never use but would rumple the bed and wet the towels. Hiring a car, she would drive to the city where he was. Most times they would sleep together, but that was far less frequent now much to her relief. Unlike the beginning of their relationship, if she could even call it that, he had difficulty getting and keeping it up.

The next day she would return to her arrival airport, take a plane to another city, stay a night than fly back to Boston. Nor did she know or care where he was before or after their meetings.

This would be the only phone contact.

Nine months…

She wasn't sure she wanted another assignment right now or ever.

In nine months, she could be a mother and a wife. Maybe it was an omen that she should take Jonathan up on his offer.

She took out her phone. When he answered, she said, "Get a cup ready and make an appointment at a clinic."

# 28

Chantal's Notes: Florentius Volusenus also Wilson Florence (1504-1547 maybe on both dates). We've the first page only of a manuscript 1574 from Florence of his De Animi Tranquillitate. Wish we had one from the Lyon 1543 printing. For illustrations we can do a lot with the story (real?) that the idea of an abode of a tranquility came to him when he had a dream. The legend went that the dream followed a conversation with a student as they sat on the banks of the River Lossie where it was said that he was born.

His life was interesting because he tutored Cardinal Woolsey's son. Woolsey was an agent of Thomas Cromwell and well-travelled. He was a philosopher, knew Hebrew as well as Greek and Latin and can be described as a Christian Humanist and ...

\* \* \*

Chantal had taken almost a half hour working on those two paragraphs. She would pick up her pencil and then put it down again as her mind wandered. She wanted this poet as part of the museum and their ownership of one of the manuscripts was her best argument for including him.

She glanced at her watch. Damn! She didn't have that much time before the morning board meeting. She was grateful to Roger for taking care of Blane, even if it meant he could do nothing related to the investigation of Duncan's death for the day.

The board, which was annoying her more than usual, was split two/two Peter and Janis yes: Jackie and David no. But Peter especially might sway Jackie. If only she had crammed it through last meeting before Hamish died. He would have been on her side.

How to get beyond the idea that he was too modern. Her ability to summon new arguments was failing her. Lord, politics in such a small environment was exhausting and a complete waste of time and energy.

Because it was a morning board meeting, Chantal had provided the members with scones, cream, preserves, coffee and tea. All edibles were still in the bags from the bakery and she still needed to make the coffee and brew the tea. She began to set the table, hoping it would be inviting but not so special that they would spend time on it rather than business.

None of her board were morning people. Maybe, just maybe, this meeting hadn't been such a good idea. She should have waited until afternoon, but none of them were available the same time on the same day. No general had to strategize a battle plan like she did to arrange a meeting. At least she was dealing with four, not five difficult people. That made her feel badly, knowing that Hamish was in his grave.

"Yo hoo! Jackie Ferguson, the first to arrive, had a voice that penetrated. Chantal suspected the woman was going deaf. Over the year, they'd been working on the project, her voice kept getting louder and she needed statements repeated more often.

"I'm in here." Chantal turned, the carton of cream in one hand, the pitcher in the other as the woman bombed into the room.

Jackie Ferguson eyed the cream reminding Chantal of a person who had just come across a rotting corpse. At sixty, Jackie was still thin, no thickening of the waist the way many her age had suffered. Chantal doubted there was waist-keeping plastic surgery, but if there were and Jackie needed it, she would have it. As always, she was perfectly dressed.

Sometimes, Chantal wondered how expensive her nightgowns

were and what labels were on them. Jackie once explained that if she were writing shopping novels, she had to do lots of research. It wasn't her fault that the research ended up in her closet.

As Jackie poured herself a coffee, David Jones slouched in. He looked hung over.

Chantal knew David spent a lot of time hanging out in pubs and letting the women fawn over the famous writer. "I'm a male Enid Blyton," he'd boasted at the last meeting. "Isn't that a great pick-up line?"

It was Hamish who had chosen the board, his right as the mover-shaker behind the museum and as the largest donor, and he'd thought having a younger person would increase the chances of catching the interest of Gen W or as Hamish had said, "Whatever damned letter is being used these days, Z, X, Y, M to describe them."

That David cared diddly dam for literature other than the writing in his bank account didn't help.

Peter McEnroe entered the room carrying his beaten-leather briefcase with his initials next to the lock. He put it on the table as if it were a baby placed in its cradle. Chantal knew the briefcase went along with some literary prize he had won early in his career, which had given him the status to find a higher-class publisher.

The locks opening made a snap. Peter removed five blue, one-inch folders. Peter, like his books, would never use one word when two or ten would do. Chantal found him unreadable even if he had been nominated for the Man Booker prize. His writing bored her.

At first, she figured it was because English was her second language, but later decided that his writing was boring because he was boring. Maybe that was why he had been through four wives—probably they couldn't stand his main topic of conversation—himself.

She glanced at her watch making a bet with herself on how long it would be before he mentioned his nomination.

Janis Aiken came out of the ladies' room. Chantal hadn't seen her enter the building. "It's looking good in there, nothing like a fun toilet," she said. "I love the mural painted over the sinks. J.J. did a good job."

"Too bad it added to the cost. Now Hamish is gone we can't count on him topping up the fund anymore." This was from Peter who adjusted his cravat and sat down.

Chantal knew the next hour would be battle about cost cutting. At one point, Peter asked, "I don't suppose you'd consider a salary cut, Chantal?"

Before she could answer, Janis spoke up. "For God sake, Peter, the woman is a single mother and we're only paying her a pittance as it is."

Fifteen minutes and thirty-two seconds into the meeting, Peter mentioned his nomination.

Chantal found the circling of words about costs reminded her of a cyclone spinning for the joy of the spin. She gave them a paper with her ideas for the opening as well as the list of places to list the museum, proposed events to attract the public as well as scholars. The last reason might be another argument to include Florentius Volusenus. Four academic papers on the poet had been published in the last two months.

"I've contacted English literature departments throughout Scotland, England and Wales to propose special seminars here. I've priced them slightly less than they would find elsewhere. Nearby there are several B&Bs, which would be willing to provide rooms at special rates during those events."

"Hmmm," Jackie mumbled something. Chantal doubted that she had read any of the poems or had even heard of the poets before joining the board. Probably she hadn't read many of them afterwards.

"And we've overlooked social media," Chantal said.

Social media had been bad words when Hamish was alive. He wrote his novels by hand and gave them to his secretary. Once when she dropped papers off at his home, Chantal saw that he still had a dial telephone on the table near the door.

The meeting rambled on until lunch, when Chantal ordered sandwiches from a nearby pub. Even that produced disagreement.

By two, they still hadn't covered the Florentius Volusenus issue, but they gave Chantal permission to set up a Facebook page and write a blog about the development of the museum. When they all wanted to approve each blog, Chantal shuddered.

Bless Janis. She proposed that in the interest of time, only she should approve it the first few months. Later they could take turns. Chantal made another bet with herself that none would want to take on the extra work. She was grateful that at least as writers they knew the importance of publicity, although none of them wanted to do it themselves.

A plan for Chantal to approach the major companies in the area for funds was approved four to nothing.

By 5:30 all of them kept looking at their watches. "That's it." David stood up and began gathering up the financial statements, drawings and other papers distributed. "I've a hot date. Good job, Chantal."

The others, except for Janis, followed. "They certainly have added to your work load."

"I still have a job."

"At the same pay, even. I sometimes wonder why I even bother with those assholes."

"You can't quit. I need you."

"Speaking of needing me, any luck on finding out more about your husband's death?"

Chantal shook her head. "A policewoman is helping my friend's husband, who is an ex-policeman. They have eliminated lots of possibilities but haven't found one good lead."

"I doubt you'll ever accept it was an accident?" Janis reached for her coat.

Chantal shook her head.

"Would it help if I joined their team, new damned eyes and all that?"

Chantal stood up and hugged Janis. "Thank you."

"For offering to help?"

"That and for being the voice of reason."

# 29

**"Oh shit!" Robina thought when** the receptionist said, "Ian is gunning for you." She had just entered the station and still wore her coat, scarf and gloves.

So far it had been a bad morning. The alarm hadn't gone off and even her cat had slept in not doing his, if-you-don't-feed-me-I'll-die-of-hunger act, the shower pressure was terrible and the sweater she'd planned to wear had a spot that she hadn't noticed. Her hair dryer broke and even with short hair the fall cold had left her chilled as she pedaled her bike to work.

She had not seen her boss since he'd come back yesterday. She'd been off with Roger. Granted, all they'd done was eliminate suspects. That wasn't entirely true. They had confirmed and reconfirmed that Duncan MacAndrew was a nice man, liked by his rugby team mates and friends.

Except for the git on the team who disliked him, no one was unhappy at giving information, useless though it might be. They still hadn't gone to the people Duncan worked with either in his current job or his previous one. That might be more difficult considering AGG had a pull in the city as a good a jobs provider.

Robina debated getting a cup of coffee, but she heard the roar from Ian's office. As she entered, she saw Ian McAlister glowering. He was a gold-medal glowerer, she thought. "Welcome back."

He stood up, leaning on his desk with his knuckles much like a gorilla, an overweight and balding gorilla. "What the hell are you doing?"

"I was going to get a cup of coffee and check my messages."

"Don't get smart with me, young lady." McCallister had made no secret of his disapproval of women police doing any work other than acting as receptionists, waitresses or secretaries. Robina had met his wife who cowered as much as he glowered.

Robina's relationship with him had been smoother when she pretended something he was lecturing her on was new information, which most often it was not. "I don't understand."

"I had a phone call from Robert McDuff. You *do* know him."

Of course, she knew him. He was Duncan's insurance agent that she'd spoken to with Roger the last time out. The agent had been at the funeral and was an old-school friend of Duncan's. They hadn't learned anything new. She nodded.

"What the hell were you doing with some Frenchie asking him about a closed case?"

Robina held her coat in front of herself, a cloth shield while she thought of how to answer.

"Well?"

McAlister repeated his question.

"I think that Duncan MacAndrew was murdered."

"He was, by a hit and run driver that we haven't been able to find."

"I think it was something more."

"It's a closed case."

"Then why had he been almost run down more than once and in London as well as here?"

"He was probably too stupid to look both ways?"

"In a parking garage?"

McAlister came around to the front of his desk, using his bulk to force her to stand straighter. "You were using your badge when you had no right to."

Robina didn't remind him that he used his badge to get parking places.

"I'm putting you on suspension as of now, while we investigate."

She knew she should keep her mouth shut but the words came out before she could stop them. "Investigate the MacAndrew killing?"

This time, McAlister screamed. "No, to see if you could keep your job. Now get out of her you stupid, stupid bitch. And hand in all your equipment and identification before you leave the station."

For a moment Robina didn't move.

"I said, get out."

She turned and walked although she wanted to run. That people had heard she could tell by the way everyone was fascinated with whatever was on their desk and not a whisper was being spoken. Usually there was a low buzz of voices, tapping of computers, people talking on the phone.

Nada!

Rien!

Nothing!

Total silence!

Robina fought tears as she walked to her own desk and gave up everything that made her a policewoman, leaving them in a line-up on the top. She put on her coat and walked out of the station.

As she unlocked her bike, Mike McNulty, who held the same rank as she did, came up behind her. "I heard."

"Who didn't?"

"I think you were right. I was never happy with the decision to close the MacAndrew case."

Thank you didn't seem appropriate, so she just shrugged.

"I've kinda been looking into it too. Maybe we could meet up."

She wanted to hug him. "Can we do it with the 'Frenchie' and Mrs. MacAndrew?"

He nodded. "It's a good idea, but I'd also like to take you to dinner."

She threw her leg over the bar. She'd always preferred boys' bikes. The last thing she needed now was a come on, even if Mike was a nice guy, widowed and cute.

"This isn't just a come on. I've wanted to ask you out for some time."

Robina wasn't sure how to answer, so she said nothing.

"Okay, I'll change the subject. "I've been doing some nosing around myself on my free time."

"Why?"

"I never felt right about this case, and I've had some spare time."

"I'll see how Chantal and Roger feel."

Only when she pushed off on her bike, did she let the tears flow. God damned bastard, she thought. It was McAlister not McNulty who was the object of her scorn.

# 30

BOSTON, MA

**C**arol Dixon woke up to the cadence of rain on her skylight. The floor-to-ceiling windows were water-streaked. She stuck the thermometer, purchased yesterday, in her mouth.

Damn, she thought after looking at the reading, I must be ovulating. What timing.

She reached into her purse, next to her bed and pulled out her cell. Jonathan was on automatic dial. He picked up after the first ring.

"I'm ovulating. Can we go to the clinic today?"

She heard him laugh. There was the sound of dishes in the background.

"Hey Seth, Carol still says yes. She's ovulating. Now!"

"Fantastic." Seth's voice came through the receiver, but fainter. She could picture them eating breakfast in the nook of their townhouse. A window that looked out on a small, brick-paved courtyard decorated with trees and plants.

Their kitchen was far better equipped than hers because both men delighted in cooking, the same way she delighted in buying ready-made meals from different restaurants.

"We checked with the clinic, but it is at least three months before we can get an appointment," Jonathan said.

Carol hesitated. She'd be in the middle of her next series of assignments. Pregnant women are even less suspicious, she thought.

Then again, it wouldn't take much to get her to change her mind and not do it all.

"Are you still there?" Jonathan asked.

She sighed.

A short pause. "Not having second thoughts, are you?"

"Maybe one-point-five thoughts."

She heard Jonathan say, "She may be thinking of backing out." The sound was muffled as if he had put his hand over the telephone, and she could hear Seth's response.

"How about we try a DIY method since I'm ovulating right now according to my handy dandy thermometer?" Carol surprised herself in saying that.

"Hold on a second."

The rain continued to batter the skylight: the sky was dark gray. She waited for their response. She heard their muffled voices and guessed Jonathan had his hand over the mouthpiece.

"Put the coffee on. We'll call into work and be over in about an hour." Jonathan disconnected.

Carol got out of bed. The under-floor heating made the walk to the bathroom comfortable on her bare feet. She showered quickly and threw on jeans and a sweatshirt. There was no dress code for artificial insemination. In the kitchen she ground the coffee beans. Because the boys were fussy about their coffee, she kept some special beans for them. Special, because they had brought them over themselves and had written their name on the bag, after she'd serve something they termed undrinkable.

She rummaged through her kitchen drawers in case she had a turkey baster and wasn't surprised that she didn't. She'd never cooked a turkey, but at one point her mother had provided her with several utensils from a gourmet cooking store as a birthday gift.

An imagined scene of telling her mother that the baby she was carrying had a turkey baster as a father made her smile.

By the time her doorbell rang she had two cups of coffee for them, which she handed them immediately. Seth held up a bakery bag. "*Pain au chocolate* in case you haven't eaten."

She led them to the oak table she'd found in an old barn in Ipswich, not the Ipswich in Massachusetts, but the one in England and had had it shipped to Boston, more to annoy her mother who balanced New England frugalness with quality and had deemed the table not worth the shipping cost, just as Carol knew she would. At times Carol felt she should outgrow the need to win her mother's disapproval: she enjoyed it so much.

The men wore suits and ties. "We should go into work after this. Otherwise we'll never catch up," Seth said.

The three of them sat at the table. "How do we do this?" Carol asked: their goal, their decision. "I know it wouldn't appeal all that much, but Jonathan, we could actually have sex."

Seth shrugged. "It wouldn't be like you were cheating on me with another man."

"Let's look on-line. I mean, we haven't had time to research this."

She brought her tablet to the table and typed in home artificial insemination into duckduckgo.com—her favorite search engine because it didn't keep records of searches and it didn't turn the information over to any spy agency. In her line of work every precaution was necessary. To the people who said that you needn't worry if you have nothing to hide, she did have something to hide.

This was her fifth tablet. Every couple of months, she destroyed her old ones, although any police might wonder why anyone would buy six tablets in a year.

"Here's what we need," she said. A syringe with a plunger that is about four inches long, a sterile collection container, tube and germicidal soap."

"I'll go to the drug store," Seth said, put his coat on and was out the door.

"Wait," Jonathan called before the door closed behind his lover. "It can't be a regular condom, the container. They have chemicals that kill sperm."

"I don't want dead or damaged sperm in me." Carol wondered if damaged sperm might lead to a freak. She had no plans on keeping the kid, but she was sure Jonathan's father would react badly to anything other than a perfect inheritor.

Seth waved his agreement. The door closed.

"This is weird," Jonathan said. "When we were in the playpen together, we never thought we'd be doing something like this."

"When we were in the playpen together, I only thought about wanting to hit you for stealing my toys."

"I didn't steal your toys," he said.

"I stole the ones you stole from me."

Jonathan began to pace. "If this doesn't work we can try the old-fashioned way although don't take this the wrong way but…"

"I know, I know. I hold no sexual appeal for you. It's okay. You're cute but you don't turn me on either. We'll leave that as a plan B."

The drug store was only two doors down from the building where Carol had her loft. When Seth came back, his hair was plastered to his head and his coat was drenched. The paper bag had almost disintegrated from the water. "If the store had been any further away I'd be shoving all the stuff in my pockets and clutching them to my heart."

"You should have taken an umbrella." Carol's tone was matter-of-fact, not accusatory.

"I was rushed." Seth handed Jonathan a cup. "Get as much as you can."

Jonathan went into the bathroom. Five minutes went by, then ten then twenty. Finally, the door opened with a small creak reminding Carol, she needed to oil the top hinge.

"I can't."

"What if you two make love, only instead of using Seth, use the cup?"

"Without you watching. We gays have our sense of privacy," Jonathan said.

"I'll go out and wait by the elevator."

Carol's loft was the only one on the floor. There was less than three feet between the elevator and her door with no place to sit. Chiding herself for agreeing, she couldn't even pace. She should have brought a book out.

I'm calling it off, she decided, but then Seth opened the door. "Done, your turn." As Carol entered the loft, he said, "I've gotten as much semen in the syringe as I can. I've made sure there are no air bubbles."

140

"Do you want us to do the next part," Jonathan asked.

"No way," Carol said. She looked at the bed. "Why don't you leave. I'll take it from here."

Seth and Jonathan looked at each other. As one they said, "We'd like to be here, it will be our baby."

"If it works," she reminded them. "Now get out."

They left, saying they'd be back soon.

She'd printed out the instructions and arranged herself on the bed with her pelvis elevated. Although she'd had several sexual partners, the act itself had never really meant that much to her. If some cases she delighted in telling the man that he was boring, and she didn't want to see him again.

The terms they used in response were not complimentary. Dyke and cunt were two of the kinder ones.

"This is a one-time deal. I'm not going through this twice," she said to the cup. "You guys better start swimming. May the best man win." With that she inserted the syringe as far as she could and slowly released the contents.

She elevated her hips even further, took the book about financial austerity that she was reading from the night stand and opened it. She fell asleep. She woke to knocking.

The clock showed she had been asleep at least two hours, certainly enough time for one of those little bastards to hit the waiting egg.

"Come in." Despite her elevated hips, she had the duvet over her when there was a knock.

Seth and Jonathan peeked around the door. "Done?"

"Done." Carol started to get up.

"Why not stay there a little longer to make sure," Jonathan said.

"I'm getting hungry." She wanted to see what they would do.

"What if I get you some Chinese food and bring it back?" Seth asked. "Jonathan can stay with you."

"Go away. This time stay away."

Carol needed to be alone. She'd had enough of their company. "I promise not to move, but later I've work to do." No way was she going to tell them what her work was.

# 31

**O**ne of my greatest talents is observation, Janis Aitken thought as she sat at Chantal's kitchen table and watched the group look yet again at the tape of the person stealing the car from the airport.

It had done her well in her fifty-one years. She'd gotten her Ph.D. based on her thesis about an American southern evangelical cult, which led to an adjunct role at two New York universities. She took another sip of the wine she'd brought to the meeting along with two kinds of cheese. The Frenchman hadn't turned up his nose, so she must have chosen well.

For a moment, her mind drifted back to her years in the States. How she had hated teaching looking at those rich kids who thought that her course was a commodity they'd bought so they deserved an A. The rest were so worn out from working all hours to pay for their education, that they were too tired to pay any attention much less care about the knowledge she was trying to impart.

There were her fellow professors who said they lived to find that one dedicated student who would be better than they were and would go on to do great things in whatever field they were in. She never found a student who fell into that category.

Her writing *Murdering for God* to amuse herself had become, much to her surprise, not just a best seller, but a multi-national best seller. Her husband, that shallow, jealous little prick, who had put her lack of academic commitment down now put her publishing success of "cop trash" down.

She'd packed up her things and returned to her native Edinburgh paying him off. He had no compunctions about taking the spoils of a lack of academic commitment.

"Run it again." She brought her attention back to the work at hand—trying to find Duncan's murderer.

The laptop was on the center edge of the table with everyone gathered in a half-circle giving some a better view than others.

The furthest away was Chantal, poor thing, a walking nerve. Who could blame her with all she'd gone through in the last few months? Chantal had told her that she looked at the damned video so often she had dreamed about it three nights in a row. Never mind that the girl had to deal with the stupid museum board. Those assholes didn't appreciate Chantal's passion for the project, so tied up they were with their own egos.

Robina was also passionate, although why anyone would want to be a policewoman was beyond her comprehension. Pretty thing, smart and probably scared the hell out of that boss, another male whose prick deflated when faced with a smart woman. No way, she could prove that, but her best guesses were usually accurate, although she would double-check her guesses when possible. This wasn't one of those times, although she imagined it would be fun to walk into the police station and asked for the "ball-less asshole" named…" only she didn't know the name, and she would only reduce Robina's chances of being reinstated.

"What are you smiling about?" Roger asked her.

"The amount of effort we're putting into this," Janis lied.

She found the Frenchie and Annie a very mismatched couple not just in age or nationality but in attitudes, yet there was an obvious love between them. Third culture kids like Annie, never really fit in anywhere one hundred percent. There were too many variables.

If she were still teaching, horror of horrors, that might make an interesting course. Better to use it in one of her books. At the moment, she was out of ideas for her next one, not that she ever had to write another word. She'd invested her earnings of her three best sellers in real estate and that would provide a modest living if she never touched another computer key, but doing nothing with her mind for the rest of her life? No way.

She zoomed in on Mike McNulty. Now that man was obviously smitten with Robina, who seemed much too interested in Annie's husband. Not that she was panting when she looked at him, but if a human put out sexual smells like cats and dogs in heat . . . well that said it all.

Was he interested? She couldn't tell. Wait, a minute: he has reached over and put his hand over his wife's. Tender.

"So, what do you think, Janis? Man or woman?" Robina asked.

"Woman, the way she walks. What about the backpack?"

"Backpack? I didn't notice much besides an ordinary backpack," McNulty said.

What Janis wanted to say, was, "Of course you didn't asshole. Your goal being here is Robina. She's so much smarter than you that you're out of your class and you don't know it. What she did say was, "Freeze it."

"I wish it were in color," Annie said. "We might be able to identify the brand, although with all the backpacks out there, it's another straw in the haystack, not a needle." She moved closer to the screen. "Can we blow it up?"

Robina did.

"We've lost definition." Annie cocked her head and moved so close to the laptop her nose was almost touching the screen. "Damn it, there's no logo."

"I'm not sure if it is my eyes or if it is fuzzy like suede," Janis said.

"Probably your eyes, not to be rude," Roger said. "Suede isn't waterproof."

"It looks like a good quality," Annie said. "Big enough to hold quite a bit: I'd bet expensive more than a kid could afford."

"Unless it was a rich kid."

"We haven't established age."

"Let's look at it frame by frame," Roger said. "Take notes."

They did click by click. Not everyone wrote down something at the same time. There was frame after frame where people wrote nothing.

About half way through there was a cry from upstairs.

"Sounds like Blane," Chantal said. "Excuse me."

"Hope he doesn't wake Sophie," Roger stood to listen at the foot of the staircase. "Thank God, she's a sound sleeper."

"Should we wait for Chantal to come back?" Robina's hand rested on the keyboard, but she hadn't advanced the video.

Trust a woman to ask that, Janis thought. She'd set in enough meetings to know that men would continue if a woman left the room, but women often waited for a man to return. If only her observation of this video was better. But she couldn't observe what wasn't there.

When Chantal didn't return after five minutes, the conversation concerned offers of more wine and cheese and quality of different cheeses, Annie suggested they resume.

That one is a leader, Janis thought.

At the end they compared notes.

More thought the person was a woman. The backpack was large enough to hold a lot of stuff and it looked heavy by the way the car thief had shifted it from her shoulders into the back seat. It had dropped fast.

No one could see how the thief had opened the car, but it was done with the speed of using a key. Janis noted that they were using the female pronoun when discussing the thief. Progress.

"Who wants to say it?" Roger asked.

No one spoke.

"We don't have enough to go on. There are no official reports of the other attempts on Duncan's life. We are sure she," he pointed to the frozen screen of the woman behind the wheel," was the driver, unless she dumped the car and someone else took it."

Everyone nodded.

"We've got the video of her raising the gate at the garage exit, but the way her hand is, we can't make out the token."

"We talked to everyone Chantal gave us," Robina said. "Nothing."

"If you continue, you will definitely lose your job," Mike said directly to Robina.

No one heard Chantal come back downstairs. "Blane's pulling

at his ear, maybe he has an infection, but he's gone back to sleep. Maybe you should give up."

Annie got up and put her hands on Chantal's shoulders. "Are you sure? Is that what you want? To give up?"

"Yes, I'm sure and no, I don't want to." There were tears in Chantal's eyes. She blinked them almost back. "You've done enough, all of you. I can't ask anymore."

\* \* \*

Roger set on the edge of the bed to take off his shoes.

Annie was already under the covers, her white flannel nightgown, slightly discolored from too many washings. was visible over the top of the duvet. "How do you feel about flying home via Geneva?"

"I wouldn't mind seeing your parents." He pulled his sweatshirt over his head. When he turned around the scar where they had stapled his chest after his heart surgery still was visible through his graying chest hair.

Every time Annie saw the scar she felt grateful he was still alive and not just because she didn't want to raise Sophie on her own. That she loved him so deeply still was a shock to her for at one time she did not think she was capable of either that strong an emotion nor capable of living as a wife or mother. *C'est la vie*, it's life, my life, *C'est ma vie.*

"I will love giving my notice tomorrow. In fact, I think I'll call it in."

"Do it however you want."

"The firm is such scumbags. They are breaking so many employment laws. I'd love to be a whistleblower, talk to some reporters."

Roger slipped under the covers. He took her head in his hands and kissed her forehead. "You don't always have to be a female Don Quixote. Leave some windmills for others."

She snuggled into his arms, knowing as soon as they were both asleep, they would move to opposite sides of the bed with their backs to each other. As she gave into sleep, she had a wave of disappointment that she had failed Chantal.

# 32

**F**our hours had gone by since she'd inserted Jonathan's semen. Carol Dixon had to pee really bad. It was uncomfortable with her hips up on the pillow. She'd put on the television, something she rarely watched, but she didn't like reading in that position. It was hard to angle the book.

The music in the soap operas was the part she found the most interesting, but a few sentences increased her understanding how people could get caught up in the stupid plots. She flipped through all the stations to find nothing she wanted to watch.

The joke about the reason so many sperm were necessary to fertilize one egg because sperm were male and didn't want to ask directions flashed through her mind. Had one brave little boy made it? There was no bang. One didn't hear the attack of an egg by a sperm. Was there already a union splitting into two, four, eight, etc.

Her bed was a king-size with the thickest and fluffiest duvets that she had been able to find on one of her trips through Austria.

She'd never had sex in that bed not wanting it defiled by a male. For a short period, she tried sleeping with any male who wanted to sleep with her hoping she would learn to like it more. She hadn't. When she had a lover over, they used the couch. Now she'd had sex with a syringe in her virginal bed.

Her tablet was in easy reach on the nightstand. She typed in fertilization process only to learn what was going on inside her,

147

assuming a sperm had hit her egg. She discovered that the kid would be only about a hundred cells in four days. How wrong she'd thought that the process was faster, happening instantly on contact. It would be called a zygote. If she had a baby, maybe they could call it Zy.

God, she had to pee, but she didn't want to wash the future-kid into the Boston sewer system. When the pressure reached the stage it was a choice of wetting the bed or flushing the semen, the flush won.

Her bathroom was on one end of the flat with stone walls, a copper tub and a European shower hose. The sink was a bright copper as well. They had no smell of copper, a bit of a disappointment. Blood smelled like copper to her. She loved that odor.

While she was up she fixed herself a cup of tea and cinnamon toast. "I'm not staying in that position any longer."

For the next few hours she started planning her trips flying into Montreal, Edinburgh then Paris training to Stuttgart and Amsterdam. With all the electronic tagging at airports, she would never go into the country where she was working by air if she could avoid it.

She always used her own passport to Montreal, where she'd rented the same B&B since she began. There she messed up the bed, put a few dirty dishes in the dishwasher just in case someone came in but not so dirty they would mold while she was gone. Using her Alice La Russo passport, she'd fly out of Montreal to the continent wherever her next assignment was and search for ground transportation.

Europe was best for that. The train system would allow her to travel between Schengen countries where there were no border guards to record her entrance. By checking to make sure there were no conventions or conferences at her destination, she could find a hotel without booking on line. Her fake passport with a real credit card matching the name on the passport allowed her presence to be undetectable.

How long that would last with Europe becoming more and more paranoid about terrorists, she didn't know. That was another good reason to retire.

Carol often marveled at her own cleverness in setting up her non-traceable system. However, today the fun was going out of her projects. She'd proven over and over she could do it—she wanted new challenges.

Reaching for the phone, she dialed her mother's landline. Her mother seldom had her cell phone on. She thought them a rude interruption and insisted that her second husband, Caleb Hancock, shut his off the second he entered the house or whenever he was with her. He might be a successful (very) hedge fund manager, but he was unable to stand up to Annabel Barron-Dixon-Hancock.

Martha answered on the fifth ring, "Hancock residence, how may I help you?"

Good old Martha, the family housekeeper from before Carol had been born. She had been Carol's refuge from a series of too-strict nannies. The night the then thirteen-year-old Carol had pushed her drunken father down the stairs, albeit a very successful banker in the old Boston tradition when he left his house but a sexual abuser of his daughter when his wife was out, Martha had come to her rescue saying they had been talking in the kitchen and neither of them had heard the fall. They had seen the body only later when Carol was in her way to bed.

"How are you, Sweetheart?" Martha asked as she always did.

Greetings exchanged Martha said, "Your mother isn't here. She went to the florist to order special flowers for dinner tonight."

"Guests?"

"Franklin and Diana Pierce."

"Really. Old Caleb is sucking up to his client?"

Martha's laugh told Carol that she was right. Franklin brought a lot of business, his and others, to her stepfather's hedge fund.

Carol pictured Martha in her practical shoes, tweed skirt and matching sweater. Only when she'd was forced into acting as cook between cooks, would she put on an apron. Carol's mother thought uniforms were for servants of the *nouveau riche* and both husbands as well as the late Dr. Barron had been old money, money that had survived from before the Civil War.

No one was allowed to mention slave trade where the seed of

the Barron family fortune had been planted. Unlike many Boston Brahmins, subsequent generations had enlarged the fortune rather than squandered it. Women married into money, first sons not up to the task were pushed aside for sons with good business sense. No one discussed this either.

Caleb Hancock's money on the other hand had been garnered from the ravishes of the family fortune. He had also been able to repair the damage done to Annabel's family money by Carol's father's and Annabel's husband's death. As an only child, she had married well, but after Banker Dixon's death, those who had taken over the family enterprise weren't family for the first time and ignored the stodginess that had kept the bank well into the black.

Had Annabel been male, she might have been trained to work, but she'd been educated at Wellesley with the goal of a FAH degree, find a husband, one from her closed Boston social circle.

Carol thought the entire structure a pile of shit that she wanted nothing to do with.

After Carol hung up, she began plotting, not her next assignment, but her next move with her mother, whom she considered an enemy and had from early childhood. Annabel had stood in the way of most of what Carol had wanted to do. She'd sent her rebellious daughter away to school.

Originally Carol thought that she'd been sent there as protection from her father, but as time went by she was convinced if her mother knew what her father was doing, she didn't care enough to stop it.

Carol's next call was to Jonathan. "I've an idea."

When she explained, he said, "Seth and I had plans tonight, but yes, I think it is a good idea."

# 33

**"A**re you nervous?" Jonathan Webster asked Carol as they walked up to the front stairs of her parents' Beacon Hill home in Louisburg Square. The house had been her father's and her grandfather's. All the houses on the square were red brick: some had bow fronts, some still had the original violet tinted glass. An iron-fence surrounded the green-treed oval grassy area in the center of the square.

"We handled a sale here, not long ago." Jonathan pointed to the attached house two doors down. "It went for eleven million."

Carol was aware that she had a good chance of inheriting the house. She didn't think her mother had put her stepfather's name on the deed nor did she think her mother would allow it to leave the family or go to Caleb's son. She'd been with Robert at Harvard. Although they had not shared any classes, they would run into each other as they crossed the campus. They were more apt to nod than talk. Now he lived in London working in The City. She was sure he was a scumbag stealing money from the poor to give to the rich.

He would never be one of her targets, she was sure, although she wondered about going freelance in his case. What stopped her was that it was too close to home. If she wanted to justify her activities, she might have said that she was removing bad guys from society, but she didn't care in the least about society, bad guys or good guys.

There were the very rare family dinners when Caleb's son, Robert was in Boston on business. They were always tense affairs where manners replaced any warmth between the people. Robert detested his father, which decreased his chance of any inheritance.

Caleb's other son, Matthew, like Carol, was a lawyer and had a storefront operation in Roxbury. At one time, she'd debated joining him, more to annoy her mother than a desire to help the poor. Maybe she would do that after she retired.

She hated the house she grew up in. Until her father had started in on her, her childhood had been neither happy nor unhappy. It was what it was. She avoided visiting now because it was a chore, like emptying the garbage.

Jonathan asked, "Nervous?"

"No." If anything, she felt pleasure at being able to dupe her mother. That was probably the best emotion she could summon.

Maybe there were cells inside her right now dividing up into different functions and hopefully the right combination of XY chromosomes were lining up together to form a male. Otherwise she would need an abortion. Not that she wanted children, but a daughter would have been preferable if she had to have a child and raise it herself. A daughter would not satisfy Jonathan's father.

Losing sleep, changing diapers, being second to another life—oh no—that wasn't for her. She smiled thinking how shocked her mother would be when she not only divorced Jonathan but gave him custody of her mother's grandchild.

Carol had not had a key to the house—ever. She pressed the bell.

Martha answered almost immediately. "What are you doing here?" A blush spread on her face. "I didn't mean it *that* way. Usually we know that you are coming... and... when we talked earlier... well you didn't..."

"I didn't say I was coming, because I didn't know it myself. Are they at dinner yet?"

"Living room. Pre-dinner drinks. I'll tell your mother." Martha took their coats.

"Don't. We'll go in."

Carol and Jonathan walked down the hall flanked by a staircase with a rich red carpet tacked down with brass holders. The living room was the second door on the left. Carol opened it without knocking.

Annabel Barron-Dixon-Hancock looked up as if she were expecting Martha and a flicker of disappointment crossed her face. Carol noticed it: no one else seemed to. Caleb, in all his full-white hair glory that made him look like a senator, had a big smile as did Franklin and Diana Pierce.

Caleb walked over to his stepdaughter and hugged her before shaking Jonathan's hand. The Pierces gave the appropriate cheek kisses and handshakes.

"To what do we owe this unexpected pleasure?" Annabel asked.

Jonathan and Carol exchanged looks. This was the moment, the drama, that she'd decided to do in advance of a confirmed pregnancy. Increases verisimilitude, they decided.

"Should I tell them, or do you want to?" he asked.

"You." Carol wanted to gauge her mother's reaction.

She wasn't disappointed. Open-mouthed than a half smile.

"I've waited a long time for this. I always knew you and Jonathan had a thing for each other," Diana said.

Why and hell would she think that, Carol wondered. It confirmed her belief that Diana was less than bright.

"Congratulations." Caleb pumped Jonathan's hand and slapped him on the back.

Franklin looked at Carol with a frown. "This is a surprise. For some reason, I didn't think you were the marrying kind." He shifted his look from Carol to Jonathan and added, "Either of you."

"We aren't getting any younger, and if we want to have a family…" Jonathan's voice trailed off and glanced at Carol.

"You're ready for children, Carol?" Franklin asked.

"My biological time clock is ringing." She took Jonathan's hand. "However, even without babies, I love him."

Caleb called Martha. "We have wonderful news. Jonathan and Carol are engaged. Would you please bring a bottle of champagne and a glass for yourself too." When Martha had left the room, he whispered into Annabelle's ear. "Martha loves her as much as we do, so she should be part of the celebration." Annabel's acquiescent nod told Carol louder than any words, that it wasn't a breach of etiquette but recognition of the place of staff with slightly fluid boundaries.

After the toast and Martha had left to check on dinner, Annabel said, "We should ask you to stay for dinner, but we've only prepared a meal for four."

Jonathan draped his arm around Carol's shoulder. "We weren't planning to stay. We have reservations at The Four Seasons."

"The lovebirds need to celebrate on their own," Diana slurred her words slightly, confirming yet again Franklin's complaint that his wife was too fond of alcohol.

"I want to use the facilities before I go," Carol said.

"I'll walk with you. I need to use the facilities," Franklin said.

As soon as the door to the living room closed behind the two of them, he grabbed Carol's elbow. "What the hell do you think you're doing?"

She rested her elbow from his hand. "You'll never know."

# 34

## EDINBURGH, SCOTLAND

It was early afternoon. The office had its usual heaviness not helped by the rain outside. Although there were no windows it seemed to Annie that the dampness seeped through the walls. She chalked it up to her imagination.

Her supervisor, Mr.-Berry-not-Jack, was walking through the cubicles muttering to the different translators. Some responded: some continued working.

After he passed Louisa MacLaughlin, the woman stuck her tongue out at his prompting a slight rustling from the others. Mr.-Berry-not-Jack turned but all he saw were eyes either on the keyboards or papers next to the keyboards.

Annie had briefed Louisa on the lack of anything that might make Duncan's murder more sinister than a hit and run when they passed each other during morning tea. Louisa had whispered that Mr.-Berry-not-Jack, had taken her aside, and warned her that Annie was a potential trouble-maker.

Annie understood. Louisa needed her job.

Annie was a trouble-maker. When she'd found several more rules and regulations violating European Union Law, she'd e-mailed Fiona Clark.

The response from HR?

Nothing, which was what Annie expected. The company didn't care.

Annie couldn't help but wonder how Mr.-Berry-not-Jack ever got his position. In the sense that the department put out the required work and met deadlines was how he kept it, she was sure. As she looked up he was hovering over her. "Do you mind? I don't like someone standing over my shoulder." The words fell from her mouth before she could stop them.

"I, I…"

"Don't hover over me."

"I'm checking your work."

"My work is fine. You're slowing me down."

"In my office, now," he screamed.

Annie saw that everyone was staring at their screens. Hands were on keyboards, but not a finger moved.

Enough was enough.

She opened her bottom left drawer and grabbed her purse. "Listen Jack, I've worked in probably forty companies. Without doubt you're the worst boss I've ever had. And this is a horrible company. It doesn't care if it breaks the law. I don't need to deal with a petty tyrant like you any more, Mr. Little Man. I quit."

With that she shouldered her pocketbook, walked to the coatroom and stormed out. She did not hit the time clock. She did not stop at personnel. Let them worry about the paperwork.

Once on the street she felt only relief.

The rain had not lessened, and she'd left her umbrella inside the building. Who cared, she could buy another.

Chantal would understand. Besides, she didn't think she could find more information to prove that Duncan's murder had any connection to work.

\* \* \*

"I know we are at a dead end," Chantal said. She and Annie sat on Chantal's bed where Roger and Annie slept. Roger was taking a shower; the children were asleep.

"I've imposed on your lives enough." She smiled at Annie. "I bet it felt good to tell your boss where to go."

"You've no idea. I did it loudly enough and I'm sure everyone in the room wished they could have done the same."

Roger came in, a towel wrapped around him. "What's up?"

Despite the feeling of failure, Annie said, "I think it's time we go on-line to book a flight to Geneva."

# 35

Three months later
Stuttgart, Germany

A lice La Russo took her passport back from the reservation
clerk who had to be in his sixties.

"How long do we have the pleasure of your company?" His accent
was as thick as the lederhosen he was wearing.

"I'm not sure."

"January is slow, so it is not a problem if you stay beyond your
four-day reservation."

The man came from behind the desk. The lobby was all carved
dark wood with designs of animals and trees. Even the ceiling was
dark, carved wood of yesteryear. Nothing indicated a chain had
taken it over. There had been a sign that it had opened in 1902.

The man grabbed her suitcase and led her across a hall and
outdoors across a courtyard. Alice glanced and noticed that there
was a large pool with more multi-colored koi than she could count.
They all swam to the edge of the pool.

Her room was modern with a thick duvet on the bed. The
bathroom featured a bidet and a rain-forest shower head.

As soon as the man left, she lay down on the bed. The flight from
Montreal was long. She was tired. At least she no longer wanted
to vomit the entire day. Some of the desire to sleep 24/7 had also
disappeared, but she wanted a long nap before she began part two
of her new assignment.

Still wearing her cotton gloves, she slipped off her skirt despite her clumsiness with the buttons. The waistband was tight.

Alice never unpacked when she on a mission. The danger of leaving something behind with a bit of DNA was too great.

When she woke, she would go on line and get her bearings on the office and home of Gunther Braun, age forty-five and chief financial officer of Wagner GmbH. She wondered why he was a target, as part of a privately-owned firm.

Part of her resented she had been brushed off when she asked the question.

Prior to leaving, she'd done her homework at an Internet café. Although she'd never been to Stuttgart before, she knew the streets and the public transportation system. For this she would not have to rent a car, but she would want to check out the Braun residence and office but not as Alice La Russo.

She had a boy's cut wig, jeans, boots and a leather jacket. She must work fast, because her bump seemed to be growing every day. Boys don't look pregnant.

# 36

## ARGELÈS-SUR-MER, FRANCE

As Alice La Russo was settling into her hotel in Germany, Annie Young-Perret saved her document entitled *Accounting Software Manual,* ASM, the same initials as the village's. She had completed her translations into Dutch, German and French and cleaned up the original English. She'd received the assignment right before Christmas and it had driven her crazy over the holidays.

Some of the sentences were so convoluted that even had she been an accountant or an IT whiz she wouldn't have been able to follow them. Thank goodness for Skype or all her project earnings would have gone into overseas calls talking with the software developers. The company had assigned a liaison engineer to her, one that could write. He in turn went back to the software developer for clarifications.

This was the fifth project for this company, and unlike AGG, she loved working for them even if the work was less interesting than from some other clients. They treated her as if she were a genius, because of her language skills. She wasn't about to dissuade them.

In one way, while working at home she missed settling into another country, another city and exploring the history, the architecture for a few weeks or a few months.

Sometimes she looked into the mirror and wondered where the old Annie went. The old Annie had been replaced with one who thought it wonderful to curl up in bed with a book, her husband beside her, or take a walk on the beach promenade, pushing Sophie's stroller.

Her office was in the home she shared with Roger. It was set back from the street with twenty-two pine trees and a kaki grove. There was also a full vegetable garden planted by her stepdaughter Gaëlle and her boyfriend Guillaume. In January, it was barren. Cold weather crops would need to be planted in a few weeks, not by Annie or Roger, but by the young couple who were at an Agricultural College.

The office was in an alcove off the couples' bedroom with just about enough space for her desk. By choice, she didn't want a window. Looking out broke her concentration.

In the living room, she could hear her stepdaughter, Gaëlle, playing with Sophie. Now that the baby was walking, no make that running, confining her to an area was harder and harder. Sophie's take on a playpen was that it was a prison and the only way to deal with a prison was to scream for release.

Gaëlle was home for a week, delighting Annie not just because the girl made a great babysitter, but because the two had formed a close bond. There were times Annie had felt like a pinball between the girl, who had been a normal teenager against an overly strict father. Annie had worried that Gaëlle would be jealous of Sophie and had asked the girl outright.

"Don't be silly. I always wanted a sister, and this one will never borrow my clothes." Gaëlle had hugged Annie. "We're good, always have been, always will be."

Annie then opened the book she was writing on Scottish poets for a final edit. Quintin was niggling her to finish. He wanted to place it in Chantal's museum when it opened, if it opened.

Annie suspected her sales on this would be even lower than the book on that stupid saint, whom she detested the more research she'd done. Maybe, besides the museum some book stores in Scotland, some English literature departments might be interested. If anyone else was, she'd be amazed.

She'd loved doing it although she'd had a problem finding material about living conditions of the time.

Good thing it was the kind of research she relished. She also had a long list of acknowledgements for the people whom she'd contacted and who had filled in the blanks.

She'd never shaken the feeling of failure that she and Roger hadn't found Duncan's killer. The whole process was like seeing a mystery on television in a program and having the electricity go off before the show ended.

She knew she wasn't alone. Robina Collins, Janis Aitkin and Louisa MacLaughlin emailed her with different theories or more likely frustrations when they didn't pan out.

Whenever Annie couldn't concentrate, she would go into various news sites: *RT, Aljazeera, Washington Post*. She also looked at alternative media. Her interest had been aroused by an article about the large number of dead bankers from strange causes: falling off roofs, smothering in their cars. The total was approaching fifty over the past few months, against three over the past five years. She felt mean thinking the only good banker was a dead banker, but she'd worked at several banks and the word scum bag covered many of the people she met—not all—but many.

Not her problem.

Her Skype flashed. Funny—she was thinking of Louisa and she'd reached out to her. Glancing at her watch, she saw that it was afternoon. She couldn't imagine Louisa was calling from the office.

She hit video call and the Scottish woman appeared on her screen. The background wasn't the office but a living room with a couch and there were toys on the couch. "You're home?"

"One of the kids has the flu. Also, does my backup babysitter."

"That must make the idiot boss unhappy."

"The good news is that he has disappeared."

"Disappeared?"

"He hasn't shown up for work. His wife says he didn't come home after work on Friday."

"Bizarre."

A small boy, dressed in pajamas and carrying a ratty teddy bear, came into view on the screen. Annie saw him climb onto Louisa's lap, lay his head against her chest, and stick his thumb in his mouth.

Louisa caressed his sweaty-looking red hair as she talked. "I told you earlier that I sometimes know things I have no way of knowing, not a second sight, just feelings I get, that are about sixty percent right."

Annie had no recollection of the conversation. She, herself, sometimes had instincts that made no sense but turned out to be right. Maybe everyone did.

"Anyway," Louisa said, "I would never make it as a fortune teller, but I tend to listen to those feelings."

"And…"

"I overheard Fiona in HR say that a lot of people who work for the company die too young. She joked about it being unhealthy—like eating too much fatty food lead to heart attacks."

"And?"

Louisa shrugged.

"I'm not sure. I talked to Robina and Janis. We wish we could follow up, but how? We need to get corporate files." Annie hoped that Louisa would use her instincts to pick up on what she wanted.

Louisa shifted her son's weight and then put him on the couch. "Excuse me, I want to get him a bottle. Maybe he'll sleep."

Louisa returned and picked him up. "We must hack into company files."

Annie pictured Louisa trying, getting caught and fired. She voiced her concern.

"Not me. We need to hire a hacker. Wish I knew one, it's not that we can put an advert in the paper."

Annie's thoughts catapulted to her friend Mark. He was a student at EPFL in Lausanne and had been her neighbor as a young boy often visiting to get the attention he lacked from his professional parents. His mother had been arrested for the murder of his father, but when the real murderer was discovered, she had been released.

Mark had helped Annie before, but she wasn't about to put him at risk. "I've a friend who might know someone."

The little boy began to whimper.

"I'd better go." Louisa's image faded.

"Where's Sophie's jacket?" Gaëlle came into the office area or rather stood at the door. There wasn't room for a second person unless Annie removed her chair and sat on the desk.

"On the rack near the kitchen door."

"I couldn't see it."

Maybe Mark could recommend a hacker. Her problem would be to convince him, it should be someone other than him.

# 37

## EDINBURGH, SCOTLAND

The light diffused by rain was the first thing Robina Collins saw through her bedroom window when she opened her eyes. She rolled over in her bed. The other side was empty.

The smell of coffee accompanied kitchen sounds. "Don't be annoyed," she told herself. It wasn't Mike's fault that she wanted tea. Some mornings she might want tea: or she might want coffee and wouldn't know which until she'd been awake for a few minutes.

The smell of bacon wafted up the stairs. Her taster was looking forward to porridge not eggs and bacon, no matter how well Mike made them. How could she be so ungrateful when a man was in the process of making her breakfast in bed?

Mike McNulty was as close to a perfect man that any woman could ask for. He wasn't living with her although he spent at least four nights a week in her bed. A few of his personal possessions were scattered around the bathroom, bedroom and living room.

She never stayed at his flat. It was too *bachelory*. How someone who could cook so well not bother to buy even basic cooking equipment was beyond her. He had done nothing else to turn his flat into a home. How much would it take to buy a bed frame for the mattress of the floor?

Other than his lack of décor, he was a great guy. Her suspension had been short. Mike had let the upper echelon know that Ian hadn't followed procedure, anonymously of course. Ian had been reprimanded, which didn't improve Robina's relationship with him.

Two months to go, she thought. Two months and Ian would take early retirement, not his choice. Who her new supervisor/partner would be was still unknown. Overall those who were up for the Ian's post were younger and not as anti-woman. The possibility that they would bring in someone from outside, was also possible.

"Breakfast, my Love." Mike carried a tray with a fry-up and coffee. He was off work today. She needed to shower for her shift. She glanced at the old-fashioned, flower-shaped clock, which she'd found at a flea market. Two hours and nineteen minutes before she had to be at work and it was only a ten-minute walk. "That's really sweet of you."

Mike placed the tray on her lap. "I'll go get mine." He knew better than to expect sex before her job, but he claimed he liked just being next to her, although she was sure if she initiated it, he wouldn't refuse. Sadly, he was a good lover in and out of bed.

Robina felt stupid, really, really stupid. Ever since she had met Roger Perret, she had had a fantasy relationship with him. Half of her blamed it on Terry, her girlfriend, who was single, contentedly single.

Terry had confessed she had an imaginary husband, Phillip, who was tall, thin, ten years older and sported a full head of graying curls. Phillip always was pleasant, shared all her household chores, never forgot her birthday and never messed up the small cottage that Terry had bought. "With masturbation, you can control when you come, and you never have to make conversation afterwards." Terry had confessed all that one night when Robina had gone to dinner and they'd had too much wine.

Roger, in Robina's mind, would know when she wanted tea or coffee. Imaginary lovers were better than real ones. They never farted under the covers and always were there to listen and to offer the right degree of commiseration.

If Robina had told anyone, they would have said she was crazy. She wasn't. She knew Roger was imaginary.

Mike was real. Everyone loved Mike. Mike wasn't at fault that he didn't create a spark in her. The cliché, a good man is hard to find, bounced around her head. "You really outdid yourself," she said to

Mike when he came back with his own breakfast and crawled under the covers with her. He didn't even slosh his coffee, damn it. "I can't tell my friends, they would be crazy with jealousy."

When Mike smiled, she knew that she hadn't lied: lying was something beyond her with the exception of a white lie now and then. Maybe a gray compliment was all right.

Her mobile rang.

"This is Paul at the station."

"They've found a body in the park around the corner from your house. How fast can you get there?"

"As soon as I can get dressed."

* * *

"It took you long enough," Ian McAlister said as Robina arrived at the murder scene. He looked gray, but he always looked gray. The wind blew his comb-over straight up.

As in most crime scenes, the tape was strung around the area. Several officers and four people from forensics mulled around the dead winter grass. Whether the forensics were men or women was hard to tell with their plastic clothing designed to reduce scene contamination.

The park itself was not that large. It was as a known gay hangout.

"Probably a puff," Ian said. Robina, would tell Mike later Ian sneered as if murdered puffs didn't deserve the same treatment as non-puffs.

"Careful where you walk," The forensics man facing her said. Robina knew she should know his name, because she'd worked with him a while back. She was better at remembering conversations with people than their names. They had talked about all the mystery series set in Edinburgh. There were more murders in mystery books set in the city than there were in real life they had laughed. Most investigations were property crimes.

Another man had his back to her. Unlike those in white plastic to reduce the chance of contamination, this person was in blue plastic. Maybe he an intern from Napier University's program. They sometimes worked with the local police. Robina had taken a couple of courses with the team leader at Napier University, Dr. Thomas.

"Who is it?" Her eyes were drawn to the blood-encrusted dent in the top of his head. She forced herself to look down the body to where his trousers were down about his ankles.

"Wallet is missing," Ian said.

"Have we checked the missing person report?" Robina asked.

Ian glowered. "Only a couple more months and he'll be gone, she thought as he said, "Thank you for that astute idea." It was more of a growl. Glowerer and growler.

The Edinburgh forensic crew was the one of the four forensic centers in Scotland. The man whose back was to her, turned around and saw her. He stood. "Nice to see you Collins. How long has it been?"

"Three years, Sir."

Dr. Thomas looked at Ian McCallister. "She was one of the brightest students I've ever had. I tried to convince her to go on and get a degree in forensics."

If Robina could guess what Ian was thinking, it wasn't pleasure that anyone would think well of her, especially a highly-respected professional.

"What did him in, Doc?" Ian asked the medical examiner who stood up to stretch after kneeling too long in a kneel next to the corpse.

"We need a full autopsy, but the fact his brains are bashed in would make me think perhaps, just perhaps that was the cause," the examiner said.

"Collins, since it was your idea, go back to the station and see who has been reported missing," Ian said.

\* \* \*

"What's happening," Mary, the receptionist at the police station asked as Robina burst through the door heading toward the detectives' area. "Was there a murder?"

"Yes, Robina said over her shoulder. She was followed by Ray, a rookie.

"Ray, can you find me the missing person reports for the last week. Any 999 calls." She was sure that the body was recent. Maybe he wasn't even reported missing. If he just disappeared it would be too soon for him to be registered. Maybe it was too soon for anyone to notice he was gone.

The man she spoke to moved away from the others and spoke into his phone.

She thought that either rigor mortis hadn't begun which meant that the body was there only a few hours. It had been blustery last night. That would slow everything down. Or had the poor man been there at least a day or more and the muscles relaxed. The medical examiner would autopsy the body and could tell if the body had been moved.

Ray came back in. "A report came in last night on a Jonathan Berry. That's the only missing man reported close to the dead man's description for the last six weeks."

As soon as she typed in the name, she learned that Jonathan Berry had not come home from work Friday, according to his wife. It was not like him. He hadn't reported to work after the weekend and he'd had a perfect attendance record, she'd claimed. His photo, if you dented his head, looked like the corpse.

Rummaging through her bag, it took a few minutes to find her phone. She dialed Ian. "I think we may have found who." She read the details and sent the photo via her mobile.

"The height and weight match. It looks like him." Ian said. "Go tell the wife."

Of all the chores Robina hated most was telling the family that someone had died. Until now the victims were from car accidents, drug overdoses or suicide. She'd never had to tell a family their loved one was murdered.

"Can we wait until we have him in the morgue, so his wife can identify him quickly, she won't have to wonder if we're right or not?"

"No."

"But…"

"No buts. You're a woman, you'll know what to say."

Her phone went dead.

Shit! was all she could think.

# 38

"**You're not going to believe** this," Louisa MacLaughlin said to Annie who was standing in her living room in France. Sophie was struggling to get down. She'd just swooped up the child when the phone had rung. There had been no hellos, no how are yous.

Sophie screamed. She was an outdoor child and resented being inside. Now that Gaëlle had gone back to university, Annie couldn't be outside when she needed to work. Roger had taken up coaching the local swimming team and was at the village pool and unavailable to supervise his daughter.

Half of Annie was happy that he had something to do that he enjoyed. The other half wanted him to share more of Sophie's care.

"Hello, Louisa?" Annie put her screaming daughter down on the floor and with one hand locked the door to the outside. Sophie stretched to reach the key but was too short.

"Yes, it's me. Call-Me-Mr-Berry-Not-Jack is dead."

Annie sat in the nearest chair. "Dead?"

"Murdered."

"Murdered?" Repeating what she heard wasn't helpful. Jack Berry was younger than she was. "What happened?"

"There was a company announcement. The papers didn't go into detail, but I talked to Robina. I've been working with her and Chantal somewhat."

"And…"

170

"We just sit around and discuss theories, sadly. I think it makes Chantal feel better. Anyway, Berry's head was bashed in. Poor girl, Robina that is, she had to go get the wife for identification. Her idiot boss thinks women are better at that sort of thing. Telling the family that is."

Poor woman, Annie thought. She remembered, or thought she remembered, he had two small children because of a photo he had on his desk.

"Robina's idiot boss thinks it was the wife. She claims she was home with the kids, but they are too small to provide an alibi."

"I thought her boss would be retired by now."

"He's staying on until there's a replacement."

It wasn't nice to think ill of the dead, but if he was anything at home like he'd been in the office, the wife might be relieved. Still, with two small children…

"Are you still there, Annie?"

"I'm here."

"That's the second death in this office that isn't normal."

Annie had one of her flashes, the type that Roger pooh-poohed. She wasn't sure for what, but not knowing what she was looking for exactly hadn't stopped her in the past. "Can you get some information on other deaths in the company?"

"Now that *Jack* isn't around, I can do more Intranet research."

"I'll do Internet searches. I think I know all the companies associated with AGG, but can you email me a complete list, in case I miss one. Do it from home." Annie wasn't sure what she was looking for, but she would know it if she found it or she hoped she would.

# 39

STUTTGART, GERMANY

**A**lice La Russo/Carol Dixon had a list of cyber cafés in Stuttgart. The one she chose was on Königstrasse and using her iPad and Google maps she saw that it wasn't that far from her hotel where she was in the double bed snuggling under the thick Eiderdown.

The room was the most modern part of the old-fashioned hotel with its white walls, white floors, white linen. The only color in the room came from the painting on the wall, ultra-modern with splashes of red and blue. It occupied a too large part of the opposite wall above the television.

When she'd come in from the airport last night, she'd taken a taxi, something she didn't like to do, but she knew with her wig and boyish clothes, she looked like nothing like her real self.

Still with facial recognition technology and international computers, she was less and less comfortable using her fake passport, although the person she'd paid a bloody fortune to for it had said that Alice La Russo had once been a real person, who was now a real-dead person and that had been her real passport.

At a price of $10,500 she only cared if it worked. Carol had researched records, which had shown her that Alice had died three months after getting her passport. Alice's obituary had appeared in the Portland, Maine newspaper. She'd died from a fall. Alice was a year younger than Carol and from the photo that appeared there was a resemblance.

There was always the danger that Alice's survivors would report the passport missing, but then again maybe it was something that slipped their minds. The passport had another two years before it expired. The only trip the real Alice had ever taken was a week to Paris. All the other border stamps were Carol's.

The gray wig was the same hairstyle that was in the passport photo, only longer. She'd paid a bloody fortune for the wig too, and in her business, she couldn't take a tax write-off although the idea of some IRS looking at a tax return where she listed her occupation as "contract killer" amused her. On the other hand, she didn't pay taxes on her commissions for her missions. The sound of commissions for missions amused her.

Most of her earnings were in bricks, gold or silver stored in a safe hidden in her apartment. She wasn't worried about thieves carrying it off, if any broke in. The safe was bolted under the floor. It was full of gold bars and a few silver ones.

Granted there was no interest being paid on the metals, and yes, she knew that the precious metals market was being manipulated, but like bricks and mortar investments, it was a solid, not a fiat currency.

She was debating buying more real estate. The agent who handled her property left her worry free.

Money had never been the reason she did what she did. Money would always be there and unless the world went completely mad, her trust fund would outlast her.

Her tastes were minimal. She didn't need a car in Boston and rented one when she wanted to leave town. Her flat was paid for. Her debts were zero. If she'd thought about it, she might have wondered how people got themselves in debt, but she never did. Other people didn't interest her much except as targets of her commissions, which were work-related.

The light filtered through the slats of the *Rolloden* that she'd closed before going to bed making shadows on the wall.

Until now, she worked because she loved the hunt. Planning was part of the fun. However, crossing borders was getting harder.

Retirement after this assignment was over looked good. The baby moved inside her again. Her pregnancy had been anything but pleasant. Throwing up and sleeping, throwing up and sleeping, throwing up and sleeping… at least that stage seemed over.

A new energy had engulfed her shortly before she booked this trip. Today, she would need it.

The room was comfortably warm as she went into the shower. She dressed in a nice pantsuit to look professional. Her Alice wig was enhanced by makeup with shading that gave her deeper cheekbones, similar to the real Alice's.

Her precautions were to cover herself with the hotel staff. Unlike the chains, there was only a staff of five. Three of those were family members. A chain might have been better, but a chain could have a centralized computer system where police could pull her name. Would there be a policeman smart enough to connect her international crimes? A stretch for any cop.

Before she went downstairs to the breakfast room, she stopped at the pool. The koi swam over to her, their mouths opening and closing as if trying to talk to her. "How's your jet lag?" They might ask.

"No problem with jet lag," she could answer. She'd adjusted time differences quickly. She'd expected her body's acceptance would take longer because of the pregnancy.

This would be her second kill on this trip. The first had been in Edinburgh. She'd been unnerved when her target had walked in front of her in a deserted place where'd she been doing reconnaissance. She'd grabbed the opportunity. That wasn't how she liked to accomplish assignments. She was out of Scotland before the body could be discovered. She would check the Edinburgh newspapers it at the cybercafé. No way would she risk having any search show up on her tablet.

She was famished. The smell of toast and bacon as she entered the hotel dining room only added to it. The room's carved wooden walls made her feel like she was in a zoo with the bears and deer in oak bas relief. Like all German hotels that she had ever stayed in the breakfast buffet contained meats, cheeses, cereals, breads, fruit. The waitress asked if she wanted tea, coffee or hot chocolate.

Supposing the milk would do the baby good, she chose the latter. She took out a paper map.

The cybercafé was about a twenty-minute walk from the hotel. There was a huge park with a pond where swans floated. A medieval *Schlöss* and a newer *Schlöss*, if one wanted to think of a palace built in the 1700s new, flanked the park.

The cybercafé had been her choice because its website said it only had the three computers. As soon as she entered the small room, she checked for cameras.

Nothing.

The smaller cafés were always better because they had less security. One computer was free, and she started her research.

No matter what she plugged in, she couldn't find a photo of her target's house. Gunther Braun's neighborhood was unlisted anywhere on the Internet. That meant on-site recognizance. Damn it.

Back at the hotel, she put a short brown wig into her backpack and an outfit that she hoped would look like a cleaning woman. She decided to change in Breuniger's Department Store bathroom than catch the Number 7 up the mini-mountain to Möhringen. She bought several cleaning supplies, which she stuffed in the backpack although she suspected it was overkill. There were probably no American cleaning women who didn't speak German.

The neighborhood itself was less expensive than she had expected: upper middle class, yes, but not where a CEO of a company might live. Herr Braun's two-story, stucco house had a small garden with a grayish-brown wooden fence with in front. Dried stems were intertwined within the cross worked slats. They probably were roses. Carol wasn't much of a plant expert, but she did know a thorn.

She noticed a Mercedes in the garage. As she walked by another Mercedes stopped in front of the house. A man, wearing the traditional dark green Loden coat, came out carrying a briefcase. With his short bristled gray hair, he presented himself as a stereotype of a German businessman. More important, he matched the photo that she'd been given.

He spoke to the driver as he got in the back seat, but she didn't understand.

One thing was certain: this was not a good place to complete her assignment unless she could come up with something original.

Until now she used different methods to complete her assignments. Not only did that offer the greater challenges that gave her so much pleasure, it reduced the chances of being caught by someone noticing identical methods. If she were a poker player she wouldn't have a "tell," that physical sign giving opponents information. However, she wasn't a poker player.

Suddenly she felt her energy drain out of her. Probably the damned baby playing havoc with her hormones. As anxious as she was to finish the assignment, rushing to the point of being slipshod wasn't an option.

The number 7 *Strassenbahn* carried her down the hill and back to Breunigers where she transformed herself into Alice.

She stopped for a cup of coffee, which revived her. Another *Strassenbahn* took her to Braun's workplace. She'd expected it to be larger, more pretentious. In reality, it was a small building in an industrial park.

If he was driven to and from work each day, getting to him would be difficult. The dossier she'd been given was less complete than any others. The normal information was there: age, wife's name and age, children (left home—one at university, two married, no address available).

She used her burner phone to text Franklin. "I need more info."

It came back, "none available."

\* \* \*

The koi no longer swam toward her but kept circling doing whatever it is koi do when they know there's no chance of food.

Carol had been watching them since she had come up from breakfast. Her project was dead, unfortunately just the project. The person she was to kill on contract was alive and well.

She had researched everything possible on Braun. An interview in *Das Spiegel* had emphasized him as a creature of habit, which should have made her assignment easy, but the article also cited that he had no hobbies, didn't eat in restaurants, go to movies, plays, or sporting events, and lived only for his work where he was considered brilliant.

Failure was not her style. Once she tried something she would work at it until she succeeded.

Her last job would be a failure. Franklin was and always been her only client, and that was a fluke.

As a little girl, she didn't think about being a killer as a career path.

Franklin was also her ex-lover, something that no one, not her parents, not his wife even had heard a whimper of a rumor about. They'd been in bed after sex which neither thrilled nor displeased her, other than the satisfaction that her mother would have a shit hemorrhage if she knew, which was enough of a reason for Carol.

He came to her place as always, saying the simplicity of her loft compared to his antique-laden home was a joy. At the beginning of their affair, he'd shown up unannounced until she said she'd stop seeing him if he did it again.

"You've someone else." He had pouted.

She thought a pouting man only slightly younger than her father was disgusting. She pinched his lip.

He'd yelped.

She didn't love him. She wasn't sure she even liked him. She slept with him because she could.

Their first business discussion was February 11, five years ago. She could see the snow coming down through her skylight. Even though there was no way anyone could see in, he wanted her drapes—or rather her bamboo curtains—dropped.

He had said he would love to find a new source of income. His main topic of discussion was business after they'd had sex. Earlier he'd been talking about a young employee that had had a heart attack. "It had to be a birth defect. Too bad it was his wife that was insured. Low premiums, big payouts."

"Good for her, though."

"Too bad, I wasn't the beneficiary."

"Why couldn't you be?"

"How would I know who has a birth defect?

"If you did you could have them killed."

He'd sat up in bed. "Great idea in theory."

"No, set up a dummy company. Have the person insured by that company for that company and voilà."

He reached over and looked at his watch. "I'm late."

Six months later he had set up the company. She'd volunteered to be the killer for a percentage of the insurance.

# 40

## ARGELÈS-SUR-MER, FRANCE

"**W**hat are you doing?" **Roger** asked. He entered Annie's work area to find her on her hands and knees with file cards spread out on the terry cotta tiles. "You're a computer girl. I didn't know you knew what paper and pencils still were."

She rose to her feet without disturbing any of the cards. "Louisa gave me a list of the people in the various AGG companies who've died."

"What have you found?"

"Not much." And she hadn't. Some were natural deaths, one was a suicide. Duncan's was a hit and run and Jack Berry was a murder. A couple she couldn't find anything at all, not even an obituary book listing from a funeral home.

"I've been trying to find a common denominator." She debated telling him about the high number of bankers' deaths, but he would point out that none of the people who were dead were bankers and some seemed to be from natural causes.

"You never were good at math," he said, confirming she was right not to say anything until she had something more substantial, if there was anything more substantial.

Sophie propelled herself into the room, scattering the cards before Roger could grab her.

She looked at the mess her daughter had created and then at her husband. "Why don't you do lunch? In fact, cook Chinese, today."

He frowned. Roger had never been near a wok in his life.

"Translate that into you're taking me to the Chinese buffet in the industrial zone.

\* \* \*

The Chinese restaurant had typical décor with big fans and lots of red enamel.

Roger, Annie and Sophie were ahead of the normal lunchtime crowd. The waitresses, who were Chinese, not a large population group in Argelès or even in nearby Perpignan, were still setting up the tables.

Unlike many of the restaurants in town, this was new. The family had only been there twice before, so they were not known. Annie found it a bit strange to be in a local restaurant where she didn't know the just staff but the staff's life story.

A woman, perhaps no more than thirty, greeted them. She wore the high-neck Chinese tunic costume in a blue silk. On the way to the table, she paused to pick up one of the high chairs off to the side.

"No chair!" Sophie said.

"Yes," Annie, who was carrying her daughter, said.

*"J'ai dit NON!"* She reached for her father. Although she was two and three months, Annie marveled that she directed English at her mother and French at her father. When it was the three of them she would use whatever language they were using. Her vocabulary was about twenty to thirty words in both languages, many of them negatives. No and *non, veux pas* and won't were the most frequent lately.

*"Tu n'as pas un choix."* Roger took his daughter from Annie.

It took both parents to put their screaming twisting child into the high chair. One couple walked into the restaurant, looked at the tantrum-throwing kid, turned and walked out. Annie thought of all the times she'd wondered why a parent didn't control their kids. She issued a mental apology to them all.

"Now you see why I said Gaëlle was enough." Roger was speaking through his teeth.

"Ignore her," Annie said.

Easy enough to say, but Sophie started to climb out of her high chair. Roger put her back, took off his belt and belted her in. The child continued to howl.

"Go get your food from the buffet." Annie did as he said. Glancing back, she saw that he had turned his back on their daughter. By the time Annie returned with her plate strategically piled, Sophie was sniffling.

"My turn," Roger said.

Annie placed a spare rib, an egg roll and pieces of pineapple on Sophie's tray. "Eat," she said. It helped that Sophie loved spare ribs and pineapple. Her nose was running. Annie wiped it despite the twists and turns.

As they ate, Roger asked, "Why do you think there's a connection with all those deaths?"

If he brought up the topic, then she would go into it. "I don't know, I just feel it. If I try hard enough, maybe I can find the connection."

"Even though the defuncts worked in different jobs at different levels in different places?"

Annie used her chopsticks to pick up her soy-sauced soaked noodles. "If I get to know the people enough, maybe I'll figure it out."

"You are the proverbial dog with the proverbial bone. Why don't you try telephoning them?"

"They are dead."

"I mean their families."

# 41

Carol spent at least twenty minutes watching the koi circle in their pool. The outside was more like a New England stone wall and was at least fifteen by fifteen feet, not bad for a captured fish. The evening's cold had frozen the puddles on the stonework making up the courtyard, but the pool must be heated, she thought.

She cursed herself for deciding to give the killing one more try. She had no hopes of getting Braun alone. Although she was an excellent markswoman, there was no way she could get a gun.

For one job where she had to travel by plane, she'd taken two suitcases with the parts of a Glock 17 divided between them. She had worried the entire time that someone in security would notice the main part of the gun in her larger suitcase, but they hadn't. If they had would they have checked her other luggage? When the job was done, she'd taken the gun apart and scattered it in garbage bins in three cities before flying home. It was the last time she shot someone.

Carol didn't like guns despite her proficiency. Subtle means such as hard to detect poison were far more challenging. She'd learned to make HCN (Hydrogen Cyanide) first but preferred potassium chloride injected into the armpit where the hair would hide the needle mark.

Bombs were out because she didn't have the technical knowledge. The possibility of blowing herself up was too great. One way she had never killed was by fire. Something started in the middle of the night might be a challenge, but she might take other people with her target, which wouldn't be fair.

Even if she could set fire to Braun's house when he was alone, the logistics would be difficult. She would have to get the fuel to his home, which would involve a rental car. If the gas were to be spilled in the car, then it might be traced back to the rental agency. Then again, she really was good at stealing cars.

How much gas would it take to destroy a house? The damned German homes had so little wood in them that they wouldn't go up like suburban New England houses would.

Still, despite all the negatives it might make a great challenge for her last mission. She wouldn't end her career with her first failure.

She hadn't wanted to spend this long in Germany. She was tired of heavy food and guttural speech even though most Germans spoke more than passable English.

The drizzle was too cold for her to stand looking at koi.

Back in her room, she made a list.

The room was warm. The maid had not yet made up the bed, which was fine with her.

She took out her notebook and began:

- Find plans for house (government office that issued building permit)?

- Find fuel type and amount needed (cybercafé, go to several)?

- Check to see if the house is alarmed (not sure this can be done)?

- Automatic lights outside?

- Patrols for the neighborhood?

- Best place to steal a car?

Damn, it would be easier if she spoke German or at least read it. The neighborhood wasn't the type where a person hanging around any amount of time wouldn't be noticed.

Unlike her other assignments which she had relished, this was a chore.

She wanted to be back in Boston in her loft.

One of her professors, who had quit teaching despite being an excellent lecturer, had said he was leaving because he was burned out. "Everyone burns out if they do something long enough," he'd told the class.

Maybe she was burned out. Maybe the idea of burning down a building had caused her to finally burn out. The irony amused her.

She put down the pencil.

Frankly she didn't give a flying fuck if Franklin was happy with her or not. He'd made a fortune from her work, not that she hadn't boosted her net worth too. It had been fun. It just wasn't fun anymore.

# 42

Dr. Marianne Morella sat at her kitchen table and looked out at the swirling snow. The coffee in her favorite, violet-decorated mug was cooling.

No way was she going to be able to do hospital rounds today. She'd already called in saying it was impossible to drive into the city. The doctors already there knew they'd be stranded on duty. In the last storm, she'd been the one who stayed.

A week ago, the governor had told everyone to stay off the roads as this storm piled more snow on the already high banks from the last two storms.

Her only hospitalized patient was a six-year old girl who had thrown up from the flu so heavily that she had to have IVs to replace the lost liquid. The nurses had her home phone if the doctors on duty had any questions.

As for her patients with whom she had appointments at her office in the afternoon, they'd had a good laugh when she telephoned each one to say her office would be closed. The idea of leaving the house was pure fantasy.

Back in the old days when her son was young, snow days were joyful. They would do jigsaw puzzles as her parents had done with her and brothers and sisters. The little boy who would climb into her lap was now a teenager that topped her five-foot eight height by four inches. At least an inch of that happened from the time she'd left him for his last year at Phillips last September until she picked him up at Christmas.

Sean had refused to come home at Thanksgiving. He tried to avoid Christmas. Marianne forced him to face the house without his father, reminding him that his father was away on business more often that he was home. She had felt, even when Jamie was alive, that she was mother and father to the boy, which was why, despite her and her husband being from big Italian families, that she wouldn't have more than one child.

In one way, she was looking forward to this snow day.

Since Jamie had been killed in St. Petersburg, of all places, the house hadn't seemed all that different. Between their two careers, they hadn't seen all that much of each other. When they did, they made love, chatted a bit about inconsequential things, caught up on chores. She hadn't been unhappy: she was sure he had been equally satisfied. If he weren't, there was nothing she could do about it now.

For a doctor and a successful businessman, their Cape Cod style house perched on a hill with a long driveway through pine trees was unpretentious. Neither had wanted to get on the upgrade treadmill that many of his colleagues experienced. To justify the decision to them, who saw his unwillingness to buy a McMansion, he claimed that his wife was too busy with her career to go through the work of moving.

Her intention today was to read a good mystery, stay in her sweats and *not* use the extra time to do paperwork, laundry or household chores that the cleaning woman didn't do.

Rather than drink another cup of coffee, she decided the book needed a hot chocolate and a fire in the fireplace to be properly enjoyed.

Since Jamie's death, she had assumed the husbandly role of things like bringing in the wood from where the delivery man had stacked it. When he was alive, he would often forget, but she and Sean had made sure there was a good supply before he went back to Phillips.

The house had been remodeled inside. Walls had come down so the first floor instead of having a separate dining, living room and kitchen was one big room. The brick fireplace had been replaced with a wood-burning stove. Between that and the solar panels, she could keep the house comfortable.

His colleagues were only business acquaintances. Their wives didn't mix except for forced social events. In many ways, except for business dinners, her life went on much like it had before Jamie was killed. In all possible scenarios of how her marriage would end, murder was never one of them.

She was almost through chapter five of the mystery and thought she'd figured it out, when the phone rang. The screen didn't show a number. She hoped it wasn't a marketing call.

Maybe it was the hospital, maybe Sean. Her social life had been nonexistent since James died. The neighbors, with whom she had little contact because of their busy schedules, had contributed a few casseroles after the funeral.

"You don't know me, but I would like to talk to you about your husband's death, his murder." The voice had a local accent. "I'm calling from southern France. My name is Annie Young-Perret."

Carol's first impulse was to hang up. This must be a cruel joke or a scam like the kind you get supposedly from a friend who is in Wales and has lost her pocketbook and passport and needs money wired to her immediately.

"How do I know you are who say you are?"

Annie rattled off a lot of information, including her book on Amazon and her telephone number. "You can call me back. Or are you on Skype? My husband is an ex-policeman in Argelès-sur-mer."

Marianne took Annie's Skype details without giving her own. "I'll do some research and if I want to talk with you, I'll call you back. What's your number?"

Annie gave both her landline and her mobile.

After hanging up, Marianne sat in her chair. Scum had formed on her hot chocolate which was no longer hot. She went and poured it down the sink before dropping a capsule in the coffee maker. She took the cup to the computer.

She used one of the search engines that didn't report to the NSA, not that she had anything to hide. There was little need for the government to know what journals she read. Pediatric disease articles indicated nothing detrimental to United States security.

There were two books that Annie had written. One was on Kindle and she downloaded it. From "About the author" she learned that the information she'd been given by the voice on the phone matched that in the book.

She went to Facebook. Annie didn't have a closed site and most of the things posted showed a cute a little girl. Much of what was there was in French which Carol had studied in high school but names of bones, muscles, diseases, had long since pushed the French out of her head. There was no point calling the police on the other side of the world.

She issued an invitation on Skype. Within minutes her Skype was lighting up. Although the picture was less than perfect she saw a pretty red-head. In the background was a bookcase. In between the books were sculptures of small animals.

Neither the woman nor her environment seemed threatening. Nor did it seem like a scam. As she watched, a little girl climbed into her mother's lap. Scammers usually didn't have cute kids with bows in their hair. "I admit you've piqued my curiosity."

She listened as Annie went into the number of young employees of AGG that had died under abnormal conditions.

"How did you find this out?"

"Research. One of my friend's husband, who worked for AGG died in a hit and run. It's a hard company to work for."

"Jamie never talked about his work that much. I can't even tell you what he did, but I know he travelled a lot. What do you want from me?"

"To be frank, I don't know."

Marianne sighed. "Who else has died?"

Annie gave her the list.

"But they are in different countries and have different deaths. And in different countries, even. I don't see how there can be a connection?"

"I don't either, other than they were too young to die and all worked under the same umbrella company. Excuse me a moment." Annie's face left the screen.

Marianne heard a small voice say, "Don't want to," and Annie say,

"You have no choice." Annie came back on the screen. "Have they found out anything about who killed your husband?"

"The police found nothing. The room was totally clean of any fingerprints. I mean clean, not even the maids who cleaned up. Not even Jamie's."

"So, the murderer knew what he was doing."

"There was a woman with Jamie in the bar, someone said. They had a drink together, but they left separately."

"Co-worker?"

"Not according to the description."

There was silence as if the pretty red-headed woman was trying to think of the next question.

"I've had my lawyer try to work with the Russian consulate in D.C. and the St. Petersburg police. The police have filed it in its non-solved file and gone on to other things."

"I really appreciate this," Annie said.

"I don't think I've been much help," Marianne said. "If I can think of anything more, I'll let you know."

"If I found out anything more, I'll get back to you. Give me your email and I'll send you a list of the people who died and the circumstances. There are people, mostly amateurs and a policewoman when she's off duty who are working on the hit and run in Edinburgh…" Annie paused. "…with not much luck."

"I'd like to see it, the list. Maybe I can think of something. And feel free to share my contacts with the others."

The screen went dead after proper goodbyes.

Marianne took her cold cup of coffee and nuked in the microwave. She walked to the window to watch the snow pile up. No need to worry about shoveling. She paid someone to plow the long driveway and to shovel the walk to her front door.

As much as she would have liked to go back to her book, her mind would not let herself concentrate. Shit.

# 43

## STOW, MASSACHUSETTS

Tom Richardson unlocked the door of his house. Inside it was completely dark. He shut off the alarm by feel and threw his keys on the table under the alarm.

The house was cold: cold from the damp from the lake that never went away, cold from the snow that just kept coming and cold from the emptiness.

The house was a building, not a home. He and Rita were never there when she was alive to do things that made it homey like the ones they had grown up in. When he flicked the light switch, he could see the mezzanine leading to the bedroom where he slept on those few nights that he didn't stayed at the hospital.

He could claim that after Rita died, he didn't want to face the bed where they had made love, but the truth was, even before she died, he'd spent more nights at the hospital than at home.

He wasn't sure where his marriage had gone wrong, if wrong was the word. Inactive might have been a better description. When they were both at Boston University, he in pre-med and she in business, a fairy tale ending seemed possible.

Perhaps it had started when he was in med school and she was working on her MBA. They both earned advanced degrees from Harvard, but her campus, even if it was on the same side as the Charles River, was not close enough so they could share even a quick lunch. So bogged down with their studies, they communicated by notes and later by texts. He would wake up to find her gone or she would be asleep when he came home.

Compared to their parents, they were success stories. Like his father, he worked with his hands, but not tinkering with engines. His hands pulled babies from women. Rita, who had loved her mother, had sworn she would never be a stay-at-home wife.

He had learned NOT to deride her corporate world as being inferior to his although his opinion hadn't changed.

It had been his idea to buy this house. Maybe, just maybe, it was to show off to their parents, when they had them for Thanksgiving dinner. He was never able to finish a meal for the three Thanksgivings they'd hosted their families because patients went into labor.

The doctors and nurses had been kind about his wife's death.

"Too young."

"Such a bright future."

"She was so beautiful."

What followed the condolences he termed as the "you shoulds," he ignored. What bothered him most was he didn't miss her. He'd loved her once, but she had not really been a part of his daily life for some time.

One of the "shoulds" was "you should not to do anything for a year." He wanted to sell the house and buy a condo near the hospital. He disobeyed that "should": a realtor was coming tomorrow to check the place for listing.

He knew it would show well. Maybe the realtor would be one of those that would add flowers and bake bread before a showing. She might light a fire in the large stone fireplace opposite the floor-to-ceiling windows.

Upstairs, he noticed that the landline was blinking. Unusual. As a couple, they had no social life. His parents, the hospital, and his secretary always called him on his mobile.

He listened.

"Dr. Richardson, I'm Annie Young-Perret again and I'm calling you from southern France. I want to talk to you about your wife's death. There have been a statistically unrealistic number of deaths of young AGG or its subsidiary's employees and we think there's been some foul play. Could you please call me at the number I left on earlier messages or Skype me."

"Stupid," he thought.

There was no evidence of foul play in the hotel room where his wife had died. An autopsy had shown a heart attack, unusual at her age but not unheard off.

He erased the message.

# 44

**"You failed." Franklin Pierce stood** at Carol's door. His black woolen overcoat was glistening from melted snow.

Jet lagged and in her pajamas, Franklin was one of the last people she wanted to see.

"Aren't you going to let me in?"

She stood aside. He brushed by without touching her unlike when they were first lovers way back when. Then he would sweep her up in his arms and carry her to bed. That he no longer wanted her didn't bother her at all. The only thing she had really appreciated in their love-making was the release and a certain sense of power it gave her over him.

Unlike many mistresses, instead of begging him to stay, she would tell him to leave: she had other things to do that day or night, whenever.

"Only fifty percent. I got the one in Edinburgh."

"You messed up on Braun."

Carol didn't like being reminded of her failure. She'd worked out elaborate plans to set his house afire, but nothing would have been workable. Anyone getting near the house at night would immediately trigger lights on the front and side doors. Braun was never without either his muscular driver or his bodyguard.

"You have to try again." He threw his coat on the chair and poured himself water.

193

"No, I don't."

"You don't expect me to pay you, I hope."

"I expect fifty percent for the Edinburgh kill."

"When you do the other one right."

"It is a person-by-person deal."

"That was the first double kill. What do you intend to do about it?"

Stupid, little man, she thought. He wasn't that much taller than she was. Her affair had been partially a lark and partially to get back at his wife Diana who always asked Carol when she was getting married.

It wasn't that Carol needed the money. It had never been about the money, but she knew the money was important to Franklin. It was he who indirectly got the insurance money through the sham corporation.

They'd dreamed up the scheme together, one night after making love. It had started as a *what if*. Most of the ideas had been hers.

"If you're not happy, get another killer," Carol said. Thinking of herself as a killer always gave her a tingle. She was a serial killer as well, but unlike most, it wasn't sexual or deviant. Her pleasure had been, notice the had been, she thought, devising new and better ways to kill. It had been fun studying poison books, learning about guns, stalking victims.

The fact that she killed in different places and then left those places except for her Boston kill, meant the police, who usually looked at family members, would never trace her.

Franklin, you will pay me. She lowered her voice.

"Or what?" he put his empty cup down on the counter top. "You can't go to the police."

"I suppose I could go to your wife." She realized she wasn't being very smart. Franklin wasn't a man to be cornered any more than any wild animal. She laughed.

"What's funny?"

"We're at each others' throats over money. It's silly. I don't need the money. I can't implicate you without implicating myself and vice versa. It's not worth it."

He frowned. "You are being sensible, almost too sensible."

She rested her hand on her stomach. "With the baby and all, I've been thinking it is time to retire. And there's the wedding to think of."

Her mother was planning a rushed wedding in two weeks. That her daughter *had* to get married wasn't as shaming as her never being married. A small, tasteful wedding with a loose-fitting wedding dress was fine.

"You're really marrying that faggot?"

"What a terrible thing to say about my beloved." Her voice was almost a coo as she kissed Franklin.

He resisted, but not for long.

About the moment she had an orgasm, Carol realized that she did need to do one last kill to be safe. This would be hard because she had a connection to the victim.

# 45

Jenna Johnson looked out her window at the sun setting over the Rockies. Her house, a converted ranch—a real ranch—not the suburban idea of a ranch, that had belonged to her grandfather, was located just outside the village.

Back when she'd grown up in this town, Manitou Springs was even smaller than it was now with its current population of about 5,000 people and its split personality between being a tourist destination with its cowboy character and a real place to live. Manitou Springs was part of her soul.

The years when she'd followed her Air Force officer husband around the world, she would dream of being in Manitou Springs and looking at this very view at the end of each day. Not that some their assignments hadn't been interesting: Japan, Germany, California, North Carolina. The best assignment had been Oslo where he'd been an attaché at the United States consulate, especially during the long summer nights where the sun barely set. She'd paid for it in the winter, when daylight was almost an unknown quantity.

These experiences she'd enjoyed, but only because she knew some day she could go home, her real home, not some temporary officer quarters on an Air Force base that looked like the last base where they'd lived and the one before that and the one before that. She would have her own furniture, or at least her family's furniture, not government-issue that was the same old, same old.

She'd done her bit as an officer's wife, entertaining other officer wives, smiling at the bitchy generals' wives and not getting caught in gossip about who was sleeping with whom on the base. She swallowed her complaints much more than she would have liked. It worked until Bob had retired as a full bird colonel with the eagle replacing what she called the flower. She knew he had wanted to get at least one star, and have people call him general. High blood pressure followed by a leg injury had forced his retirement, but not before he was eligible for his full pension.

In the early days of their marriage, it had been fun exploring new places. Unlike many officers, Bob had enjoyed going "out on the economy" and intermingling with the locals, whenever he could. Part of the fun was the knowledge that one day, she would be back home in Colorado.

The house where she grew up had been redone. It still retained some its rustic character with eclectic bits of furniture, paintings and memorabilia. The small windows had been replaced by large ones. Solar panels covered the roof.

The corral had been rebuilt to keep the horse she'd dreamed of having for most of her married life.

Her children were grown. Her daughter lived nearby in Woodlawn. She considered herself lucky that her home had escaped both the big fire and the floods that had almost devastated the area before she moved back.

Some of the kids she'd gone to high school with had reconnected with her, but their life experiences had been so different from hers that they didn't share much in common once they got past the "remember-when" chatter.

Over the years, she'd made friends with other service wives, a few of which she chatted with on Facebook or Skype. Others were Christmas-letter friends.

If she thought about it, she would say she was lonely, but only a little. When her kids were growing and her husband was away, she'd run the family alone.

Sometimes she was angry, furious even, that they had been denied the retirement they'd planned, not travel as many older couples did because they'd done that, but to stay home to build the small ranch together. Maybe it had been her dream that even if her husband had lived, it would not have worked. He'd been a city boy, although he'd loved the holidays when they visited her grandfather. She would never know now.

He'd become too involved in building a contracting firm to provide bodies to the government for its endless wars. He loved the schmoozing at government functions necessary to win those contracts.

She was good at schmoozing too, only she hated doing it.

At that point, she'd rebelled. It was her turn. He'd had his for twenty-two years. Her ultimatum had shocked him. She was shocked that he was shocked. Hadn't she been saying what she wanted for at least the last eight years? Hadn't he been listening at all?

Thus, she'd said, "Colorado or a divorce." He was on his way home the night he died to discuss their future be it together or apart.

The car accident had ended the two alternatives for them as a couple.

The coroner had ruled he had fallen asleep at the wheel. That was unlike Bob. More than once she had known him to pull off the road to catch "forty winks" until he had the strength to continue.

The moon gave a curious light to the snow on the window frame. Already the night arrived later and later.

Her suppers were always light: an apple, a yoghurt and if she felt like treating herself, perhaps a few shrimps.

Tonight, it was a half-cup of leftover lentil soup, which she held in her hands as she watched the horse turn around in the corral. In a little while, she'd go out and put her in the stable.

With Bob gone, she seldom felt the need to fix meat. She carried the cup into her bedroom, which doubled as her office. Her desk with her laptop was between the two windows. Even if there were no neighbors around, she closed the curtains.

This was her time of day to check Facebook. Strange that some of her friends were people she'd never met, but friends of friends and sometimes friends of friends of friends. She also could track what her daughter and grandkids were doing refraining from any critical comments when she disapproved and adding happy remarks when she did. Her son-in-law said she was a great mother-in-law. She tried. She tried.

The first thing she saw was her six-year old granddaughter in a tutu.

Then she noticed a message. She clicked on it and read, "You don't know me, but my name is Annie Young-Perret. I wanted to telephone you, but your number is unlisted. If you are the widow of Bob Johnson, I think his death may have connection with several others. My Skype name is my full name. My telephone is +00 33 4 555-12 81. You can also check me out on the Internet. Please, please contact me."

For the next hour, Jenna researched the woman. She'd written two books, neither of which Jenna had ever heard of. She had a blog although she didn't write in it often. It did tell about her life in France, her husband, her daughter, her work as a translator. Sometimes she wrote about how she felt that her upbringing in several countries made her feel she would never belong one hundred percent anywhere. Now, that, Jenna could understand.

Should she call?

A three-three number was France, which matched the blog and Facebook information available. France was what—seven hours ahead.

It was something she might do tomorrow after she'd slept on it. When she took a sip of her lentil soup, it was cold.

# 46

## EDINBURGH, SCOTLAND

**"A**re we late?" **Robina Collins** asked as Chantal MacAndrew opened the door. Mike McNulty stood behind her. The wind was blowing. The umbrella did little to protect them from the rain.

"Come in quick." Chantal pulled Robina in. The door opened directly into the kitchen where Janis Aitken and Louisa MacLaughlin were nursing mugs of hot spiced wine. Its smell perfumed the air. "Take off your coats, and I'll get wine to warm your insides."

Robina noticed that the kitchen even with people was not all that warm, but she knew with the financial problems Chantal had, she'd keep the house as cool as possible. All of them were in heavy wool sweaters over jeans. Robina had even put on a pair of thick tights in preparation for the meeting.

Clean dishes were in the drainer. A pot, which contained the wine, was on the middle burner of the stove top. The room was not well lit. A single light fixture hung over the table giving a ghostly glow to the faces that might be more appropriate for a séance.

The writer, Janis Aitken hugged Robina and Mike once their coats were removed and hung on pegs near the door.

Louisa MacLaughlin waved from where she was seated. Robina thought she looked tired, more tired than usual. She'd learned enough about Louisa to know juggling a job, kids and as much freelance work as she could find was a position that she hoped never to be in. She glanced at Mike and for a second pictured him picking up their kids after the divorce. Stupid, she thought. We aren't even engaged, and I've already made him the bad guy in our divorce.

"Let's get started," Chantal said after the customary remarks that were more politeness than any real sharing of information.

They all sat on the side of the table with their backs to the stove so they could see the opened laptop in the middle. Notepaper was in front of Robina and Mike. Louisa had an iPad that she used for her notes.

Skype rang on the laptop. Annie Young-Perret appeared on screen. "Hi from Southern France."

"Don't tell us how warm it is there," Mike said.

"The Tramontane is blowing. Warm isn't a word I'd use. We'd better get going, because we've lost electricity a couple of times today."

Murmurs of approval came from the group. "How did you make out contacting the next of kin of the victims?" Janis asked.

Robina liked that the mystery writer didn't use weaselly words like alleged. Annie was the same way. Louisa, not so much, which Robina chalked up to worry about her job.

"All are interested in pursuing it except one. Tom Richardson, the husband of the murder victim in Boston, never got back to me. I've left several messages on his landline with contact info."

"Nothing?" Janis asked.

"Not a whimper, but then again, he might not think of Rita's death as a murder," Annie said. Her image blurred.

"And the rest?" Louisa asked, "Especially Call-me… er, Jack Berry's wife. I'm sorry, I shouldn't disrespect the dead, even shitheads like him."

"I haven't contacted her because the investigation is ongoing. I thought Robina could do that," Annie said.

Robina thought that would really piss off her boss, who was being a bastard right up to his retirement date.

More than once Mike had felt her fury. "Why take it out on me," he'd ask.

"Because you are the only one nearby," she'd answered. Thinking how patient Mike was, she reached for his hand.

He squeezed it. "What we lack is a common thread despite them all working for the same company or the same company's subsidiaries and being too young to die naturally."

More murmurs of agreement.

"We need to get their personnel records," Annie said. "There has to be something that covers it all."

Louisa sipped her wine. "I can't do diddly damn about the Boston and Colorado deaths. Those files would be in the U.S. offices." She took a drink of her wine. "At least I think so. I've heard that they are trying to consolidate records, but it could be a rumor."

"But Duncan's and Jack's? You could get those?" Annie asked.

"I could try, but it's dangerous to my future employment."

Robina leaned into the range of the view finder on the laptop so Annie see her. "Hi Annie."

"Hi Robina. What about you? A warrant?"

"My boss would never go for it if I suggested it."

"What if I do," Mike asked.

"Maybe a fifty percent chance," Robina said. "I suppose it's better than waiting till Ian retires in April."

"Do you think that if Louisa could get something about Jack and Duncan, a warrant would cover the other deaths?" Chantal asked.

"It would increase chances but trying to explain how we got them would be difficult. We couldn't use them in court, if we ever get that far, unless the information was swept with a warrant," Robina said. "Still if they could pick up the same information after a warrant than it would be useable."

"No, it doesn't. Annie, I think it is okay for you to contact Jack's wife," Mike said. "Robina will get in more trouble if she does it."

The screen went dead as Chantal spluttered, "I feel awful. You are all doing this to help me, and I'm not holding up my end."

Robina's immediate reaction was to get up and put her arms around Chantal. "What you need is a hug and more hours in a day. If the police had done their jobs properly this wouldn't be an issue."

"Let's try Annie again," Janis said when they saw that Annie went offline. "She warned us about electrical problems, but I'd think her computer might have a battery backup."

"It might be the entire system that's down," Louisa said.

They waited for thirty minutes, trying to call Annie periodically, but there was no response.

Finally, Robina stood up and Mike followed her. "We'd better get home," they said at the same time.

The rain was still pouring as they walked to the tram. He pulled her into a doorway of a closed shop. She wasn't sure what kind of shop and didn't really care because of his kiss.

Strange, she thought, how much he'd become part of her life.

# 47

## EDINBURGH, SCOTLAND

Janis Aitkin was the last one to leave after the Justice for Duncan meeting, as the group had named themselves, although with each passing meeting they were more convinced that Duncan's death wasn't a one off.

She and Chantal sat at the kitchen table. Wine glasses, the remnants of several cheeses, cracker bits and a few grape stems were among the wine glasses that hadn't been quite finished. A few dregs were left in the wine bottle.

"You look like hell," Janis said to Chantal. The writer pushed her graying tangled hair back from her eyes. The streaks looked as if a hairdresser had put them in, but it was nature. She reached out and covered Chantal's hand with her own.

"I think my bones are tired," Chantal said. Her French accent was more pronounced, as it always became when exhausted. She feared Janis's sympathy would cause her to cry.

She'd almost reached the point where she would call her parents and ask if she and Blane could come live with them until she could find a job in Geneva.

Almost.

Not quite.

Although they had pretended to accept Duncan, they'd considered her choice to live in Scotland somewhat uncivilized. It was so un-French. As for her choice of career, it wasn't real world. Not that they said it. It was the cock of a head, a murmured "hmm" that "spoke" disapproval.

After Duncan's death, her father had said he would help her, but only if she returned home. He didn't understand Edinburgh was her home, not just because of Duncan, but because she loved it from the castle on the hill to the scones. She'd even learned that tea could be as good as coffee and a kilt was not an affectation but a statement of national pride.

She had friends here. No one questioned that she was Swiss-French—she was Chantal: mother, museum worker, friend, widow. It was the widow part that was appearing in her nightmares.

The museum opening was two weeks away. The finishing touches were being put on the building. The press had been invited for a pre-opening event.

Several members of Parliament had been invited in the hopes of getting more public funding. They'd accepted.

The budget needed three months of a certain number of entrants and events a day. She'd coerced groups to hold events: a wedding, bi-weekly poetry classes, two club luncheons and a tattoo group's annual general meeting. Had the Scots not been so enamored of their history, she doubted she could have convinced any of them to enter the halls.

There was no budget for a public relations person, but Janis had paid for her own publicist to send out press releases, including what photos to catch an editor's eyes. The art work had shown up in the local paper.

The publicist had worked her connections to convince the BBC to do a segment on their opening. A BBC radio interview had been set up for two weeks after the opening. The woman had pointed out, it was one thing to get people in the door the first couple of days, but they needed people to come regularly.

Chantal did not expect locals to visit regularly. The museum was too focused, but she hoped that tourists might be tempted. Poetry was never overly popular as evidenced by the number of starving poets or those who wrote poetry after work. Janis had pointed out it was even harder to earn a living as a poet than it was as a fiction writer.

Chantal's biggest problem was time to cram everything she needed to do and still give Blane the attention he should have. The expense of the nursery wasn't helping her worries.

"Someday, you'll look back at all this, and think what a great job you did," Janis said.

I should live that long, Chantal thought. "Promise?"

"Promise." Janis started to clear the table, but Chantal waved her away. Janis ignored her until all the dishes were in the dishwasher. She kissed Chantal on the top of her head, picked up her coat from the pegs by the door and said, "Get some sleep."

Chantal didn't get up to lock the door. This part of the city wasn't dangerous. The alley entrance was too out of the way to attract burglars, although she wouldn't have gone to bed without locking up. She sat almost too tired to get up and go to bed.

The Skype flashed.

"Everyone gone?" Annie asked as she came up on the screen.

"Yes."

"Tell me, how are you *really* doing."

Chantal said nothing, but she teared up.

There was a long silence. "I'm coming over for a week to take care of Blane and whatever else you need done."

"What will Roger say?"

Roger appeared on the screen. "One of the reasons I married Annie is that she is a specialist in friends. I can manage Sophie for a few days."

"I'll tell you when I'm arriving. Now go to bed." Annie disappeared from the screen.

Chantal knew she should put the dishes away because she wouldn't have time in the morning, but she was just too tired.

Rather than undress, she just crawled under the covers and prayed that Blane wouldn't wake too early.

# 48

Frannie Berry watched *The Chase* on the telly. This was her time of day. Three-year old Helen played quietly in her room. She never understood how she produced such an easy child to raise. The little girl had almost foregone the terrible twos although that didn't mean that she didn't test Frannie's patience in asserting her own will over certain foods or clothes.

It was almost as if Helen knew that her mother had enough to handle with her father.

After the funeral as people were issuing almost formatted condolences, it was all she could do not to laugh, dance and sing, "I'm free! I'm free!"

Marrying Jack had been a major mistake, brought on by panic of spinsterhood. Now that was an old-fashioned word, she thought, as a contestant decided to go for the smaller amount offered by the Chaser. She wanted to concentrate on the program but couldn't.

Had Jack still been alive, she'd be rushing around like a crazy person, making sure everything was perfect for his dinner including having the table properly set and the kitchen being clean. No one else she knew ever sat down to dinner with all the pots and pans used in their meal preparation sparkling and in their proper place in the cupboard.

She'd realized her mistake within two weeks of returning from their honeymoon, or better to say that the confirmation of her fears had happened within two weeks of returning from her honeymoon.

"You should live with him first," her mother had cautioned, but

Frannie, who had never been asked by anyone to even date regularly, had been afraid he'd get away.

It wasn't that Frannie was unattractive, although she was nothing special, a bit overweight with a skin that still broke out if she even walked by piece of citrus. Her brown hair wasn't thick: she wondered about those hair commercials where the model swung long locks so shiny that one almost needed sunglasses to look at them. She'd tried them all and the only thing that changed was the degree of dull.

What Jack had described during their much too short courtship as paying attention to detail she learned on their honeymoon was closer to OCD. She'd given it three months. At the end of that time, as she was wondering where she'd go, because she didn't want to go back to her mother's I told you so. Then, she discovered she was pregnant.

The word *trapped* didn't begin to describe how she went thru the pregnancy. He'd been thrilled and insisted he set up the nursery. When she'd rearranged some of the furniture to what she thought would be easier: he'd moved it back and put tiny drops of paint to mark where it should stay.

When the police had come to announce his death and probable murdered, she almost said, "Thank you!" but she knew that could put suspicion on her.

AGG had carried enough of an insurance policy that going back to work could be postponed for a few months, although she'd already started to hunt. The house had been his, but it was mortgage free. His cheapness meant there was a large savings account. He hadn't been adventurous enough to play the stock market, a good thing, too, she thought.

She had no idea why anyone would murder him, but if he acted at work as he acted at home, she felt that any of his direct reports might have fantasized it. She'd never met any of them. Jack was determined to keep his home and work lives as separate as if they occupied different continents.

The phone rang just as The Chaser was one behind the contestant. She lowered the volume and flipped on the subtitles then answered.

"You don't know me, but I once worked for your husband. I'm Annie Young-Perret."

"Poor you." The words slipped out before she could stop them. "I suspect he was a hard boss."

"That isn't why I'm calling." Annie went on to explain that it seemed strange that so many people who worked for AGG had died before their time.

Frannie at first wasn't sure how to respond. Then she said, "Does it matter. He's still dead?" As the words slipped out of her mouth, she thought how bad they must have sounded.

"There's group in Edinburgh who were looking into Duncan MacAndrew's death… The VP of HR. He was a hit and run. You did know that your husband had been hit on the head before he fell into the water."

"A robbery?" Frannie wished she cared more, but she didn't. His death had freed her and if someone had killed him, she was grateful. The confused feelings made her think of herself as an awful person, which she wasn't most of the time. She was a good mother, a good daughter. She went to church at least once a month and she had worked in a soup kitchen on weekends until she married. Jack had stopped that. He'd sulked until she'd quit her as a secretary in a real estate office.

"How do I know you are who you say you are?"

Annie rattled of her home phone, her mobile, her URL, her blog and Chantal's number. "Check me out. Call me back, or if you give me a time, I'll call you back. We can also Skype."

"I will. Call me tomorrow," Frannie said.

By now The Chase was over, and she hadn't seen who'd won. No matter.

Helen was still playing in the other room, her voice in conversation with her imaginary friend, Tiger Lion. Frannie had grown used to Tiger Lion being another member of the household. Jack had been so against Tiger Lion that Frannie and Helen had told the creature to hide when Jack was home making a game out of it when they heard his car pull into the driveway.

When Helen learned that Jack wasn't coming back, she'd said, "That means Tiger Lion doesn't have to hide anymore?"

Frannie sighed as she dialed Chantal's work number.

"Early Scottish Poets Museum, how may I help you?"

"Chantal MacAndrew, please."

"Speaking."

"I hate to bother you, but my husband worked for AGG as your husband did. Both seemed to have died in extraordinary ways. Do you have a minute to talk?"

"I'm in the middle of something, but this is more important. What was your husband's name?"

"Jack Berry. Anne Perret-Young asked me to talk with her. I'm checking up on her.

By the time Frannie hung up, she was willing to help, not because she loved her husband, but because she thought there was something wrong. She didn't give a damn about justice for Jack, but Chantal seemed like such a nice person with such a sad story.

Even if it was a foreign call, she called Annie. A man picked up and handed it over.

"I will help. Have you talked to Fiona Clark? The HR person?"

"No."

"She came to the house and was really helpful to me. She seems like a nice person."

"Thanks for the name, and I'll try. I'm going to be in Edinburgh in a couple of days. The group that is working on this will be meeting at Chantal's. Would you like to join us?"

Frannie hesitated then said, "Why not?"

# 49

Louisa MacLaughlin had gone from work to a café with Internet for a half hour the last five nights, trying to hack into the AGG databases. She wasn't alone, but had a friend from university, Dan Regan, who met her each night to help. There would be no way to trace a hack back to her home computer if anyone tried.

Babysitting was the problem. Last night her baby sitter told her if Louisa couldn't make it home earlier, she'd have to find someone else.

Damn it! She hated letting down the team.

Tonight, a friend was relieving her regular baby sitter. When her friend said, "no rush," Louisa appreciated the extra time. Still, there were limits of what she could ask of friends.

She and Dan sat side-by-side in the coffee shop. Most people had gone home for dinner or to a pub for a pint.

"They lack good cybersecurity, your company." Dan reached for his coffee on the table.

"Hello Louisa."

Louisa and Dan looked up. Jason Colter, the AGG hot-shot IT guy was standing there, his hands in his jeans pocket. His long hair was in a ponytail, but a few strands hung over his cheeks.

Louisa moved to change her screen, but Jason grabbed her hand. "My God! I come in for a cup of coffee, and totally by chance, I find out who the shit is trying to hack our system." He looked at Jason. "Or should I say shits." He reached over and brought up the screen that Louisa had tried to hide. "This is my fucking lucky, lucky day."

Louisa exchanged looks with Dan. There went her job, fired for cause, her chance of ever getting a recommendation and another job at zero. "It isn't like it looks."

"Tell me how it fucking looks to you."

"Sit down. We're trying to solve a murder… murders."

"Jesus Christ, now that's a good tale, if I ever heard one."

"Really, sit down."

"I'll sit. This must be better than anything on the fucking telly tonight." He sank back into the soft seats that surrounded the low table that held the laptops and their coffees.

Louisa talked as fast as she could, trying to judge his reaction. When he unfolded his arms, she thought she might be gaining ground until he said, "That's the bull shittiest load of crap, I've heard." He started to get up.

"Wait. Look at these newspaper articles on the other deaths."

"So what? Some fucking top execs get themselves dead in other places in the world."

"All AGG employees or subsidiary employees," Dan said.

"We're trying to find out if there's any connection by going into their personnel files, but we can't find them."

"Of course, you can't. They are in a separate database." He stood up. "I gotta go."

Louisa stood. She was almost his height. "Don't tell on me. I need this job."

"You hack into the company database, and you expect me to be quiet?"

"Think of the reason at least." As much as Louisa hated to grovel, she would grovel like she never groveled before, if it meant keeping her job. "Maybe you could help us."

"You're nuts." Jason picked up his coffee and left.

# 50

**"Leave me alone, Mother." Carol** Dixon said. She and her mother Annabel Baron Dixon Hancock were sitting in the library of Annabel's Beacon Hill house. All the spare walls held floor-to-ceiling bookshelves filled mostly with hardbacks going back to the turn of the century, twentieth not twenty-first. The forest-green, damask drapes were held back by lighter green tassels. Some light seeped through the bow windows.

"You shouldn't be wearing jeans and a sweatshirt. It isn't proper. But that's not as important for us to discuss for now. If we don't do something soon, people will think you had to get married."

"Jeans and a sweatshirt are comfortable." She held up the sweatshirt to show her mother her growing bump. See! I'm pregnant, Mother. Four months. Even if they've done wonderful things medically, the chance for a premie of four of five months surviving are almost impossible."

"Pull your sweatshirt down. If you have a full wedding, it will put a better face on it." Whenever Annabel was upset, she always tugged at the black pearl necklace that she wore with her gray sweater set. Any other day she would have on her white pearls, which she would pull the same way. Her hand barely left the necklace.

"Jonathan and I are going to City Hall, with his parents and you, if you want to come: and Caleb, of course." She was tempted to say, that besides inviting her stepfather, whom she did like much more

213

than her mother and her dead, but not loved father, they would invite Jonathan's live-in lover, but she suspected that her mother would pull so hard on the pearls that they would break and she didn't feel like crawling around the floor, trying to find them.

Martha, the housekeeper forever, knocked on the library door. "Telephone, Mrs. Hancock." Annabel refused to have a phone in the library. She felt the one in the hall, her husband's office, the kitchen and their bedroom was more than enough. She did have a mobile phone, but the number was given out to only select friends. Her friends were selected by a process that made emission into an Ivy League school seem slipshod.

"Anything I can do?" Martha asked. She'd been more of a mother to Carol than Annabel ever had been to a point that she and the nanny had a fought a war while keeping the animosity from Mr. and Mrs. Dixon.

"I think an ultimatum is in order," Carol said. "When mother comes back can you bring some tea?"

Martha timed the tea perfectly. Annabel had just seated herself when Martha appeared with the tea tray, which included a pink flowered pot and matching cups. "The tea, Mrs. Dixon, just like you asked."

Carol poured the tea in the formal manner on which her mother insisted, handing her the cup while resisting the temptation to spill it on the gray sweater.

"I can get King's Chapel," Annabel said. "I spoke to…"

"City Hall, Mother."

"But…"

"City Hall. We'll tell you the date."

Annabel put down her cup on the side table. "That is…"

"That is what it will be." Carol reached for the plate of fresh-baked lemon cookies. Annabel would never have allowed a store-bought cookie in the house. The cookies were almost transparent. Long ago, Carol would sit and watch Martha as she mixed the dough. She would leave some dough before baking saying, "It doesn't matter when you eat them, before or after baking."

"We'll tell you the date." Carol looked at her watch. "I'm late for meeting Jonathan."

Her mother held her cheek up for a kiss. Carol obliged.

\* \* \*

"So how did it go with the wicked witch of Beacon Hill?" Jonathan asked. He kissed her on the cheek before she took off her coat. They sat in the bar of Four Seasons.

The walk from her childhood home across Boston Common to the hotel, had given Carol a chance to calm down. "Don't let her get to you," she chanted under her breath so people wouldn't think she was crazy. Maybe they would think she was just another one of those people talking on their cell phones through a discreet mike.

"As you'd expect. As my stomach gets bigger, she'll be less likely to watch me waddle down the aisle. I gave her a put-up-or-shut-up."

She climbed on the stool with a back. She hated backless stools. "We need to set a date with City Hall."

"Hello, you two soon-to-be marrieds." They could see Seth Jacobson, Jonathan's lover in the mirror behind the bar. "Mind if I join you or do you lovebirds want to be alone? There was no malice in his teasing tone.

"Did you show your father the sonogram of the baby?" Carol asked.

"I did. He was ecstatic. No queer was ever so happy to see a penis as he was."

# 51

Louisa MacLaughlin was afraid when she held her key card to the door of the AGG offices, she would be denied entry. Jason Coulter could have already shut her off before going to Human Resources with his discovery.

Everything was normal in the Tech Writing/Translation offices. Productivity had increased since Berry's death although the atmosphere had relaxed.

She brought up her screen and then the in-house email. The first message was from the HR person, Fiona Clark. "See me at 9:15, please."

Shit, this is it, she thought as she read the message asking Louisa to come see her as soon as possible.

Trying to figure out how to pay her bills, how to get another job swirled through her mind as she walked to the Human Resources Department. Unlike the night she and Annie broke in, she didn't skirt the security cameras but strutted. She would not be cowed, or at least she wouldn't look like she was being cowed. Her mother had instilled in her the crude saying so unlike her mother, "Don't let the shitheads get you down."

The receptionist, yet another new one, had her sit and didn't offer tea or coffee. Was that a bad sign? An HR magazine was on the coffee table in front of the mustard yellow chairs, which reminded her of children's nappies after a bad bowel movement. The birthday party for her son would have to be cancelled. No money for extras after she was made redundant. She wasn't sure whether she preferred that phrase or the American one, fired.

Fiona didn't enter the reception area from her office, but from outside. She still wore her coat. "When will I learn NOT to bring my car? Parking." She smiled at Louisa. "Did Adrienne tell you I was tied up in traffic?"

Adrienne had the decency to blush.

"I've just got here, and she was on the phone." Louisa lied to give the girl an out. Even if she were preparing her out-going paperwork, she'd remember her kindly.

She followed Fiona into her office. The woman indicated Louisa should sit.

"I suppose you're curious why I've called you in."

No, Louisa thought, I think you're going to make me redundant and/or press charges against me.

"I've good news," Fiona said.

"We aren't going outside to find a replacement for Jack, Jack Berry. Between your CV and job performance reviews, we'd like to offer you his post, with a three-month trial. Others might fuss that it wasn't posted, so we will say it is temporary, then post it and give it to you."

Louisa didn't know what to say so she said nothing.

"You do want it. It comes with a £30 weekly rise."

Louisa knew from rooting around in the personnel files that Jack Berry made £75 pounds a week more than anyone in the tech writing/translation pool." Still she couldn't let on that she knew. How long would she have the job, once Jason squealed on her? "I'll take it."

* * *

"Lunch?" the message from Jason flashed on her screen, some minutes after her temporary promotion had been announced. Some of her co-worker congratulations were obviously of the why-not me category, which she would have to deal with. Others seemed sincere.

Everyone seemed relieved that Berry was gone and his replacement temporary or not was known, not anal and competent.

Louisa didn't plan to plan her course of action for the department until after lunch.

The morning dragged. At any moment, she expected her access to be shut off, but then again, if Jason was doing her in, why would he want to have lunch with her?

\* \* \*

The cafeteria still was quiet at 11:45 when Jason and Louisa met. They took their trays and ordered the daily special of macaroni and cheese.

After settling at a table in the furthest corner, the same one that Louisa and Annie used when being overheard was undesirable, Jason smiled. "Congratulations."

"Thank you."

Louisa was afraid to say anything. She hated it when other people had power over her, and he held the biggest hammer that anyone could ever have wielded in her life.

"Relax, Lady. Your secret is safe with me."

"Why?" She hadn't meant to blurt it out.

"Because I did some research and those deaths are weird. I want to join your group."

# 52

EDINBURGH, SCOTLAND

Annie Young-Perret followed Fiona Clark into her office still surprised that the Human Resources granted her an appointment. The vibes put off by Fiona were cool at best, for which Annie could not fault the woman. After all, she had walked off her job at AGG without even a wave good bye at HR.

However, she learned that if you don't ask, you will never get a positive and often she was amazed when she thought she didn't have a snowball's chance in hell, she get what she was looking for.

Fiona was dressed in the same business suit she'd worn the day she'd interviewed Annie. Annie wore the black dress she bought for the opening of the museum but "*businessed* it up" with a scarf and jacket.

Never in her life had she done something like that, just walk off a job, but it had felt good, really good to tell off her idiotic boss not just for herself but those that didn't have the luxury. To her it would make no difference. She'd never had trouble getting clients. In her work, it didn't matter if there were gaps between jobs. Her credits spoke for themselves, and more than once clients came back to her with another project, some several times.

She had more work than she wanted, so much so, that she sometimes felt that her original goal of only working six months a year was drowning in assignment opportunities. At the same time, she hated turning down work in case clients would not come back

219

to her. The good part was she did most of her work at home, making Roger happy and herself as well. She didn't want to be away from Sophie. She reminded herself whenever she might allow a moment of self-pity, which was infrequent, that most people would love to work as she did.

Fiona sat behind her desk and waved her hand at a chair.

Annie sat. She wasn't there to make amends: she was there to get information.

Fiona picked up a pencil and began fingering it. She rocked back in her chair and looked at Annie without saying anything.

This was not the first time that someone had played who-could-blink-first trick with Annie. She was damned if she would be the first to break the silence. A trick that usually worked was to get up and leave, but this time, she couldn't risk failure. Another was to look at her watch, which she did, pulling up the jacket sleeve with a flourish.

"I've never had someone walk off the job, before," Fiona said.

"I never walked off a job before."

Fiona cocked her head. "Interesting. Want to tell me why?"

"Just because Berry is dead, didn't make him any less of petty tyrant when he was alive," Annie said.

Fiona nodded several times.

A knock at the door was followed by the receptionist who stuck her head in, "Don't forget your meeting."

"Is that the old, don't-forget-the-meeting trick, to guarantee I'll be ushered out quickly?"

Fiona laughed. "You're certainly not like any employee I've ever dealt with."

Annie took a deep breath. "Actually, I was here under false pretenses." She then explained how they were convinced there was a problem with the deaths in AGG and that Duncan was one of the casualties. She'd provided two other names that Louisa had given her.

Annie watched Fiona's reaction. Except for a widening of the eyes, there was none.

"None of that makes any sense, any sense at all," Fiona said when she finally did speak.

"Which is why I'm here. Maybe Duncan found out something, a

220

connection, a reason the company would profit from their deaths."

Fiona picked up a pencil and turned it front to back, front to back before she spoke. "Annie, you seem like a nice person. Your work here was certainly exceptional, but this is crazy." Fiona looked at her watch. "I really do have a meeting."

Annie rose and walked to the door. "There has to be an explanation, Fiona. Whatever it is, I hope you aren't part of it, because you seem like a nice person, too."

\* \* \*

After Annie had left, escorted by the receptionist, Fiona sat in her chair. She was shocked to discover that almost a half hour had gone by when the receptionist reminded her, there really was a meeting. "Send Bill in my place," Fiona said.

What to do next. She had not thought she was doing anything wrong when Franklin Pierce had approached her. Granted it was a bit unusual for the CEO of the company purchasing her old, decrepit firm to take out insurance policies on executives at subsidiaries around the world. He had explained they were doing it for tax reasons, which she understood absolutely: replacing management was difficult.

What was stranger was that the company also had taken out policies with the company as beneficiary on lower level, younger employees. Cost was minimal. They had lost a secretary to cancer at thirty-six. The benefit to the company more than covered the year's payments to the insurance company. Ghoulish, she thought, but still, profit was profit. Wasn't it?

She had pointed that out to Franklin. He had paid off her house, which she thought also strange, but not having to worry about her mortgage, certainly made her life easier. After Stephen had left her for a younger model, keeping up payments had been a constant worry. How Franklin Pierce knew that she had no idea, but people in powerful positions didn't get to high places without being thorough.

He also had made her his mistress, which she knew was stupid. But after Stephen had left she needed a lover to convince herself she was attractive. Forty wasn't old to a man in his late fifties like Franklin was. To him she seemed young and beautiful. She also suspected she wasn't the only woman he slept with. Not quite like having a woman in every port, but a woman in every AGG office, maybe.

From time to time, Fiona would think of Franklin's wife. She'd checked the Internet to see pictures of the couple at charity dinners in *The Boston Globe*. Franklin said from the beginning, he'd never leave his wife. This made Fiona happy: he would never do to his wife, what had been done to her.

How guilty should she be? Franklin came to Edinburgh maybe every six weeks, sometimes less.

For a week, she'd weighed her choices. Insurance policies were not illegal. Being mortgage-free was a bonus.

Then Franklin had asked her to make sure that all employees had insurance policies with a subsidiary as the beneficiary. After saying it was AGG's world-wide policy, he showed her an article from two business magazines talking about the practice.

Her job was to include the applications into the hiring package where employees signed form after form. They could be selling their children for all they knew. They weren't the only ones who never bothered to read what they signed. She always checked the box on the Internet that said she'd read and understood the rules for the site although she never did.

She took out her mobile, the one with the red case, not the one she used every day. There was only one number she ever called and dialed the international number.

When a male voice that she knew both in and out of bed answered, she said, "Franklin, we may have a problem."

# 53

" **I need to go to** the men's room," Jonathan Webster IV stood, leaving Jonathan Webster III with his fiancée Carol Dixon. That annoyed her. He knew how much she disliked his father and didn't want to be left alone with him.

Carol watched her fiancé weave around the few tables in the restaurant with the stereotypical red-checked-clothed tables. The less time she spent with III, as she thought of Jonathan's father, the better.

The restaurant was in Boston's North End where, despite gentrification of the old brick warehouses and homes, a large percentage of Italians still lived. Shops that made spaghetti and dried it over twine strung from one end of the shop to another, restaurants like this one that had individual owners were still possible to find. Old men gathered by the statue of Paul Revere to play boules or chess and solve the world's problems.

III put his hand over Carol's after moving his wine glass so it wouldn't spill. "I can't tell you how relieved I am that you are marrying Jonathan. For so long I was convinced he was a puff."

Why III used the English expression, Carol didn't know. Normally old Boston families were not the least pretentious. Maybe it was because III had been the ambassador to King James Court under one of the Bushes that certain British phrases had wormed into his vocabulary.

"And if I needed any more proof he is straight, I'd just have to consider my grandson that you're growing."

Carol would have loved to have told him about the syringe conception, but that would be too costly for Jonathan and her.

"Will you sell your apartment?"

"I doubt it. Maybe I'll rent it," Carol said.

"I assume that the poof Seth will move out of Jonathan's."

"He's looking for a place."

"Who is looking for a place?" Jonathan IV sat down placing the napkin he'd left in his chair across his lap.

"Seth," III said.

"There's no rush," Jonathan said.

"But you will be married next weekend. I assume you won't live in Carol's," III said. He had turned his nose up figuratively and literally when he saw her studio. The smell of paint from the flat below had come through the ducts. He had expressed concern for his grandson's welfare until his wife told him to mind his own business. III had said, "My grandson is my business."

"We've talked about switching places for a while," Jonathan said.

Quick thinking, Carol thought. The three of them had plans to leave enough of her stuff in Jonathan's place and hide Seth's in case Jonathan's parents dropped in. She had decorated the nursery in the traditional blue for boys. Both sets of parents to dinner had been invited to see it.

She had no intention of living with Jonathan and Seth any more than they intended to not live together. The fiction would be kept up as long as necessary: long as necessary was defined as the checks clearing.

Seth and Jonathan would set up their own law practice, but not in Boston. As new parents, they no longer wanted to put in the seventy to eighty hours required in a high-pressure practice. They'd found a town in Maine where the one lawyer was retiring to Florida and was selling his practice.

"Aren't you afraid of being outcasts as gays?" Carol had asked. She didn't want her two friends to be hurt by rejection of a narrow-minded community. At the same time, she didn't want the cell-set what she was just beginning to think of as "the baby" to be unhappy.

"Strangely enough, this little town has both an artistic and a gay community. Not as much as Provincetown, but enough that we can build a life," Seth had said.

She could imagine the explosion from both sets of parents when the truth came out, but she really didn't care. III would have his grandson, Jonathan and Seth would have a life together. She would have a bit more money, although that didn't appeal all that much to her. Unless she did some stupid things, she had enough to live on modestly for the rest of her days.

What her next step in life would be was so unclear. Often when people asked her what she did, she wanted to say hit man or hit woman to see their reaction. They wouldn't believe her anyway. Boston Brahmins weren't hit men, especially female Boston Brahmins.

When the waiter cleared the dishes, she ordered espresso.

"Is that good for the baby?" III asked as she took a sip of Jonathan IV's wine.

"My gyn doesn't have it on the forbidden list."

"I have to get back to the office. You too," III said to IV.

"We need a couple of minutes to make sure I can attend the birthing classes Carol has found."

"Men didn't do that in my day." III put his napkin next to his empty demitasse. He folded the copy of the sonogram which had showed his grandson's baby penis and put it in the inside jacket next to his heart. "Don't take too long."

When he left the restaurant, Jonathan said, "Billing hours. I don't make money sitting here." He too put his hand over hers. "I can't thank you enough for this."

"What are friends for?" Carol meant it.

# 54

**"You really messed up." Franklin** Pierce stood at Carol's door holding his hat in his hand. It was the type of hat that men wore throughout the 1930s, although that was long before Franklin would have been even in baby bonnets.

Carol had been curled up in her bed with a book. She preferred reading in an almost prone position with a couple of pillows propped up on the headboard of her bed. The knock at her door disturbed her.

She ignored at first. It meant that someone had been let in by one of her neighbors. Let them try someone else.

The knocking continued.

Shit! Her book fell of the edge of the bed onto the floor. She picked it up and turned a corner of a page marking her place. "I'm coming."

Discovering Franklin standing there, turning his hat around and around in his hands, pleased her even less than being disturbed.

He pushed past her. He took off his coat wet from the melting snow that must have landed on him as he made his way to her front door. Carol was sure that his chauffer had let him off a block or so away both for parking and anonymity reasons.

Although he was a frugal New England Yankee, he did have a driver to run him from his Financial District Office to his Brookline home, but his car was not a limousine. It was a quality Volvo. Pierce kept the car in top condition for years and years.

226

Using his handkerchief, which bore his initials, he wiped the moisture from his face. She knew he wasn't here to discuss the weather.

Then he took off his suit jacket, loosened his tie and stamped to the refrigerator leaving his footprints. When he and Carol had been lovers, she'd always stocked his favorite wine, beer, coffee, and eggs. After making love he wanted to have a fried egg sandwich. Because it was so out of character, it had always amused her that he made them himself.

Having him as a lover had amused her.

He was barely the type of man for a family or any other human that took his time. Business oozed out of his pores.

She'd dropped off some papers about her trust for her step-father to sign. Franklin had been there for some reason: she neither knew nor cared what it might have been. As debonair as he might appear, his pass was not much different from those she'd known in high school. He had told her that she was his first and only mistress. She had no reason to disbelieve him. In reality, she didn't care if she were the first or the hundredth.

Once he got over his nervousness, he had turned into an all-right lover, nothing special. He could provide an orgasm without her having to do much work on the relationship.

Only a year into the relationship did she discover that she had been wrong in thinking he wasn't the type of man for mistresses. He had been in the shower and his phone had rung. She read it. The message was from a woman who obviously was more than an employee. After listening to the message, she'd erased it.

The fact that he had lied to her didn't bother her. She had so little invested in him other than an orgasm here and there, that what else he did with whom, when and why had no importance.

What she liked more were their conversations about business, which were fascinating. Because she'd chosen not to work didn't mean that she didn't follow business news, not just press reports, but the story behind the story.

About a year into the affair when they lay side by side in her bed, he was wondering how he could bring in more money but without using the normal financial channels, it was she who suggested the insurance scheme where all employees would be insured. He would be the beneficiary through a straw company.

At first, he was shocked. Then he set it up.

Then he collected one million from a middle-level manager of thirty-five who had a heart attack while jogging.

One night he complained the young didn't die often enough.

"Hire a hit man," she said.

It took her at least six months to convince him and another three to give her a trial reminding him that a hit woman would be less-suspect.

For her it had been a great challenge not unlike passing the bar. Her research into weapons, fake identities, Interpol had kept her busy for several weeks, working a good eighteen hours a day. Her computer knowledge wasn't quite as strong as she would have liked, but she made sure that anything on her computer was erased so an ordinary scan would never locate her searches. Than she destroyed the hard drive and bought a new one.

It had been fun.

Had.

It wasn't anymore. She looked at him and thought, little man. She knew he would hate that designation. He thought of himself as a powerful CEO and to those that worked for him, he was. But his prick was small and his ability to satisfy her had more to do with his tongue than his manhood.

He stood by her refrigerator leaving the door open. She walked by and closed it.

"Franklin, you've got to go. I'm tired."

"Not until you listen to me." He stood by the table where she ate her meals. She sat while he remained standing as she sighed. It would be quicker for her to listen than to fight.

"Women are asking questions in Scotland?"

"I'm sure a lot of women ask questions in Scotland."

He slammed his hand down on the table. "This isn't funny." He proceded to talk about Annie, Louisa, Robina and Chantal, all names Fiona had supplied after launching her own investigation.

She stood up next to him. They were almost the same height. Few people talked back to him, she knew.

"Don't worry, I'll take care of it."

"You'd better." He picked up his coat from where he'd tossed it and slammed the door. She heard his steps going down the stairs.

After he'd gone, she threw herself on the bed and lay there before picking up the book. Like Scarlett O'Hara, she'd think about it tomorrow when she was fresh, but she knew where she would start.

The last thing she wanted to do was go to Edinburgh, but it didn't seem as if she had much acceptable choice now. There was a choice to everything, she knew, depending on the price one was willing to pay. No one had to take the dog out for a walk if they were willing to clean up the mess caused by the dog's limited ability to hold its bodily functions.

First, the research: this was not the time to start getting careless.

# 55

**"There's nothing to be nervous** about." Annie arranged another tray of champagne glasses.

"Nothing? Nothing?" Chantal smoothed the black dress she'd bought at the charity shop. It would have cost four figures had she bought it in the original dress shop: it was only £52 at the charity shop, still more than she could afford. As museum director, the last thing she could afford was to look tacky. Thank-goodness the black heels, which were already killing her feet added to the look.

"You've thought about everything possible for the opening."

Chantal wished she was as sure as Annie was. Before she could say anything more, Janis Aitkin came through the door. She carried three large stacked trays each covered with aluminum folder. "I've never made so many nibbles in my life. I'm a writer, not a caterer." Her smile belied any real annoyance. The budget for the opening had been extended by every way possible including having the board chip in with food and champagne.

Chantal knew Janis would be the only writer who made things herself. "If we'd had a large budget we could have done things from the period."

"Since it is winter, porridge, bread, rotting apples, leeks... that would be wonderful," Chantal said, but the muscles in her face relaxed.

The culture editor of the local paper was coming. The Lord Provost, who had backed out at the last minute was sending his deputy, at least. Tomorrow, the host of a popular antiques show, was coming to interview her about the museum. It would be the feature between where experts talked about the value of antiques and an auction of the items selected.

One of the draws for the general public was a chance to meet the writers on the board as well as their well-known writer friends who had been coerced into attending. Poetry might not be all that popular, current or medieval, but mysteries were, and locals were proud of the authors who called Edinburgh their home.

Writer David Jones arrived at the same time as Peter McEnroe. Their individual styles of arrogance made her prickle. Even if David wrote teen mysteries and McEnroe still considered himself the prose Shakespeare of his time they agreed on wanting the museum to work. For this she ignored her dislikes.

Three women with musical cases walked in and asked where they should set up. The poetry would be read alternating with folk music of the period.

"Hello Annie."

Chantal looked around to see who was calling out to her friend to see a drop-dead handsome man. He would have been perfect to play the romantic lead in any Italian comedy, preferably showing up on a motor scooter, taking off helmet and shaking out his dark curls.

"Quentin," Annie squealed as she threw her arms around the new arrival, who had been followed by another man, not half as good-looking. Both were dressed in jeans, dress shirts, blue jackets and scarves looped around their necks. Annie led the two men over to her.

"Chantal, the director, Quentin, my editor, and his friend Serge," Annie said. They did the ritual handshakes. "Quentin brought Serge here. He wants to look around to see if the poets could be some sort of cartoon series. He does a lot of educational production."

"Most of which you've never seen," Serge said. "But I make a great living selling materials to schools around the world."

Chantal knew Annie's editor worked on half a shoestring: she wondered if his friend was the same. It didn't matter if they could get positive publicity.

People started filtering into the museum.

"Showtime," Annie whispered into Chantal's ear. "Break a leg."

A blur was the only way that Chantal could describe the next two hours as she talked with the press, political figures, educators, and poetry lovers. They had not expected as many people to accept the invitations. One woman, a slightly-pregnant American journalist, said she hadn't received an invitation, but she'd heard about the opening from a friend. She said she represented a small literary magazine in the US.

Chantal had insisted that the music and poetry readings be spaced out. J.J. Harris would also give a brief explanation of his artwork in each room between the music and readings. The board were the readers.

Each made a plea for sponsors or memberships.

By nine twenty people began to drift away corresponding to the dearth of anything left to eat and the last dribbles of champagne having disappeared until only Annie, Chantal, Harris and the board were left.

"We did it," David Jones said as he left. McGregor nodded as he buttoned his overcoat. "Nice work Chantal."

Clean-up was left to Annie, Janis and Chantal who had kicked off their shoes and were padding around the room in their stocking feet. "I don't care if they are plastic, save the champagne glasses," Chantal said.

"I'm saving the napkins too," Janis said. "The clean ones."

It was closer to midnight when Annie and Chantal were back at Chantal's, paid-off the baby sitter and were in their pajamas sitting on Annie's bed dissecting the evening.

"Even with all the symposiums and everything booked, we still don't have enough to survive," Chantal said after Annie congratulated on pulling off a tremendous accomplishment.

"Are you going to bail?"

Chantal thought it a good question. "Not until I have to. You work that hard to put something together, it becomes part of you."

After Annie headed to the couch downstairs, Chantal wished Duncan had been there to see what she'd been able to do. People had told her that the emptiness would go away, but so far it had only been muted.

# 56

Carol Dixon's name tag read Leslie Maginnis, Editor, *Tuscaloosa Literary Magazine.* She had sent five copies in advance to the Early Scottish Poets Museum when she requested an invitation to its grand opening adding she would retrieve it when she arrived, not to mail it, because she was travelling.

This mission had felt different from the others she'd done. Those were exciting, a joy at facing the challenge. This was a chore, much like cleaning up an egg that had dropped on the floor.

Usually when she went through customs with her Alice La Russo passport from Canada to wherever she was heading, she felt smug at beating the system along with an amount of gratitude to the real Alice La Russo.

These days, although the passport was for a genuine person, albeit it a very dead one, with all the electronic surveillance, she wondered if a border guard might discover a dead person taking flights all over the world.

And then there was facial recognition equipment, which was why she always wore makeup that gave her slightly better cheekbones or thicker eyebrows. Dark glasses were too obvious, but she did have colored contact lenses, wore her hair so much of her face was covered. Sometimes she stuffed those cotton rolls that dentists used in her mouth. Still there was only so much she could play with because of the photo in the passport. Total appearance change was out of the question.

Tonight, she was trying to look like Leslie, an American Southern belle with a literary bent. She'd put in a temporary brown dye and wore her hair in a tight chignon. She'd always been good at accents and when she picked up her nametag at the door let out as good a Southern drawl as she'd ever heard from British actresses on PBS. Of course, she had trouble understanding some of the local Scottish accents and she was equally sure those gathered at the museum opening wouldn't know a genuine Alabama accent from a fake one. They would just think it was American.

Still, attention to details was the most important part of her success. Just because this was going to be her last job, it didn't mean she could be sloppy. Being caught now, well that would be ironic, and irony was not something she needed.

Holding a glass of champagne in her hand, she examined the painting of a very large and saucy rabbit.

"What do you think?" a man asked.

She jumped. "I like it. I think if captures the spirit of the poem." She had read the poems before coming. If anyone asked her, it would look as if she knew what she was talking about. No one did, which meant that she didn't have to lie or say how the real magazine that she didn't work for was thinking about doing a special issue. As a non-reader of poetry, she thought it might be hard to believe, except she knew that poets did take themselves seriously enough, that they might swallow the lie.

"Thank you." He stuck out his hand. "J.J. Harris, painter of said rabbit."

"It must have been a fun project," she said.

Carol really didn't want to spend time talking to anyone. She was here to identify Annie Young-Perret. After Franklin had left her loft in Boston a week ago, she'd spent hours in different Internet cafés searching for the woman that had been nosing around too much.

Franklin had emailed her a photo of Annie taken by the Edinburgh AGG security cameras. She arranged a meeting and chastised him severely. "No traces, including email," was something she had warned him about more than once in other assignments. He might run a company, but the man could be incredibly stupid sometimes.

Annie was all over the web. Her Facebook page was public, which was how Carol knew for certain that she would be at the museum opening. She had a website where she advertised her translation and tech writing services and her two books were prominent on her publisher's website. Carol had ordered both from a bookstore under the name, Diane James. They hadn't arrived by the time she'd left. Damn it! She wouldn't be able to get any idea about Annie from her writing.

With her curly red hair, Annie was almost easy to spot, although there were several other natural redheads in the room. This was Scotland. Right now, Annie was chatting with her publisher. Carol knew who he was because his photo had been on the publisher's website. Then they picked up trays and started walking around offering them to guests.

"Champagne?" Annie asked, looking Carol directly in the eye.

"Thank you." She took it and turned away and headed into where Janis Aitken was beginning to read something by William Dunbar.

"*Quhy was thou blyndit, Resoun? quhi, allace!*" Janis said. Her voice was clear even if the words could have as easily been in Chinese or Swahili for all that Carol could understand.

"How many of you understand?" Janis asked.

Smiles, but only three people, all whom looked professorial, raised their hands.

Janis continued. "I only understand Middle Scots when I hear a translation. I love the sound though, a bit like an Indian melody. Not something we're used to. Let me try it in modern English, 'Why were you blinded, Reason? Why, alas!'"

Only in "The Dance of Seven Deadly Sins" did she find herself paying much attention. Sin she thought was a phony concept designed to keep people in line. Even the Ten Commandments were a control mechanism and she would not be controlled by anyone. Ever!

"Do you like how I have the sins dancing?" J.J. Harris handed her a glass of champagne. He pointed to the wall. She pretended to take a small sip, because she wanted to stay clear headed.

Tonight, she had no plans to kill Annie, but merely needed to see her target up close. There was a certain daring to be where Annie was. If the police were to check the guest list after she killed Annie, they might discover that although the literary magazine was real, but the real editor had not been there that night. She imagined the editor getting a phone call from Scotland asking about a murder some three or four thousand miles away.

Carol wasn't sure she was going to kill Annie right now. There were still too many unknowns. What was wrong with her. Usually at this point, she had the kill worked out.

Franklin was being over cautious. Killing Duncan's wife or the woman cop made more sense. Once she would have argued with Franklin. He would say she was looking for more commissions: she would say she was being thorough.

His final argument was that if Annie died than Duncan's wife would give up. How he knew that she didn't know. For all his Boston Brahmin upbringing, he had somehow become caught up with a shady side that seemed at odds with his ever-so-staid Republican Washington connections. Although somewhat curious, she wasn't curious enough to ask.

She was leaning towards poison and was fully prepared to do so if she could create the right conditions. Hit and runs were difficult, although it was her preferred method. Something about the bump of the body against the metal of the hood and even the slight lift of the car when it rolled over the body appealed to her.

Although she was a crack shot, she didn't want to risk getting her hands on a gun, especially in Scotland. This uncertainty reconfirmed her belief that she should retire from her hit woman career.

Part of Carol's love of her work had been the challenge in trying different techniques. She wanted to do her kills with the class of her heritage, not some Italian mafia creep.

She felt a ripple inside her stomach? Was that the baby? Shit, this was not the time to go all baby machine.

"Do you like how I have the sins dancing?" J.J. Harris repeated.

Too many people were in the room for her to have noticed the panels of strange creatures cavorting in a woodland setting. "I'm not sure I know which sin is which," she said.

He laughed. "There's a clue. People are standing in front of the name of the sin written at the bottom of the panel. If I yelled fire, everyone would rush out and you could see."

"Perhaps I'll come back tomorrow when it is empty," she said. "A wiser course, don't you think?"

As he nodded, she excused herself to amble through the room listening to other conversations. One man was boasting about his own writing; a young couple was saying that they were proud of Chantal's accomplishments, even if they had nothing to do with it.

A comment about being on duty the next morning and a mention of the police gave Carol a momentary shiver. Police traditionally were not interested in poetry, but then again, they might be Chantal's longtime friends.

Carol shivered. She looked at the woman, talking with some high mucky muck. She could tell because the man was important because he wore a metal shawl of what were probably fake gold squares with a jeweled square in the middle. Somewhere she remembered that officials in the United Kingdom wore those goo-gahs on official occasions. Strange world, she thought. The Boston mayor would be laughed out of town if he showed up sporting one.

As she watched Chantal work the crowd, Carol thought, I made that woman a widow. She didn't feel guilty, powerful, sad, or happy. It was a matter-of-fact realization. It also added many, many ounces of gold, which was how she took payment, despite Franklin deriding the payment method.

She preferred the metal to the crazy economy. Even if the price fluctuated, gold had been worth something from the beginning of recorded time. No need to explain it to the tax people.

"I can pay you in gold certificates," Franklin had said, "if you must have gold."

"No, you can't," she'd replied. "I want to feel the metal." Almost half a million in gold was now stored under her beautiful wooden floor in her flat as safe from robbers as possible.

Carol had no plans for the money. She didn't need it. At least the bastard of her father had left her financially independent, something she hadn't cared about when she shoved him down the stairs. Freedom comes in many forms, she thought before bringing herself back to the museum.

What a boring evening. As soon as people began leaving, she too drifted to the coat room. If she stayed too long, someone might remember her. She worried that the artist might, but she noticed that he had been talking to everyone. Unfortunately, she was the only American there other than Annie. Except for the taking the champagne from Annie, she'd avoid any direct contact with her and she also made sure she didn't speak to Chantal.

Outside there was a light drizzle. By some miracle, she had found a parking spot to the left of the entrance of the museum with a clear view of everyone who came and went. It took another hour before almost everyone was gone, but her target and the widow were still inside. Cleaning up?

Before leaving Boston, she'd reviewed her poison guidebooks but that implied opportunity. From her research, it seemed as if Annie was seldom alone.

Again, the idea of a gun ran through her mind. A bullet hole, unless done at a certain angle would look like what it is—murder. That's why she preferred car accidents and hard-to-detect poisons. Pathologists might not think people falling from high floors might be a murder but suicide. Duncan MacAndrew's hit and run was considered a crime by his family causing her nothing but problems, leading to Franklin's concerns. Had she found a subtler way to kill him she'd be a "happy" bride-to-be, mother-to-be back in her own flat in her own city.

Why was Annie taking so long to leave?

This was boring.

As she sat in the car getting colder and colder, she noticed the closed café next to the museum had a free Wi-Fi sign in its window. She reached into her bag and brought out her iPad and logged in. Long ago she had learned to hack into people's accounts and she found Annie's.

She was booked to fly to Geneva in two days. Why Geneva? Then she remembered that Annie's parents lived there according to Annie's blogs.

Before she could book her own flight to the Swiss city, she saw four people leave the building and lock the door behind them. It was Annie and Chantal. A couple was with them, the one that was talking about the shifts that she had guessed were police. She wondered if they had investigated on Duncan's death.

The women hugged each other as the man stood to one side.

"You will come for Easter or Carnival, won't you?" Annie said. Argelès is wonderful?

"We've holiday time to take and it would do Robina good to be away the last couple of weeks of her shithead boss's reign."

"I know you can't get away Chantal, but can you convince Robina?"

"I'll try." Chantal held onto the railing with one hand as she exchanged her high heels for a pair of flat shoes.

"Are you girls okay to walk home alone?" Mike asked.

"We are. The fresh air feels good," Annie said. "It was stuffy in there."

"And wet," Robina said. "Take my brolly. I can huddle under Mike's."

Carol could barely believe her good luck. She started the car and began following the two women. All the time her mind was working. The car was rented to Alice. Her mind clicked into gear too on her next steps. Unfortunately, she hadn't worn gloves, so she'd have to clean the car so thoroughly, but a rental car, and this one was not brand new, would be full of DNA and prints anyway of the other renters.

She revved the engine, but the women turned into an alleyway too narrow for a car.

Shit!

# 57

## EDINBURGH, SCOTLAND

Robina watched Annie and Chantal disappear into the mist. Few cars were on the street: one had seemed to be following the two women, but since both were on the main road, it didn't make sense. She chalked her reaction up to over-copdom, a phrase she conjured up when she felt her work had taken over too much of her head.

Mike put his right arm around her as he held the umbrella over their heads. She hooked her right arm around him burying one hand in his pocket, one in hers. Because she'd forgotten her gloves, her hands were cold. She didn't mention it. He would tell her it was her own fault. It was.

Roger would never do that. In fact, he would keep an extra pair in his pocket for the times she would forget hers. Now, that was beyond fantasy, she chided herself.

The walk to her flat was about twenty-three minutes, which would have been lovely on a summer night, far less so on a rainy, not-yet-spring night.

The only thing she heard were their footsteps on the pavement and the rain. She would have loved to chat about the evening, the readings, who was there, what people were wearing and the art work hat J.J. had done. Talking about the poetry wasn't on her list.

From experience, she knew Mike hated small talk. He would consider an evening recap of events small talk, tiny talk, minute talk even, but he would rehash sporting events with his mates play-by-play—so very, very male.

In her imagination she thought that Annie's husband Roger would have been willing to examine every little detail. She was realistic enough to know that the Roger she'd created was a fantasy. Still she'd been disappointed when Annie said that he had stayed in France taking care of their daughter.

She no longer wanted Roger to be real. He would never, could never live up to her fantasies. The one great thing about fantasies was she could put whatever she wanted in them.

If she and Mike had a daughter would he be the kind of father that would stay home while she was out? When he was with his nephews, he would go out in the front garden and throw a ball with them daZ The boys and Mike would wrestle on the floor until his sister-in-law would call time out for the sake of the lamps and knickknacks. How would he handle a daughter?

She was sure he was planning to ask her to marry him. She'd heard him checking with police policy on married couples. "So, you accommodate where you can, but we can't work together." As she walked by, he'd said he'd call back and hung up.

Living together was going smoothly. They worked out a pattern of his getting up to start the coffee while she took her shower. When she'd cook the evening meal: he'd clean up and vice versa. He left the kitchen cleaner than she did. Those days were when they were on the same shift.

Sometimes, they would pass each other on the street or in the station as one was going on duty and the other off. She wondered if anyone had guessed their relationship. Even when they went for a pint after work, they made sure to sit far apart and leave at different times. She wasn't ready to go public. They never discussed when they might.

Her mother said to determine if someone would make a good mate check how he treated his mother. Mike called his mother regularly and drove to Aberdeen once a month to see her, not that she was an invalid.

Although she was retired, she ran two miles every day, ran a book club and volunteered in the charity shop twice a week. She didn't look sixty-five, although Robina wasn't sure how sixty-five was supposed to look: certainly not with a great figure and a stylish haircut.

Mike's father had been a policeman. He had been killed when Mike was ten. Although he refused to talk about his father, he always praised how his mother went on with her life, raised Mike and his brother while working as a secretary for a company supplying oil rigs.

"What's there to tell?" He would ask when Robina probed him on any personal subject beyond the barest of information.

If he did propose, she wasn't sure what she would say. As her own mother warned, she wasn't getting any younger. She didn't want to bare her first child during menopause. Nor did she want people to think she was the granny when she picked up any future offspring at school. Was the concept that she could do a lot worse good enough to build a life on—she wasn't sure.

Maybe she was just imagining Mike's plans.

They'd reached her flat. Although Mike hadn't moved in officially, he never went back to his place which was a hundred percent man cave with a mattress on the floor, a table, two chairs, no curtains on the windows and a kitchen that had absolutely no cooking utensils.

"Yours is a bit nicer," he'd said after the one time she'd been there. By now most of his clothes were stashed in her closet and chest of drawers.

He held the umbrella over her head as she struggled with the sticky front door key.

"I'll get some oil for that," he said.

A man who kept her dry, fixed things, was a good lover—maybe it would be enough. Mike was more real than her fantasy Roger.

Inside, Mike turned on the electric blanket. "Tea? Cocoa?" He was great at getting beverages.

"Tea." She slipped off her shoes. Her stockings were wet, her feet cold.

By the time she slipped into the warmed bed, Mike came into the room with two mugs. He set one down on her night stand, the other on his.

"So, what do you think?"

"About what?" she asked.

"Visiting Annie and Roger in Argelès for carnival or Easter?"

"Why not?" It would be great to go from dreary Edinburgh to the sunny South of France. Maybe if she saw Roger on his own turf, she would realize that what she had was better than what she couldn't have: birds in hand rather than flopping around in bushes and all that.

# 58

## EDINBURGH, SCOTLAND, GENEVA, SWITZERLAND AND ARGELÈS-SUR-MER, FRANCE

**Carol Dixon had an hour** before her flight was to leave. On her previous trip, she had found a restaurant that served great eggs benedict. There was time to eat before she needed to go through customs. Once seated, she felt the baby kick. If it kicked this hard, she could imagine what it would be like in a few months.

Probably the brat didn't like eggs benedict. Or maybe it felt her worry about her fake passport. In any case, Alice La Russo was retiring. Any future trips would be under her own name—less exciting but excitement was boring when overdone. She paid for breakfast and headed for the departure gate.

She held her breath as the Edinburgh customs looked at her and Alice La Russo's passport thoroughly. Border security was getting tighter and tighter, another reason to move on with her life, now that being a hit woman was becoming more challenge than fun. Or rather, the challenge was no longer fun.

Carol had always believed the time to quit was when she was ahead. That she wasn't back in her Boston loft annoyed her. There were moments when she wondered if this loose end was really all that loose and in time, Annie, et.al. would accept Duncan's death and get on with her life and Duncan's widow would find someone to marry and would forget about her first husband's death.

She brought her attention back to the man as he flipped through the pages of her passport. The red hair and freckles were the stereotype of a typical Scot. If he hadn't been in uniform, she suspected he might be wearing a kilt. His blue eyes were behind thick glasses, but he still squinted as he thumbed through the pages.

"You travel a lot, Miss La Russo."

"I love travelling," she said.

"What is your line of work?"

All the times she's gone through customs, she'd never been asked that. She should have been prepared. "I scout location for the movies." Stupid, she told herself as soon as the words were out of her mouth. Movies were glamorous, and that would increase the chances that the man would remember her if it ever came down to it. She really was off her game.

"But you come from Montreal."

"They have a local film industry as does Vancouver." Both statements were true. For a moment she had been tempted to say, the films are mainly in French, but thought the less she talked the better. She looked over her shoulder. A line was growing. The guard's eyes also flicked to the line. He stamped her passport. "Good luck."

She sat five rows behind Annie to make it easy to follow her after landing. Outside the arrival gate, an older couple ran up to her and hugged her in turn. As Carol walked by, she heard the woman say, "I'm sorry you can only spend one night before going home."

That must mean Argelès, Carol thought.

"I need to be back. Robina and Mike will come for carnival this weekend," Annie said as the man, her father? slung her carry-on over his shoulder.

Damn it, Carol thought. More travel. All she really wanted to do was be back in her own flat. Even being near her mother would be better than this.

She took a ticket for the bus downtown from the machine between the two exit doors.

The number 10 bus would stop at the station, and from there she could train south. It didn't matter if she arrived before or after Annie. She would be able to locate her.

So much for the sunny warm south of France in late winter, Carol thought, as she stepped off the train in Argelès-sur-mer. The train was a newer one with the exit almost equal to the platform, not like the old cars with steps planned for giants.

A wind almost blew her over. She hadn't noticed the trees on either side of the tracks were bent as if in the middle of exercises. The sky above was brilliant blue and cloudless.

There had to be a hotel somewhere in the village. And since it was off season, there should be vacancies. The lack of preplanning was not the way she liked to work, but then again, this was her last job. However, that was no excuse to be careless.

The killing itself she had preplanned, at least down to the last detail on the best method to kill Annie. She would use poison in a way she hadn't before. All her studying of different poisons had paid off before, and it would again. Unlike many serial killers, she preferred to try different methods, meaning even if police from different countries connected the deaths, they wouldn't find a consistent method.

She had obtained two tiny pellets a good year ago as an alternative killing method if needed from an underground contact. For a moment, she imagined her mother, a Boston Brahmin discovering her daughter had underground contacts. It would be beyond her comprehension. At the thought, Carol laughed, then looked around. She didn't want anyone to think she was crazy, but there was no one else braving the wind.

Each pellet had small cavities where ricin was inserted.

Carol liked the foolproofness of her plan, content with the knowledge there was no known antidote, although in her research, Carol had heard a Swiss company was in the testing phase. Even if it were diagnosed and even if the doctors knew about the possibility, the fact that some mice had survived wouldn't help Annie.

The pellets even had a sugar coating to keep the ricin inside the pellet until body heat melted it. All she needed was to get Annie in a place that she could inject her without anyone noticing.

Annie might think she had been bitten but it would not have an immediate result. People inoculated with ricin could take a few days to die of what looked like blood poisoning. By the time Annie felt sick, Carol would be on her way to Spain if not already back in Boston.

Her original idea to do it at the opening of the museum didn't work, which hadn't surprise her.

When Annie had said friends were coming for carnival, Carol smiled, picturing more than one opportunity.

As she saw a church tower, she guessed that was the center of the typical French village with its old houses and narrow streets. The locals must love gardening, because even where the front doors touched the narrow sidewalks, there were planters filled with flowers. Carol had to leave the sidewalk to maneuver around the planter with her suitcase.

She came to a traffic light. There were small shops, a bakery and a green grocery. At the next corner, she saw a sign for a hotel. She walked past the church and found the door locked.

She rang.

A man answered. "Yes, we have rooms available," he said to her question.

The first thing Carol did was take a long, hot shower. The wind, whose howls she could hear outside the window overlooking a small square, had left her chilled. Tomorrow, she would do the research she normally would have done before coming. She needed to know where Annie lived and when and where the carnival would be.

Because it was a small village, she didn't want to spend too much time outside where she might be remembered. God, she was exhausted. Whoever said energy returned in the second trimester of pregnancy lied.

The bed was comfortable. She slept before she could plan tomorrow.

# 59

**" A bowl?" Mike looked at** his tea. They were seated at a long, oak trestle table in Annie and Roger's kitchen. Sophie was busy taking pots and pans out of a bottom drawer, which Annie called the baby's drawer.

"You're in France, do as the French do." Robina picked up her bowl and drank deeply ignoring that it was too hot for comfort, but not quite burning.

Mike didn't seem to be adapting well, she thought. It was his first trip out of the UK. It showed. Having Roger so close wasn't helping her accept Mike's, well she wasn't sure Mike's what: lack of sophistication, uncomfortableness with something new?

Although she'd caught Roger looking at her longer than necessary, or so she hoped, she was also aware how well he and Annie related to each other, almost like they had secret brain-to-brain signals. When she first met Roger, she thought she'd felt a sliver of interest, but as she observed her hosts, he and Annie seemed to be a rock-solid couple.

Last night, Roger had walked her around the property, showing her the pool, the kaki and orange trees, the pines, the smaller building which housed a sheltered eating area and a barbeque. As she was thinking, no policeman should be able to afford such a place, he said, "I picked it up at a bargain because the previous owners were divorcing." He sighed. "And because of my first wife's life insurance and the sale of my Paris flat, I never had a mortgage."

Robina remembered Annie talking about Roger's first wife being killed by a man Roger had sent to prison. Sympathy only made him more attractive and his French accent didn't help her ignore his general sexiness. That was the stupid thing about crushes, especially crushes that had no hope of turning into anything else. She was too old to play the lovesick teenager mooning over someone unattainable. Her attention returned to the kitchen.

Fresh croissants and a baguette that Roger had picked up from the bakery an hour before were on the table. Annie had warmed them and put everything in a napkin-covered basket. Butter and fresh jam were next to apples, bananas and clementines. The glass teapot had only a dredge of the liquid left. Annie stood up to brew another. Freshly squeezed orange juice from their own fruit completed the *petit déjeuner*.

They two couples sat at Roger and Annie's kitchen table. Although the house was of modern construction, copper pots hung from the wooden beams.

The wind still blew through the many pines surrounding the house, but not as hard as it had the day before. "The forecast says this is the end of the Tramontane," Roger said. Everything should be better for the parade tonight."

"I hope so," Annie said. "I can see flowers flying off the floats." She turned to Robina, "What do you guys want to do today?"

"How 'bout a tour? Maybe we can decide to come back for our summer holiday or our honeymoon," Mike said.

Robina, who had the tea bowl half way to her mouth, put it down and stared at Mike. "Is that your idea of a proposal?"

"I took our marriage as a given." He reached for another croissant. "You want to marry me, don't you?"

Robina wasn't sure how to answer that. Before she could, Mike dropped to his knee, pulled a small box out his pocket, and opened it to show a ring. She'd seen movies where men had dropped rings in glasses of champagne.

"Please say yes."

"Yes."

"Wow," Annie said. "This calls for champagne. I don't care that it's only nine in the morning." She produced a bottle from the *frigo* and four glasses.

Robina watched Mike. His face could only be described as radiant. In every couple one loves more than another. She thought of all the dip-shits she'd dated over the lifetime. Mike was what her mother would have described as good-husband material. And she did love him. As he slipped the ring on her finger, she prayed that the love seed would bloom.

The landline, in the room Annie used as an office two doors away, rang, and Roger excused himself to answer it. When he came back, he was shaking his head. "That was Antoinette. She has the flu and can't babysit tonight."

"We won't be able to find another sitter. Everyone will be at the parade."

"Why not take Sophie with us?" Mike said.

Annie and Roger shook their heads at the same time, further confirming Robina's belief of the strength of their couple.

"First," Annie said, as she poured champagne into each glass, "My daughter is one of those rare children who falls asleep around seven even if we want her to stay up."

"And secondly," Roger said, lifting his glass, "Some of the floats and costumes will give her nightmares. I can stay home and the rest of you go."

"Go?" A young woman had walked into the kitchen.

"Gäelle!" Annie jumped up to hug her stepdaughter. "What are you doing here?"

"Guillaume has a major project this weekend, I'm all caught up on my studies, so I thought I'd catch a train to see the old folks." She went over and scooped up Sophie, who threw her arms around her big half-sister.

Robina looked at the young woman, whose dark hair fell in shampoo-commercial perfection to her shoulders, nothing like the wild colors and cuts Annie had talked about when she'd mentioned her stepdaughter in a conversation when they were all in Scotland. She guessed that Annie was referring to a younger version.

Annie explained everything including the reason they were

drinking champagne so early in the morning and their cancelled plans for the evening.

"No problem," Gaëlle said. "You wrinklies go. I'll stay here and lavish affection on the younger generation."

Robina didn't know if she liked being referred to as a wrinkly by someone she considered almost of her generation, but maybe Gaëlle had thought they were all old like her father. Damn it, she thought, I've had a crushed on a man at least twenty years older than I am, unattainable. She held her glass out to Annie to celebrate her engagement to a good man.

# 60

Carol had bought a wolf costume complete with mask from the *marché*. One of the stands located between the flowers and cheese stalls had carnival costumes, confetti, and that stupid colored string that sticks to your clothes when it is shot from a can.

Carol wasn't planning on the costume itself. It would be too easy to identify. The mask she would put over her head. To his point, she'd worn her wig, but once she'd stuck Annie with the poison she would be able to take the mask off and reveal her real hair.

The hotel was practically deserted. Carnival was obviously a local event: this was not tourist season. When she'd gone out last night to see a movie at the theatre two streets from the hotel, she'd never seen the hosts. Nor had she'd seen them when she'd come back from dinner. Maybe if she had gone down to breakfast, she might have. It was hard being anonymous in a five-room hotel. Each night she'd selected a different restaurant.

As she ate, she wished she had a book to read, but that might make her stand out more than just a woman eating alone. An English book would make it even more obvious, and her French was rusty enough that she received little enjoyment from reading one. Fortunately, her six years of French in boarding school and two at university always taught by native French professors who insisted on perfect pronunciation made her origins doubtful. She could be from another region.

Carol was tired. Damn the carnival parade wouldn't be starting until nine and if she knew the French it probably would be later than that.

She had learned where Annie lived. She knew two Edinburgh police were with her. Now all she had to do was find Annie in the crowd.

The sloppiness of this entire hit still displeased her. She wanted to be home in her own bed in her own loft with her own things around her. She was tired of planes and plans. This was the first time she used ricin and she thought she was doing it the safest way possible.

Annie might or might not feel the prick. She would slowly feel sick, then sicker over the next three days as her body parts shut down. No one would be able to figure out why.

She'd take off the mask, go back to the hotel and cut it into hundreds of pieces and leave it in garbage cans that were in front of almost every village house.

While Annie was busy dying, Carol would be busy going home.

There was a train to Toulouse at seven. She'd spend one night there and then fly to Montreal before heading back to Boston and the rest of her life. Franklin, if he wanted any more projects done, would have to find someone else.

Screw him. She smiled. She had screwed him and if he wasn't that good a screw, he had provided her with some of the most exciting moments of her life. In a way, she knew she would miss the research, the chase. Only twice had she seen life leave someone's face when they took their euphemistic final slumber. How wonderful knowing she'd done it.

As she left the hotel, she noticed the wind had died down. People were milling around. For a small town, she thought it would be a small parade, but as she watched the people lined up, she realized that it started at the *mairie*, went up over the bridge and circled three blocks.

Damn it!

Twice she walked all the streets, dodging children in costume and adults trying to keep track of them. Needle in a haystack, she thought, but the then she saw the two policemen. The man had just bought the woman a pony balloon. A man and a woman were next to them and the woman's woolen cap did not hide the mane of curly red hair.

She stood back. It seemed as if they had chosen that place and planned to stay there.

Annie wore jeans and a jacket, but her neck was exposed. Good, Carol thought.

The parade began with a man, who Carol guessed might be the mayor. He sat on the back of a convertible and waved.

Next came a series of floats, which looked as if they used colored tissues to make the flowers.

There was a boat with some cartoon character that she felt she ought to know but didn't, and a tractor covered in tissue flowers.

A marching band wore the same colored black sweatshirts and jeans.

She pulled her attention back to the job at hand and worked her way through the crowd until she was at Annie's right. People were pushing and shoving to have a better view.

Using her hand to hide the syringe, she raised her arm as if she wanted to wave. Just as she was about to inject the ricin into the neck, someone jostled her. The needle went into her palm instead.

Annie turned to Carol who was off balance, and helped steady her before turning her attention back to the parade.

Carol's hand was numb. She headed back to the hotel after throwing the syringe in one of the garbage cans, put the do not disturb sign on the outside door knob, and lay on the bed and thought about how her disappearance would affect people. She considered the what if her final pleasure.

# Epilogue

T he Argelès police never discovered the identity of the body found in the hotel during carnival. An autopsy showed she died of ricin poisoning, which caused a sensation in the local papers but since it was the only death of this type another story about a mayor of a nearby village committing suicide took its place.

The woman's passport was proven to be a fake.

In Boston, Carol's mother and stepfather never solved the mystery of her disappearance. They cringed whenever *The Boston Globe* did an article.

The only person who might have had any idea on Carol's whereabouts—the AGG CEO Franklin Pierce—was properly sympathetic with the family. He did not give up taking insurance out on his employees, but only collected on those that died of natural causes.

Jonathan and Seth gave up trying to find another surrogate mother and concentrated on trying to get his father's acceptance. So far, it hadn't worked.

Annie, Roger and Sophie never became involved. Annie regretted letting Chantal down in not finding out who really killed Duncan, but she was too occupied with a major new assignment despite the feeling all the deaths were associated with AGG.

Chantal, thanks to the money left by author Hamish Browne, made ends meet. Having spent so much of her energy on setting up the museum, she wanted to stay and turned down a slightly higher paying job at a museum in Glasgow.

"Feeling and proving were two different things," Roger kept saying when Annie would bring it up again, usually when the two of them had turned out the light and they were having a last chat before falling asleep locked in each other's arms.

# About the Author

**D**-L Nelson is an American-born Swiss writer and author of seven Third-Culture Mysteries to her credit. She considers herself a Third-Culture Adult, having lived in several countries. She currently lives in Switzerland and the South of France with her husband Rick and her dog, Sherlock.

www.ingramcontent.com/pod-product-compliance
Lightning Source LLC
Chambersburg PA
CBHW061606100726
47898CB00002B/547